P9-CFO-874

EAGAN, MN 55123

"Melissa Mayhue rocks the Scottish Highlands."

—*A Romance Review*

"You can't go wrong when you pick up one of Ms. Mayhue's books."

—*Night Owl Romance*

WARRIOR REBORN

"Melissa Mayhue does not disappoint. . . . A wonderful continuation of this series."

—*The Reading Café*

"Enthralling characters with a splash of Fairy magic and a dash of heart-pounding romance . . . Melissa Mayhue truly knows how to captivate her readers."

—*Sassy Book Lovers*

"The characters are rich and sensual, enriched by the lush background of the Highlands. . . ."

—*Tea and Book*

"Magic, mystery, time travel, and a beautifully written love story. . . . *Warrior Reborn* is amazing."

—*Storm Goddess Book Reviews*

"Melissa Mayhue entrances the reader with the settings and characters of a time-travel novel. . . . The romance is palpable. . . . Entertaining and beautiful."

—*Reflections of a Bookworm*

DAKOTA COUNTY LIBRARY

WARRIOR'S REDEMPTION

Winner of an RT Seal of Excellence Award

"Melissa Mayhue brings the Scottish locale to life with a colorful vividness. . . . Unforgettable characters and a magically imaginative premise."

—*Single Titles*

"Characters of vastly different backgrounds—Nordic and Texan—emotional turmoil, magic, and an ever-expanding love coupled with an unusual plot make this an extraordinary read."

—*RT Book Reviews*

"A little bit of magic, a little bit of Faerie, a little bit of time travel, and a whole lot of Highland Warrior made for a wonderful romance story."

—*Another Look Book Reviews*

"A wonderful job . . . fun, filled with action and danger."

—*The Reading Café*

"Marvelous, magical mayhem."

—*Genre Go Round Reviews*

"With strong characters, witty dialogue, and an easy to follow plot, what's not to enjoy? A must-read."

—*My Book Addiction Reviews*

"A refreshing breath of fresh air."

—*Novel Reaction*

PRAISE FOR
THE DAUGHTERS OF THE GLEN SERIES

"Deeply moving characters, fraught with emotional turmoil, the subtle entwining of Faerie magic and a highly charged, ever-expanding romance. . . ."

—*RT Book Reviews* (4½ stars)

"Wonderful. . . . Melissa Mayhue captures the complications and delights of both the modern woman and the fascination with the medieval world."

—*Denver Post*

"If you love time travel, you should be reading Ms. Mayhue's books. If you're into Scottish historicals, you too should be reading this series. Heck, every romance reader should be reading these books just because they're great stories. You will become a Melissa Mayhue fan in no time at all."

—*The Good, the Bad, and the Unread*

"Time after time, Mayhue brings her readers tantalizingly close to emotional satisfaction."

—*Publishers Weekly*

"Absolutely riveting from start to finish."

—*A Romance Review*

"A delightful world of the Faerie. . . . Snappy dialogue and passionate temptations . . . are sure to put a smile on your face."

—*Fresh Fiction*

ALSO BY MELISSA MAYHUE

Thirty Nights with a Highland Husband
Highland Guardian
Soul of a Highlander
A Highlander of Her Own
A Highlander's Destiny
A Highlander's Homecoming
Healing the Highlander
Highlander's Curse
Warrior's Redemption
Warrior's Last Gift
Warrior Reborn

MELISSA MAYHUE

WARRIOR UNTAMED

Pocket Books

New York   London   Toronto   Sydney   New Delhi

The sale of this book without its cover is unauthorized. If you purchased this book without a cover, you should be aware that it was reported to the publisher as "unsold and destroyed." Neither the author nor the publisher has received payment for the sale of this "stripped book."

Pocket Books
A Division of Simon & Schuster, Inc.
1230 Avenue of the Americas
New York, NY 10020

This book is a work of fiction. Any references to historical events, real people, or real places are used fictitiously. Other names, characters, places, and events are products of the author's imagination, and any resemblance to actual events or places or persons, living or dead, is entirely coincidental.

Copyright © 2013 by Melissa Mayhue

All rights reserved, including the right to reproduce this book or portions thereof in any form whatsoever. For information address Pocket Books Subsidiary Rights Department, 1230 Avenue of the Americas, New York, NY 10020.

First Pocket Books paperback edition December 2013

POCKET and colophon are registered trademarks of Simon & Schuster, Inc.

For information about special discounts for bulk purchases, please contact Simon & Schuster Special Sales at 1-866-506-1949 or business@simonandschuster.com.

The Simon & Schuster Speakers Bureau can bring authors to your live event. For more information or to book an event contact the Simon & Schuster Speakers Bureau at 1-866-248-3049 or visit our website at www.simonspeakers.com.

Designed by Jacquelynne Hudson

Manufactured in the United States of America

10 9 8 7 6 5 4 3 2 1

ISBN 978-1-4516-4089-2
ISBN 978-1-4516-4092-2 (ebook)

For all the readers

Acknowledgments

My thanks to all the talented people at Pocket Books who helped bring this story to life.

Special thanks to my agent, Elaine Spencer.

WARRIOR UNTAMED

One

IF ANY HARM had come to Bridget MacCulloch, there would be hell to pay.

Not that he had personal feelings for the MacCulloch woman one way or another. He absolutely didn't. The very last thing he needed to complicate his life was a woman. Especially a woman as stubborn and undisciplined as Bridget.

Halldor O'Donar had determined long ago that he'd hold tender feelings for no woman. Unless a man was of a mind to settle down with a wife and raise a family, a woman had but one purpose in his life. And Hall was not of a mind to marry. Besides, no Mortal woman would have the least bit of interest in him, once she learned what he was and how he was destined to spend his life.

His vow regarding Bridget's safety was made for no other reason than that he'd hate to have wasted all the time and effort he'd put into saving her life in the first place. Not to mention that enlisting the aid of the Tinklers to spirit the woman away from the clutches of Torquil MacDowylt had put him squarely back in the debt of the Fae.

It rankled mightily that he'd barely settled one debt to them before incurring another.

Thunder rumbled overhead, and Hall's companions cast worried looks to the skies.

"Unusual weather for this time of year," Eric Mac-Nicol mused. "But unusual tends to be the order of the day when I'm in yer company, does it no, my friend?"

"Only Thor himself has power over the weather. This is no fault of mine," Hall muttered, though the words he spoke weren't completely true.

Not even years of training and solitude had succeeded in giving him complete control over those unruly emotions of his.

Hall's second traveling partner, Patrick Mac-Dowylt, younger brother to the laird of the Mac-Gahan, reined in his horse and stood in his stirrups. "Look down there," he directed, lifting an arm to point into the distance. "Unless my eyes deceive me, we've finally found them."

Hall jerked his attention to the spot Patrick indicated. Even from this distance, there could be no mistaking the bright colors of the Tinkler wagons. With a kick to his horse, he lurched forward in full gallop, the knot in his stomach still balled up tight.

The Tinklers were several days overdue. Until he could see with his own two eyes that Bridget was unharmed, he couldn't bring himself to start his quest to find the sword and the scrolls that had been taken from Tordenet before Chase Noble's battle with Torquil MacDowylt. Without those treasures, there was no hope of defeating the monster that now possessed the MacDowylt laird's body. And if the monster couldn't be defeated, the world as they knew it faced an unholy change.

"Aho, warrior!" The elder Tinkler, William Faas, drew his wagon to a stop and rose from his seat as Hall approached, waving a hand in welcome. "We'd no thought to be seeing you out here upon the trail."

Damned careless of the Tinkler to greet riders in such an open fashion. And exactly what Hall would expect of the Fae and their chosen people. He hated how they blundered through the Mortal world, acting as if they were impervious to danger. They, of all beings, should know that appearances meant nothing. He could have been anyone. Or anything.

"You worry too much, mighty warrior." William's wife, Editha, reached out to pat his arm as he pulled his horse up next to their wagon. "I felt yer presence long before we saw you and yer friends. The one you seek is in the back of the second wagon."

Editha was more than Tinkler. Of that, Hall had not one single doubt. It was she who had convinced the others to help him spirit Bridget to safety away from Tordenet. And it was to her that he was now indebted.

Damned difficult Fae. A fine trick fate had played

on him, repeatedly weaving the path of his life with that of the Fae.

Hall kept those thoughts to himself. At least he hoped he did. With a respectful dip of his head, he turned his horse toward the next wagon, anxious to reassure himself of Bridget's safety. Only then would he ask what had delayed them.

Bridget leaned out from the interior of the wagon. He could tell the instant she spotted him because she gathered her skirts and hopped down, striding toward him in long, sure steps. Even clothed in the colorful Tinkler garb, she looked every bit the warrior princess. Determination and self-confidence shone in her every move.

An unfamiliar excitement rumbled through his veins at the sight of her. Relief, like as not, that his efforts to save her hadn't gone to waste.

She stopped and rested her hands on her hips, waiting for him to reach her, her chin lifted as if for confrontation. For some odd reason, he'd expected a smile to greet him. Odder still was the twinge of disappointment he felt when she didn't offer it up.

"He's dead, then," she said with great finality, as if there could be no other outcome.

The Shield Maiden was single-minded, bent on revenge for her father's death at the hands of Torquil MacDowylt.

"Not exactly. At least not yet."

Trapped in the burning tower, Torquil should have died. Would have, if he'd been only himself.

But the evil that possessed him could not be killed so easily.

"Not yet?" she repeated incredulously. "Then what in the name of the Seven are you doing here, lollygagging about?"

Good question. Now that he'd found her safe, his business here was almost finished, and as soon as his questions were answered, he'd be on his way.

"Hunting for you." When he should have been on the trail of the missing treasures. "Where have you been?" he demanded. "The whole of Castle Mac-Gahan is disquieted with worry over your safety."

"The whole of the castle?" she asked, a trace of a smile lighting her eyes. "Would that include you as well, big man?"

He snorted to cover his surprise. "I'm not *in* the castle, now, am I, little one?" It was answer enough and all that she would get from him.

Any sign of her smile retreated behind the hard mask of a warrior. "Perhaps you'd like to explain to me why the MacDowylt still lives. Why did you allow him to escape, when you assured me that if I went quietly with the Tinklers and left it all to you, you yerself would deal with the man."

As if she thought her staying behind wouldn't have made everything twice as difficult as it had been. His work in seeing to the safety of Chase Noble had been fully cut out for him. Still, she deserved an explanation for what was clearly his failure.

"The Beast now possesses what was Torquil

MacDowylt. You must have recognized that much for yourself. The Beast can only be killed using the Sword of the Ancients, which has gone missing."

For a moment her mask slipped, and one hand fluttered up to cling to her throat.

"Would that be the sword I saw in Torquil's tower?"

"One and the same."

She sighed, shaking her head. "If it's gone missing, I'd lay wager it's that damned greedy Hugo MacFalny what has it. He and his brother Mathew snuck off on our first night away from Tordenet. Once we discovered them gone, the Tinklers thought it best we seek protection for a few days at a place they called Rowan Cottage. Just in case the thieving minstrel should try to lead the MacDowylt laird back to us."

So that was where they'd been. Holed up with Orabilis. He'd assumed the old woman was nothing more dangerous than a witch, but she was obviously much more powerful than that if the Tinklers sought shelter under her roof.

"You'd lose that wager," he said at last, remembering the minstrel's fate all too well. "Hugo had a rather messy run-in with the Beast. His thieving days are a thing of the past now."

A shiver shook Bridget's body, a sure sign that she understood the implication of his words.

"And the brother?" she asked quietly. "Mathew's but a boy."

"No sign of him. So, as he's our most likely candidate to have disappeared with the treasures, it's him I'm off to find now."

And he hoped he could find the lad before the Beast did. For Mathew's sake as well as for theirs.

Bridget nodded her agreement, lifting an arm to him. "That's a wise plan. Help me up. I'm coming with you."

Like hell she was. The task ahead of him was daunting enough without his having to watch over a woman. Especially a woman who thought she could take care of herself. They were the most dangerous kind of all.

"You'll do no such thing. You'll continue on with the Tinklers to Castle MacGahan. I'm sending Eric along with you to make sure of that."

Her hands fisted once again on her hips. "You canna think I'll sit back and let you do this on yer own, big man. You failed me the last time. I'll no be shuffled off to safety again."

"You will, and that's the end of it. And don't even think," he cautioned as she started to protest, "to give Eric any trouble. The poor man has a new bride waiting at home for him, and he wants nothing more than to get back to her. Now go on with you, and do as you're told."

"Do as I'm . . ." She sputtered to a stop, her eyes wide with indignation. "You must listen to me. There are things I can tell you—"

"Enough!" Hall interrupted. "I've listened all I care to. My mind will not be changed."

He turned his horse and headed off at a canter, anxious to get on with his quest. Anxious to put distance between himself and the angry woman behind him.

"You canna leave without me!" she yelled after him. "I willna be treated like some delicate flower!"

What possessed him then, he had no idea. But he drew up on his reins and turned his mount back toward her. The satisfied smile on her face when he reached her side this time was everything he'd expected when he first arrived.

She lifted an arm up to him but he pushed it aside to lean down and wrap his hand in the silky length of her braid. In a single move, he pulled her close and fastened his lips over hers.

Coming to his senses, he broke the kiss and pulled away. Bridget stood, full lips parted, eyes closed, her face tilted up to him as if captured by some magic spell.

Magic he quickly dispelled. "Just this one time, Bridget MacCulloch, try to do as you're told without a blighted argument. And, for the record, there's little chance of your being mistaken for a delicate anything."

Her angry screech reverberated in his ears as he rode away.

"I'll no forget this, Halldor O'Donar!" Bridget called. "I'll no be forgetting you, you great bristly-faced ogre!"

With the feel of her burning on his lips, it wasn't likely he'd be forgetting her anytime soon, either.

THE NERVE OF that man! The unmitigated gall! To leave her behind as if she were some . . . pathetic weakling woman. And to kiss her like that! Like he had the right to do it! How *dare* he?

Brie's whole body trembled with anger.

That he'd saved her life back at Tordenet was all that kept her from wishing a pox to fall upon his head. Lucky for him her bow lay in its corner at Castle MacGahan, or she'd be tempted to . . .

Brie took a deep breath and blew it out with great deliberation, forcing her clenched fists open. How many times had her father counseled her on controlling her wild temper?

Losing herself to fury wouldn't accomplish anything. There was nothing she could do right now. She had no horse and she had no weapon. But things would not always be this way.

"So be it," she ground out, turning to find all her traveling companions staring in her direction. "So be it," she repeated, this time on a huff of breath meant to calm her as she mentally wrestled the red haze of anger flooding her mind into a small, manageable ball.

If only Hall had listened to her, she could have helped him in his quest. What she knew of Mathew MacFalny and Eleyne, the cousin he'd left behind with the Tinklers, might have saved him days in his search.

But no, he'd left her behind with a stinging insult ringing in her ears.

If only he hadn't kissed her. If only he hadn't made it feel so—she touched a finger to her lips—so *enjoyable*.

Next to her, Eric cleared his throat. "The sooner yer back in the wagon, the sooner we can be on our way." His horse pawed at the ground as he spoke, as if the animal could feel the emotions roiling within her.

The animal was obviously smarter than his rider, since the annoying man could barely hide his grin.

Bridget locked her jaw to keep from swearing aloud and strode back to the wagon to climb inside.

Patience, her father had always counseled. She wished to the Seven that she possessed even some small measure of that elusive virtue, but it just wasn't a part of who she was. Determination was what kept her going.

For now, her path was to return to Castle Mac-Gahan. Perhaps her brother would be there by the time she arrived.

Things would be different when Jamesy came home. Together, they could set out to track the sword themselves. They would find it, and they would put an end to both Torquil MacDowylt and whatever creature lived inside him. Revenge for her father's murder would be hers.

And as for Halldor O'Donar?

Turning to look over her shoulder, she cast one last glare in his direction. As she'd promised, she wouldn't forget this latest slight, his sending her away for a second time as if she were some fragile maid in need of his protection.

By the Seven, he was the most arrogant creature she'd ever met. But she'd show him. She'd track him and find him, and when she did, she'd give him a piece of her mind.

"What's got that silly smile upon yer face?" Eleyne asked, her fingers twitching at the blanket covering her lap.

"I'm no smiling," Brie denied, carefully wiping all expression from her face.

And even if she had been, it was only the thought of getting even with O'Donar that made her smile. Certainly not the prospect of meeting up with him again.

Two

Fingers splayed, the hand reached out to cover the meat in front of him. With little effort, the fingers closed around the morsel and efficiently brought it to his mouth.

This body, this vessel that had become Fenrir's new abode, was becoming his now, responding to his thoughts as if he had been born in this form.

A pity this casing was so weak and vulnerable.

Fenrir bit into the hot mutton and shivered, longing for the banquet tables of old in his home world. He longed for raw meat that dripped warm blood, fresh from the kill, rather than this pale, tasteless cooked fare that these creatures insisted on consuming.

Those days, like his original form, were long gone. But if he had his way, they wouldn't be gone forever.

He was Torquil MacDowylt now. Laird of the MacDowylts of the North. And in this guise, he would soon rule all he set his sights upon. Nothing in this world could stop him.

At least, not once he regained possession of those treasures that were rightfully his.

What little appetite he had for the tasteless swill in front of him disappeared completely at the thought of his missing treasures, and he tossed the overcooked meat back onto the table.

With the scrolls gone, it was as if a large chunk of him were gone as well. The most powerful of his ancient spells had been locked inside those pages when Odin had bidden the Elves of Niflheim to imprison him. And now, finally, after more time than he could gauge had passed, now that he once again had hands to hold those scrolls, they were gone!

The scrolls and the jewels that were the keys to unlocking his Magic from its prison. The scrolls and the jewels that were the means to imprison him again. Gone. Taken by some pathetic, putrid little human.

And the sword!

He forced himself to breathe, drawing air into the pitifully small lungs this body afforded him.

The Sword of the Ancients could not remain adrift. Steel forged in the fires of Asgard, honed on the bones of the warriors filling Valhalla, this was a weapon he must possess. This was a weapon, the only weapon, he feared. It alone had the power to steal his freedom. The power to end his life.

Not just the life of this pathetic body he inhabited, but his, Fenrir's, very existence. It had been created for that purpose.

The legs of his chair scraped loudly across the

stone floor as he pushed away from the table to stand, fury beating in his chest. Around him, the insignificant mortals who assumed he was their laird stilled, turning their frightened faces in his direction.

They should be frightened. Though they knew it not, their lives were no longer their own. Their laird had been a formidable tyrant, but at his worst, he was a frail maiden compared to Fenrir in full ferocity.

Without a word, he strode from the great hall and up to his bedchamber. Once there, he sat upon his large bed and removed his shirt, dropping it next to him.

He had sent a party of men in search of his treasures days ago, and he needed to see what progress they'd made. He needed to see if he could yet break through the mental barriers of the one who had stolen what belonged to him. Once he accomplished that step, it would be easy enough to direct his warriors to the exact location of the wretched thief and reclaim his rightful belongings.

He rubbed his hand over the smooth skin of his new body, still somehow surprised at the lack of fur. He glanced down as his fingers encountered a twinge of pain where five oozing, festering marks circled his heart. He didn't know what Torquil had done to damage their body in this fashion before he'd taken control of it, but he'd been unable to heal this unusual wound, no matter what he'd tried.

It was a mystery he would have to deal with at a later time.

He lay back and nestled his head into the pillow beneath him. Eyes closed, he retreated into his mind, ignoring the piteous cries coming from behind the black door deep within the hidden recesses there. Plead as he might, what was left of Torquil MacDowylt's soul would remain in that place until Fenrir no longer needed this form.

Calming his thoughts, Fenrir set them free, flying through the world of the between in search of the sparkly bits of stone he sought.

Only when he found them did he slow, taking care to avoid their siren pull upon him. As long as the thief kept them all together, he had no chance. But once they were separated, their power was his.

He was in luck. Carefully, slowly, he fit his essence inside the one jewel that had been separated from the others. Beyond the red shimmer of the ruby's walls, he could just make out the shadowy, wavering form a man.

"There you are," he growled, pushing his voice beyond the stone, into the cold night air. "Did you think to escape me so easily?"

The young man yelped in fright, whatever he'd held clattering to the ground at his feet.

The thief was little more than a terror-stricken boy? He couldn't have asked for better luck. Since his power rode the wings of terror, this was going to be much, much easier than he had expected.

Three

MATHEW MACFALNY STEPPED out of the small house and into a narrow, dirty alley deep in the bowels of Inverness. He didn't have to count the paltry sum of coins in his sporran again to know he'd been cheated.

The old merchant's eyes had lit with greed when Mathew showed him the jewel. He'd closed down his stall and brought Mathew here, to his home, where they could conduct their business in private.

Hugo had often said he trusted no one. Though his brother had been sorely lacking in scruples of his own, he'd been right on that count. Because of his brother's training, Mathew had split up the treasures the night before he'd reached Inverness, carrying only one of each in his sporran and hiding the others in the small pack he carried.

When he'd first approached the old merchant, something about the man's attitude had warned him this wasn't the place to present all the treasures he planned to sell.

He'd shown the old merchant one single jewel

and one ancient scroll, claiming they were all he had left in the world to support him and his poor family of orphaned brothers and sisters.

And still the old man cheated him.

Mathew had no doubt the merchant was, at this very moment, cackling in glee over the bargain they'd struck, knowing he'd fetch a much higher price than what he'd paid for Mathew's lovely bauble.

But the transaction hadn't been a complete loss. The coins in Mathew's sporran were enough to provide him with a mount and the provisions he would need to reach Dunvegan Castle.

Besides, he was more than ready to have that blighted ruby out of his hands. Let the merchant deal with the vengeful spirit dwelling inside it. It would serve him right for his cheating ways.

Freed of that burden, Mathew was ready for his next step. Although the merchant had had no interest in the scroll he'd hoped to sell, he'd told Mathew that the laird of the MacLeod was said to desire such things, willing to pay good silver with no questions asked. The great laird was also rumored to harbor a particular interest in Magic and the Fae.

Once the merchant had assured Mathew that the markings on the scroll were none he'd ever seen before, Mathew had determined that Dunvegan would be his next destination. With a story already brewing in his mind, it should take little effort to convince the MacLeod laird that he'd discovered the scrolls lying on a tuft of grass just outside a Faerie

Circle, as if the Fae themselves had accidentally left the scrolls behind.

Mathew's mood lightened as the tale seemed to take on a life of its own, weaving itself ever more intricately in his imagination. Perhaps now that he'd left his pipes behind, he should consider becoming a troubadour, weaving stories to delight the crowds.

That or any other future would depend upon how successful he might be when he met the Mac-Leod laird.

He needed a good horse underneath him, so he'd look less like a boy on the run and more like a man worthy of an important business deal. His body might be that of a sixteen-year-old, but the last few days had aged his mind and soul far beyond his years.

With a fine mount, a story such as he'd invented, and the MacLeod laird's penchant for Magic and Faeries, Mathew would be a wealthy man by the time he departed Dunvegan.

With wealth came power, and power was exactly what he needed most desperately.

Power would enable him to find his cousin, Eleyne, and take her home where she belonged. Power would enable him to stand up to his uncle and demand his rightful place at Castle Glenluce.

Such worthy goals should certainly override the tang of dishonor that clung to the way the treasures had come into in his possession. After all, the things he'd taken from Tordenet were no more than the just payment he deserved for what the evil laird there had done to his brother, Hugo.

He shuddered at the memory of his brother's mutilated body, struggling to push it from his mind's eye.

Wealth was what he needed now. Wealth and power.

Perhaps with enough wealth, with enough power, he might even drive away the nameless fear that haunted his every dream.

Four

BRIE'S HEART POUNDED in her chest as the Tinklers' wagon lumbered under the open portcullis and through the long, tunnellike gate at Castle MacGahan.

She spotted him the instant they pulled into the bailey.

Her brother had returned! At last she would have a partner in her quest to avenge their father's death.

Jamesy stood at the top of the great stairs, flanked by two men she didn't recognize. Hands on his hips, his long brown hair ruffling in the breeze, he looked the very image of everything she'd ever imagined in a Pictish king.

Thank the Seven he'd returned. For the first time since her father's death, she felt as if she weren't alone.

Next to her, Eleyne gave her a little shove as she tried to push in front of Brie. *Tried*, but didn't succeed. It would take more strength than the tiny blonde possessed to move her out of the way.

"Who is *that*?" Eleyne asked, peering over her shoulder, her gaze clearly fixed on the stairs where the three men stood.

Brie ignored her, intent on climbing down from the slow-moving wagon. She hit the ground lightly, but stumbled as she started forward.

"Bollocks," she grunted, recovering her balance and gathering up the layers of skirts that composed the Tinkler costume she wore.

The dress might be pretty, but pretty was hardly practical.

Jamesy met her halfway, wrapping her in his arms, hugging her close, and lifting her inches off the ground just as their da had always done. If she closed her eyes, she might almost believe her da had returned.

Though it wouldn't surprise her if she and Jamesy had themselves a fine, rowdy argument before the sun set on their first day together, it was beyond good to have her big brother home again. He, like no other here at Castle MacGahan, was true family.

"You've been gone too long," she proclaimed, returning her brother's embrace. "You canna believe how I've missed you."

"What I canna believe is how you've filled out in just a year's time. No wonder they tell me the castle's larder is low."

Her older brother had always had the ability to annoy her more than any other person she knew.

Though the big warrior Halldor O'Donar was running a close second of late.

"Those look to me to be curves," one of the men who joined them commented. "And none too excessive to my way of thinking."

"Did I forget to mention how it would be best for you to keep yer eyes—and yer thoughts—to yerself?" Jamesy growled, completely ruining the effect of his threat by giving her a wink as he ended their embrace.

"Once or twice, mayhap," the other responded, his voice reflecting his lack of concern over his friend's bark. "But it's yer own fault, Jamesy Mac-Culloch. When you spoke of a little sister, we all imagined a wee bit of a bairn, no a full-grown beauty such as this. You should introduce us."

Jamesy grinned down at her before turning to face his companions. "Well, then, Finn, you imagined wrong, did you no? And while we're about it, I'll thank you to keep my sister out of any further imaginings you might have, aye? She's no meant for the likes of you."

"Friends of yers, are they?" she asked, studying the face of each of the men. They had to be, or Jamesy would have taken the mouthy one to the ground by now.

"Aye," her brother agreed with a roll of his eyes. He wagged his thumb to indicate the man who'd spoken. "The noisy one with the ragged dog at his side is Finley MacCormack. And the quiet one back there is Alexander MacKillican. I couldna shake the two of them from my heels when I left Edinburgh, so I'd no choice but to let them follow along. Like lost sheep, they were."

"Allow us?" Finn snorted his disbelief. "We couldna trust this brother of yers to stay out of trouble without us. It's we who had no choice in the matter but to leave our studies and trail along after him. Am I no telling the God's honest truth, Alex?"

Alex shrugged. "We've a bond, for a fact. Harm one, harm us all."

Brie acknowledged the two men with a dip of her head, then turned to her brother, catching up his hand in hers as the four of them made their way toward the great stairs.

She had so many things to tell Jamesy, so many plans to finalize. Chief among those things was determining when they would leave to find the sword they needed to confront their father's killer.

Jamesy stopped, his gaze scanning the wagon and riders in the courtyard. "Patrick dinna return with you?"

She shook her head. "He and Halldor continued on after they met up with us."

Continued on their own merry way, leaving her behind as if she weren't every bit the warrior they were.

"Halldor?" Her brother turned a hard, questioning gaze her direction. "That would be O'Donar? He's the one who managed to spirit you out of Tordenet in one piece, is he no?"

He'd gotten her out of there, but he'd failed as miserably as she had in her original purpose in being there.

"He is. But my escape from the castle came at a price. Torquil MacDowylt still lives, Jamesy. I missed my opportunity to kill the bastard."

All traces of humor left her brother's eyes. "So Malcolm has told me. And now I hear that, thanks to some mythical beast, the MacDowylt laird is even more powerful than he was before."

Though she felt no trace of rebuke in what her brother said, she felt the guilt of having failed more sharply than if he'd accused her in plain words.

She'd been in the room while Torquil slept. She'd stood over him, that fancy sword of his within arm's reach. It had called to her to take it up, to use it as her own, but she'd lacked the nerve. Had she but plunged the weapon into his heart then and there, she might have prevented the battles that were to come. She certainly would have had her revenge.

But she hadn't. What she had done was take the coward's way out. She'd tucked tail and run from his castle like nothing more than a frightened—

"Did you hear me?" Jamesy pulled at her arm. "It was foolish beyond measure, what you did, running off to Tordenet like that. No one had any idea where you'd gone or what peril you faced. And then you tried to gut the man with naught but a wee dagger at his own table in his own hall, surrounded by his own men?"

It had been the best plan she could come up with at the time. And it might have worked, too, if not for the strength of the Beast inside him. All too well she remembered the evil red glow shining from Torquil's eyes as he'd pinned her to the table and gone for her throat. If not for Halldor's intervention on her behalf . . .

"Are you listening to me? Yer no to ever put yerself in such danger again. With Da gone, it's me you'll need to answer to now, and on this matter, I will accept no quarrel. You'll do as I say."

She could hardly believe what she'd just heard. Jamesy's voice oozed with entitlement, and for the first time ever her brother's words sounded more like those of their uncle than of their father.

Bridget MacCulloch was no delicate maiden to be hidden away before some hearth and protected by men far weaker than she. Warrior blood coursed through her veins, just as it did through her brother's. She was the last daughter of the House MacUlagh, descended from the Ancient Seven who ruled the land when not even the Roman invaders dared challenge all the way to the Northern Sea.

Yet Jamesy spoke to her as if a year away had caused him to forget that.

She pulled her hand from his and stepped back to glare at him. "Yer hardly in any position to be telling me what I can and canna do, Jamesy MacCulloch. You forget yerself. You forget who and what I am. When you leave here to go after the MacDowylt, it's me what will be riding at yer side, weapon at the ready."

"No," he said, matching her glare. "I forget nothing, little sister. And dinna you be giving me that face. I'm all too familiar with the look yer wearing, and I'll no be having any of it. Torquil MacDowylt is far too dangerous a quarry for me to give you yer head on this one. I dinna begrudge the way Da allowed you to grow up, acting as if you were as much a brother to me as a sister, but this is no the time for such pretense. If Da were here now, he'd say the same."

"If Da were here now, there'd be no need for me to go after the murdering bastard what killed him, now, would there?"

The hurtful words were out before she thought. Jamesy flinched as if she'd landed a physical blow and a tremor of guilt ebbed over her. The loss of their father had to be as difficult for him as it was for her, but she couldn't afford to backstep. One sign of weakness and he would pounce, declaring it reason enough to leave her behind. She must present her strongest side to convince him otherwise.

"You need me in this quest, Jamesy. You need the knowledge I have to find the sword."

"Do I? And what knowledge might you hold that would be so dear to me?" He crossed his arms in front of him and waited, the familiar stubborn expression she recognized from childhood hardening his features.

"I'm the only one here who's seen the sword. I'm the only one who can easily recognize it." Her gaze lit on the Tinkler wagon and the blonde perched on the seat staring curiously at them. "And I ken that the lad who's taken it is too close to his cousin not to come looking for her." She pointed toward Eleyne, feeling confident she'd made her case.

"Perhaps you have a point, Brie," her brother acknowledged, a smile breaking over his face as he reached out to tug on her braid. "And now that you've shared yer knowledge with us, it seems that wee golden-haired lass looking in our direction might be the one we need at our sides to help us capture our thief, rather than you."

Brie stood rooted to her spot in disbelief, her mouth open, watching as her brother and his friends left her behind in their haste to reach the Tinkler wagon.

Damn him! Damn them all if they thought she'd give up so easily. If this was how it was to be, she didn't need them. Not any of them. If she'd learned anything from her harrowing experience at Tordenet, it was that she was much stronger than any of them knew. Stronger even than she had known.

With a deep breath, she lifted her chin and squared her shoulders before starting toward the keep.

Jamesy's rebuke was but a minor setback, of no more importance than Halldor O'Donar's refusal to take her with him. She didn't need either one of them. She could do this on her own. Once she was rested she'd figure out a plan, and then she'd be on her way to find Mathew and retrieve the sword.

And if doing that meant going it alone, so be it. She'd show them that she wouldn't be left behind.

The fact that it was Halldor's face, not her brother's, that she saw in her mind's eye as she stomped up the stairs to the keep of Castle MacGahan was something she refused to waste her time worrying over.

Five

"Now that I think upon it, mayhap I do have a memory of the lad you mention." The old stable keeper gazed down at the coin cradled in his dirty palm, his toothless smile almost invisible within his grizzled beard. "It was a fine mount I sold the lad. A fine, fine animal."

Hall studied the other man's eyes, noting the deception pooled there. Whatever he learned from this conversation would have to be well vetted before he acted upon it.

"And?"

He expected better than that poor tidbit for the money he'd just handed over.

The stable keeper scratched his whiskers, nodding as if to himself. "And? There is no *and*. That's all I ken of the one you seek. The lad left here on an excellent steed, headed for I know not where." The man's eyes darted over Hall's shoulder, and he shook a fist. "Out of there, you lazy cur! Get back to yer chores!"

Hall turned, catching sight of a young boy scurrying out through a small door at the side of the stable.

"Damned worthless stableboy," the old man grumbled. "Not worth the oats it takes to feed him. Always sneaking around, listening in on me. Like as not, he steals me blind when I'm no watching."

"Perhaps if you were to think harder," Patrick suggested, encouraging the old man back onto the proper topic. "Perhaps then you might remember something else about our friend. Perhaps even the direction he took when he left."

Hall's companion held out another small coin.

The stable keeper allowed Patrick to drop the coin in his palm but continued to hold the hand open, as if he waited for more. With his other hand, he continued his incessant face-scratching.

It was clear to Hall they'd about exhausted this source of information. The old man might know more, but he obviously wasn't going to share that knowledge.

But perhaps there was another resource close at hand.

"I've a need to relieve myself. Maybe by the time I return, your memory will have improved."

Outside the smelly stable, Hall quickly caught sight of the real reason he'd come outside. The stableboy squatted near the corner of the building, his hand outstretched to offer a bit of food to a mangy dog.

"You there," Hall called, striding forward as the boy jumped to his feet. "What are you called?"

"Donald," the boy answered, shrinking back as Hall neared him.

"Well, Donald, I need your help. I'm searching for a friend of mine. A young lad not too much older than you. Your employer remembers selling him a fine, fine mount. Unfortunately, that seems to be about all he remembers of my friend. Can you help me, do you think?"

Hall reached into the bag at his waist and pulled out a shiny coin, holding it out to the boy.

Donald's eyes rounded and he snatched the coin before once again backing away.

"I remember him, right enough. Though it was but a runted palfrey my master sent him out upon, no a fine steed as he claimed."

Hall had guessed as much from the old man's demeanor.

"Did my young friend happen to say anything about the direction he traveled?"

Donald looked down to the coin clutched in his fist before lifting his gaze to meet Hall's. "Will you be telling my master about this?"

"I see no need to tell your master. The coin will be our secret, boy. A transaction between you and me for any information at all you can remember of my friend. It's most important that I find him, and any little thing he did or said could be of value to me in my search."

The boy chewed at the corner of his mouth, eyes downcast, some internal debate weighing heavily on him until at last he made his decision.

"Well enough, then. Yer friend traded me a sweet

for an extra bag of feed for his horse. He said the ride to Dunvegan would be a long one and he had concerns about the animal lasting the whole way there."

Dunvegan. It was the confirmation Hall needed.

He and Patrick had begun their day in Inverness at the marketplace, quickly locating the shopkeeper who had purchased one of Mathew's jewels. In his babbling about having bought the bauble fair and square, the merchant had mentioned the MacLeod stronghold.

With some strongly worded persuasion and more of Hall's silver to grease the path, the rat-eyed merchant had turned over the jewel that now resided safely in Hall's sporran.

"Anything else?" he asked, focusing once again on the boy. "Anything at all you can recall."

"Only that I dinna tell yer other friends as much." Donald grinned and touched the pouch where he'd tucked away his coin. "But they were no so generous as you, good sir, so I dinna feel as obliged to help them in their search."

"Other friends?" There were no other friends. "Tell me about these men, lad. When were they here?"

"They came through yestereve seeking yer friend, no even taking the time to feed and water their horses. When they left, they separated into two groups, each one headed in a different direction." Donald leaned forward and lowered his voice as if to share a confidence. "In truth, I was glad to see them gone so quickly. Beggin' yer pardon, good sir, but fair odd they were, the lot of them."

"Odd, were they?" Hall leaned in conspiratorially. "In what way?"

"Oh, aye, odd indeed. No expressions on their faces, no a one of them. Their eyes all strange and staring, as if they dinna even see what was before them, but looked after a vision of some sort." Donald straightened and shivered. "I've no ever seen men look like that before, no even the ones deep in their cups."

Fenrir's men, Hall suspected. Likely possessed and directed by the Beast himself.

"How many riders were there?"

The boy shrugged and lifted his arm, palm facing toward Hall. "More than I have fingers to count on one hand."

Six at the very least, then, if not more, broken into two tracking parties.

"My thanks for your help, Donald."

"And mine to you," the boy called back, patting the pouch at his hip before disappearing around the corner of the building.

Hall had known Fenrir would send men to recover his treasures, but he'd hoped to be ahead of them, not behind, in that search.

Turning back toward the stable, he filled his lungs once more with clean, fresh air and found himself scratching his own beard. Watching the filthy old man inside had made him feel as if bugs crawled on his skin, and he longed for the warm Viking bathhouse waiting for him at his home.

But such pleasures of the flesh would have to continue to wait. He had more important worries.

Before he reached the entrance, Patrick emerged, wiping a hand over his face, frustration evident in his expression.

"That one's either the greatest of fools or the cleverest of men I've yet to meet," Patrick growled, heading for his horse. "But whichever he is, he's by far the most foul-smelling of them all. I feel as though I've a layer of filth blanketing the whole of me and, worse still, absolutely nothing to show for it but a lighter purse and a passing knowledge of some fine, fine horse."

"Be of good cheer, my friend. We've plenty to show," Hall corrected. "While you visited with our filthy friend in there, I had myself a profitable chat with the stableboy, who confirmed that our young minstrel heads for Dunvegan."

"Then what are we waiting for?" Patrick grabbed the pommel of his saddle and fit his foot into his stirrup. "Skye it is."

"No." Hall stopped the other man with a hand to his reins. "Not for you, my friend. There's more. According to the boy, Torquil's men have a day's lead on us. With at least six of them on Mathew's trail, it will take more than the two of us, should we arrive too late."

Patrick hoisted himself into his saddle, nodding slowly. "You'll continue on, I suppose. While I return to Castle MacGahan for more men."

"That is the way I see it playing out best."

Hall hated dragging more men into this battle, but the one thing they simply could not afford was to allow the Elven Scrolls of Niflheim and the Sword of the Ancients to fall into Fenrir's possession.

Six

MEN WERE, WITHOUT any question, the most annoyingly arrogant creatures walking the land. And the most predictable.

"I've no changed my mind, little sister. My answer is still a resounding *no*. Yer to stay here, where you'll be safe."

Jamesy hadn't even waited for Brie to speak when she entered the stable. He'd jumped to his own conclusions and cut her off before she'd opened her mouth.

It was exactly as she'd expected he'd behave as he and the others prepared to ride out with Patrick in his quest to catch up with Halldor O'Donar.

"Ycr making a mistake. You need me with you." Though she was wasting her breath, she had no choice but to argue. Anything else would risk raising her brother's suspicions. He knew her too well.

"I said no," Jamesy insisted, softening his words with a hand to her shoulder. "What I need is for you to stay here and keep watch over Eleyne in case her cousin comes looking for her, as you claim he will. This is where you can be the most help to me."

He gave her his best smile, as if that settled everything. As if she would believe his nonsense about this being the best place for her. Here, left behind, while he ran off to stand with Halldor against the Beast's men.

Had he honestly thought she hadn't seen when Patrick had ridden into the bailey, his horse frothing with the effort of their hard ride? Had he thought she hadn't heard the impassioned arguments spilling out of their laird's solar just because she'd not been allowed to attend their meeting?

That exclusion in and of itself still rankled.

She set her lips in a tight grimace and met his gaze.

"I am no the least bit happy about this," she grumbled, drawing her traveling cloak close around her to ward off the chill of the morning. "I've every right to go with you."

"I ken you think that to be truth, little sister. But believe me, my way in this is the best."

It took every bit of willpower under her command for her to keep her mouth shut. It didn't matter what he said. Since her arguments were solely to allay his suspicions, there was no point in allowing herself to be upset by his reaction. All this was playing out exactly as she had expected it would.

"There's a good lass," Jamesy consoled, and after a quick hug he mounted his horse. "Take yer things back to yer rooms and dinna waste yer energy thinking upon any of this. Oh, and keep a close watch over the minstrel's cousin, aye?"

"I'll take care of my things once yer gone," she answered, following beside him as he made his way to join the others. "I'm headed to the wall walk first, to see you off."

Her brother's relief flashed in the smile he gave her as he joined his friends and the whole company of men headed out through the gate.

She raced up the narrow stairs to a visible spot at the wall and lifted her arm in a wave of farewell. Dutifully, she kept a smile pasted on her face until the group of men disappeared into the distance.

Men. Annoyingly arrogant, completely predictable, and, above all else, unbelievably gullible. It was one of the more valuable lessons her mother had taught her early in life.

And still her uncle had the lack of good sense to wonder why she didn't want a man of her own. Not for her. Not now, not ever. She had a much higher purpose in life than tending to the needs of some dullard.

As if to plague her, the memory of Halldor pulling her close to steal a kiss danced through her mind.

"Ha!" she huffed, smacking her hand against the stone hard enough for the sting to drive away the vision.

Of all the men she didn't want, most especially she did not want that one.

With the riders far enough away that she could

no longer see any trace of them, she hurried down from the wall walk, across the bailey and beyond, out to the small gate at the back of the castle grounds.

In Jamesy's haste to leave her behind, he'd never even noticed her horse was missing from the stable. Just as no one had noticed, in the midst of all the activity, when she'd saddled the animal and tethered him out near the back of the castle grounds.

Reins held loosely in her hand, she led her mount through the small gate and then secured it behind her before hoisting herself up into the saddle and trotting into the nearby woods.

Da had always claimed that the only thing that kept her from being Jamesy's equal as a warrior was her lack of patience and her inability to control her temper. What he hadn't counted on was her superior cunning and determination. Those traits more than made up for her small lapses of temper. Or so she consoled herself in those times when her temper got the best of her.

She traveled beside the main trail, keeping to the trees until she was far enough away from the castle to be out of danger of anyone spotting her.

Lucky for her she'd spent so much of her childhood on horseback trailing after her da. Once, when she was young, she'd even been all the way to Skye with him. The thought of again pitching across the waves on that pitiful excuse for a ferry did not appeal to her in the least, but she pushed those concerns away. That was a minor inconvenience she would deal with when the time came.

Her first priority was to catch up with Halldor O'Donar.

Finding him before the others did would be no challenge for her skills. Patrick MacDowylt was a fine warrior, but he thought in a straight line, just as her brother did. Though they'd refused her entry to their meeting, she'd listened in on them as they'd made their plans to follow the trails to the ferry that would carry them across the water to Skye.

Halldor, on the other hand, was a much more complicated thinker, more devious and cunning. She'd learned that much about him in the short time they'd spent together. He'd be keeping one eye out for the Beast as much as he would for Mathew. Especially now that he knew Torquil already had sent parties of men to find the boy.

If she were in Halldor's place, she'd figure the smart thing to do was to keep off the main trails, cutting cross-country in an attempt to catch up to the young minstrel before Torquil's men could. And if there was anything her time with Halldor had taught her about the big warrior, it was that he would do the smart thing.

Cross-country it was.

A trill of excitement blossomed low in her stomach and she pressed her heels against her horse's flesh, urging speed.

Very soon, she would once again be in her big warrior's company.

Seven

"STAY AWAY FROM me!" Mathew screamed, molding his body against the cold, hard walls of the shallow cave.

Sharp, jagged rocks dug into his back as he shrank down upon his haunches. Frantically he felt around on the ground, searching for a stone, a stick, anything he might use as a weapon against the hideous monster that advanced on him.

"Return to me what is mine!"

The demand echoed in his ears, beating at his mind. And all the while, the pulsing red eyes floated closer and closer.

What was this creature, this *thing*, that it could spike such panic in his heart and tighten his stomach in a knot of fear? It had no arms or legs to use against him, no visible way to hurt him, and yet his chest threatened to explode with his fear.

"Leave me be!" he shouted, tossing a handful of pebbles in the creature's direction.

Maniacal laughter emanated from the apparition

as the stones passed through the eyes, raining harmlessly to the ground beyond.

"What are you?" Mathew whispered.

As if in response to his question, the laughter grew louder and moved closer.

Mathew's fingers brushed against something warm and metallic and he tightened his grip around the hilt of his new sword. With a yell of triumph, he hoisted the weapon high into the air in front of him.

Instantly, the laughter ceased, and with an earth-shattering roar the glow of the monstrous red eyes blinked out and disappeared.

Mathew sat up with a start, the mysterious sword he'd stolen from Tordenet clutched tightly in his hand. His memory of the glowing red eyes clouded his vision. Perspiration slicked his face and body, and his arm trembled under the weight of the weapon as he fought to slow his racing heart.

"What are you?" he demanded aloud.

"Only Dobbie Caskie," a quavering voice answered. "And please, good sir, be so kind as to lower yer blade. I mean you no harm. As you can see for yerself, I dinna even carry a weapon of my own."

Shaking off the hazy vestiges of his nightmare, Mathew made out the form of a boy on the other side of his campsite, holding one of Mathew's bags of precious supplies open in his hands.

"You say you mean me no harm, but how am I to believe you when it's my possessions you steal," he accused, rising slowly to stand, the sword still held protectively in front of him.

"It's only food I seek and nothing more. I'm fair starved, I am."

The boy looked as if he could be telling the truth. Perhaps only a year or two younger than Mathew, this Dobbie character was thin as a rail and filthy enough that he could be living out here in the woods on his own.

"Put down my things. If hunger is all that drives you, there's food left from my evening meal in the pot by the fire. Yer welcome to that."

Dobbie dropped the bag he held and pounced on the pot, digging his first two fingers into the stale porridge to scoop it into his mouth.

Mathew sank down to sit on his blankets, unable to watch the boy's ravenous eating. He remembered all too well the pain of an empty stomach. After his father's death, when his uncle had seized Castle Glenluce, whether or not the MacFalny boys were fed was of little interest to the new laird.

This boy had all the markings of a runaway, just as Mathew had once been. Unlike this lad, he'd had the company of Hugo and Eleyne when he'd set off on his own. If not for Hugo's light-fingered gift for thievery, they all might have starved.

The memory of his brother brought a pang of loss stabbing through his heart, and a renewed conviction to find his cousin once he'd sold the treasures he carried.

Perhaps this boy shared his sense of loneliness and loss.

"What are you doing out here all alone, with no food or provisions?"

"I'm on my way to Skye," the boy answered, stopping to lick the sticky porridge from his fingers. "To my mam's folk, the MacCabes. Now that both my mam and da are gone, finding my way to my kin seemed the best thing to do. I had food with me in the beginning, but no enough to last the whole of my trip."

"Skye?" It was as if the hand of some benevolent god had dropped this boy into his path. "Will yer travels take you anywhere near the MacLeod stronghold?"

"Indeed they will," the boy confirmed, nodding vigorously as he scraped the last bits of porridge from the pot. "My uncle watches over the MacLeod's sheep. Dunvegan is exactly where I'm headed."

Fate had intervened on Mathew's behalf, sending this boy to guide him on his journey. Mathew clung to the knowledge like a lamb to the ewe's teat. He had to believe in it. Otherwise, he'd be left with nothing but the deep black worry that hung over him day and night.

"Dunvegan is my destination as well. If you'll agree to act as my guide, I'll share my provisions along the way to keep yer belly filled."

"Done!" Dobbie agreed, extending a dirty hand to shake. "And a fine deal you've struck, too, if I do say so myself. I ken the old man who ferries travelers across the water to Skye quite well and I'm sure I can get you his best rate for the crossing."

"Excellent!" Mathew tossed one of his blankets to the boy. "If you've finished eating, we should get some sleep now, aye? I'd have us make an early start in the morning."

Dobbie nodded and wrapped the blanket around himself before dropping down next to the fire. If the snores coming from his direction were any indication, the boy fell asleep almost as soon as his head touched the ground.

Mathew lay awake, staring up into the clear night sky, afraid to allow himself to fall back into the world of dreams where the hideous red-eyed monster lurked.

As he lay wide-eyed, waiting for sleep to find him, his brother's voice echoed in his thoughts.

Only a fool would trust anyone but his own self. No other will ever care for yer fate the same as you do.

His brother had lived by that motto.

"And where did that get you, Hugo?" Mathew's whispered question floated up into the dark, cold sky.

Dead—that's where it had gotten his brother. Dead, with his head thrown clear across the room from his body.

Whether or not Dobbie was a gift presented by the hand of Fate, Mathew planned to make good use of the boy. Having someone who actually knew his way to Dunvegan would save him time and effort and be well worth the expense of sharing his provisions.

To be truthful, having a living, breathing companion on the journey appealed to him, too.

Perhaps with Dobbie for company, the dark dreams that plagued him lately would cease their torment.

A yawn stretched his jaw and glassed over his vision, and for just an instant he could almost swear that two of those stars overhead glowed red, exactly like the eyes in his dream.

He rubbed his eyes with the heels of his hands, and when he looked again, the sky twinkled with only the stars that were supposed to be there.

Rolling to his side, Mathew hugged the sword close, remembering how in his dream it had been the sword that had chased the monster away. A guardian, it was, and such a weapon as this one deserved a fitting name.

Dream Guardian, he would call it, and with it at his side, he could face the world of dreams without fear. Perhaps it would even give him the courage to master the same control over his feelings in the waking world.

With one last glance up at the night sky, he forced himself not to think about who—or what—might be staring up at those same stars this night.

HALL LAY ON his back, staring up into a perfect night sky. On a cold, crisp evening such as this, the stars always seemed to sparkle much more brightly.

"Sleep," he commanded, watching his breath curl up into the air over his face as he spoke.

His body ignored the command, his thoughts flittering around like the stars twinkling over his head.

He squeezed his eyes shut, as if by sheer force of will he could transport himself into Nott's domain. But, try as he might, sleep eluded him.

He mulled over the track he'd taken so far. Cutting cross-country rather than following well-traveled trails should put him ahead of his quarry and all those who followed the boy.

Assuming Torquil's men hadn't thought to do just as he was doing. His hope was that they didn't know the back country as well as he did. There were some advantages to all his years spent serving Thor.

He knew of only a few places where Mathew could easily cross over the narrows of Loch Alsh to reach the island of clouds. There was an old man who made his living ferrying people back and forth across the waters. Likely everyone making this journey knew of the man.

As Hall saw things, he had two choices going forward. He could head for the old man and wait, hoping his luck would hold, or he could travel as he had for one more day and then cut over to the established trails, hoping to intercept Mathew.

Either way, hope was all he had to go on.

He scrubbed his hands over his face, drawing his fingers down into his beard for a good scratch. Lo, but he'd let himself become a ragged, scraggly mess over the past few years.

What was it Bridget had called him? *A great bristly-faced ogre.* He could almost hear her voice shouting the epithet at him like a curse. Not that her name-calling bothered him. It didn't. What she or any other woman thought of him was of no consequence.

His beard, on the other hand, had begun to bother him considerably.

With a resigned sigh, he sat up and reached for one of his bags. Since it didn't appear as though he was destined to get any sleep tonight, he might as well make good use of the time.

After filling a small wooden bowl with water, he pulled out a silver razor and set to work on the arduous task of removing his beard. Once he was done, he ran his fingers over his irritated skin, satisfied with his accomplishment.

He only hoped his current discomfort would be worth the look on Bridget's face when next they met. Not that he'd shaved for her. Absolutely not. He wouldn't do such a thing for any woman. No, it was standing next to that filthy stable keeper in Inverness that had convinced him to remove his whiskers. Odin himself only knew what vermin might have crawled off the old man and onto him. Without a decent bathhouse to be found for miles, it was little wonder his beard had itched.

Though he wasn't at all sure the constant itching

hadn't been preferable to the raw burn stinging his freshly shaven skin.

What he wouldn't give for a strong tisane of marigold and Jupiter's Beard to sooth the sting. But out here, in the dead of winter, he might as well wish for a pot of fresh, warm lard to slather over his face. The only thing he could do was try again to rest and put the pain out of his mind.

This time when he lay down and closed his eyes, sleep quickly encroached on the boundaries of consciousness, freeing his thoughts to drift like leaves caught in a blustery current.

Scenes flittered through his mind as he balanced on the razor-thin line separating the waking world from the sleeping one, changing so quickly he had no time to consider whether they were memories or fantasies. A setting sun painted the sky a blistering red. The sea's angry waves crashed up onto the shore. And Bridget MacCulloch, feet bare, twirled in time to the beat of an ancient drum, her body lithely twisting as if in some magnificent battle dance.

Hall toppled over the edge into sleep, a smile drifting through his mind, confident that the next time his path crossed that of the lovely Pictish Shield Maiden, she'd have to find a new epithet to hurl after him.

Eight

"WE'D REACH THE ferryman much sooner if you'd but agree to travel off the main trail." Dobbie flashed an encouraging smile and directed his steps toward the trees. "It's a much shorter distance this way."

"No." Mathew kept his gaze fastened on the path ahead. "We'll stay our course along these roads."

"Yer choice, of course," Dobbie murmured, returning to Mathew's side. Though he said the proper words, he bowed his head as if to hide his true feelings about the decision.

Mathew didn't need to see the boy's eyes. He'd witnessed the cunning expression on Dobbie's face often enough over the past two days they'd traveled together. And the premonition that overtook him each time his thoughts drifted to his traveling companion was ample warning to keep him on his guard.

Though he couldn't put a name to it, he knew Dobbie Caskie was not quite what he seemed.

Mathew couldn't always depend upon those odd

warnings coming to him, but when they did, they'd rarely been wrong. He'd had one the night his father had been killed, and again when he'd entered Tordenet Castle with Hugo.

And Hugo had ended up torn to pieces.

It was one of those feelings today that kept him on the road. An odd twitching of the skin on the back of his neck. A tingling in his feet, as if his body desperately wanted to take flight. An emptiness in the pit of his stomach that no amount of food could drive away. Either something waited for them out there in the woods, or . . .

Mathew huffed out a breath of annoyance. It was likely nothing more than the horrible dreams that had plagued him. They shattered his rest, leaving him as exhausted when he awoke as he'd been when he'd closed his eyes the night before. They'd haunted him since the day he'd walked into the MacDowylt's solar and found the body of his older brother Hugo with his head ripped from his shoulders.

With a shudder, Mathew forced the vision from his thoughts, willing himself to forget the grisly scene. He didn't ever want to see such as that again, not even in his memories. Perhaps when he rid himself of the scrolls, the dreams would be gone as well.

Mathew fingered the hilt of the weapon he wore slung across his chest. His dreams might be plagued by vicious threats from invisible foes, but as long as he kept Dream Guardian close, the hideous red eyes at least kept their distance.

"Wonder what *he's* up to?" Dobbie craned his neck, peering off into the distance, bringing Mathew back to the here and now.

Ahead of them, a horse and rider blocked the trail.

"He's new to these parts," Dobbie murmured. "I dinna think I've ever seen him before."

Dobbie might not have seen him before, but Mathew had. At Tordenet. The man was one of Laird MacDowylt's warriors. And not just any ordinary warrior, but clearly a favorite of the laird.

He was also one of the two men who'd visited the Tinkler camp the day before they'd suddenly packed up their wagons and left Tordenet with Bridget Mac-Culloch as a secret passenger.

Whether the big man waited on the trail ahead to seek his revenge because Hugo had returned to Tordenet to warn the MacDowylt of the MacCulloch woman's escape, or because of the items Mathew had taken from the castle, Mathew felt sure his being there couldn't be a good thing.

He considered turning back on the path, but the feelings that had warned him out of the forest were doubly strong from the direction he'd already traveled.

"Best you let me handle this," Dobbie whispered. "I've a way with strangers, just you watch."

"As you wish."

Mathew doubted Dobbie's ability to "handle" the big warrior, but perhaps the boy's intervention might give him time to steal away if it became necessary. Slowly, he reached to his saddle and untied one of the bags he carried there. He slipped the leather strings over his shoulder and let the bag nestle against his back. No time to remove the one from the other side. They were too close for him to make the change without his actions being obvious.

"Aho," Dobbie called as they drew close enough to clearly make out the features on the big man's face. "A fair gift it is to see a fellow traveler on the road! I'm Dobbie Caskie and this is Master MacFalny."

The churning in Mathew's stomach grew stronger, along with his need to climb up into the saddle of his horse and ride for all he was worth in the opposite direction. But that would be foolish. The animal he led beside him would be no match for the mighty black warhorse waiting ahead of them. The best he could hope for was a chance to make his way to the other side of his mount to retrieve the second bag.

"I know who you are, Dobbie Caskie. And I know what you've done. I believe you have a horse that belongs to a friend of mine. And you, young Mathew MacFalny"—the big man turned his piercing blue gaze toward Mathew—"you've taken something much more dangerous than another man's horse."

So it was the treasure that had led MacDowylt's man to find him.

"Be on your way, warrior," Mathew ordered, the cracking of his voice belying his fear. "I've taken nothing from Tordenet Castle that dinna belong to me."

"No?" The big man laughed and lifted a hand to point in Mathew's direction. "Did I make any mention of Tordenet? Don't be foolish, boy. Next you'll be telling me that sword you wear across your heart is your own."

Mathew's fingers tightened around Dream Guardian's hilt. It *was* his own. This sword was all that stood between him and the evil that stalked his dreams. He'd never give it up.

HALL COULD SEE why Bridget had expressed concern for Mathew. He was a gangly lad, all long arms and legs, as much a boy as Dobbie Caskie.

Both he and Dobbie appeared ready to bolt at any second, and that would do Hall no good at all.

Hall continued to move forward, holding his horse to a slow and measured step. He didn't wish to harm either of the boys, though he'd dearly love to bring the Caskie lad back to Castle MacGahan, to answer to Eric for the animal he'd stolen. Still, should they break and run, it was Mathew and the sword strapped to his chest that Hall would follow.

He was within one horse's length when he heard the pounding upon the earth.

Hoofbeats. Four horses, he guessed, from the sound of it. Riding hard, headed in this direction. Only the distraction of the boys had kept him from recognizing the sound much earlier.

"Off the road!" he ordered, and Dobbie dove for the cover of the trees, needing no further encouragement.

Mathew froze where he stood, his eyes rounded with his fear.

"By the gods! Move, boy!"

Hall reined his horse in front of Mathew, placing himself in between the boy and the approaching men. Four riders, just as he'd thought. Torquil's men, from the looks of them, charging forward at full gallop, swords drawn.

Poorly trained, the lot of them, to Hall's way of thinking. They strung themselves out one after another with long gaps in between them rather than forming a close, tight line to ride against him. That was a mistake for which they'd pay.

"If it's a battle you want," Hall murmured, dodging to his left as he lifted his arm to deflect the first man's sword with the flat of his blade. Only a glancing blow. He instantly recovered and twirled his weapon overhead, bringing the edge of his sword crashing down to catch his opponent across the back of his neck.

The man's head lolled forward as his horse kept running and Hall gave him no more thought, his attention already intent upon the next two men drawing close.

To his side, he caught sight of Mathew moving forward. The boy gripped the Sword of the Ancients with both hands, obviously struggling with its weight to hold it out in front of him.

"Get back," Hall barked. "Keep low and out of range."

The second man attacked, his sword meeting Hall's with a ring of steel.

His blade would be dulled after this, but he had little choice. His shield was of no use to him, hanging where he'd tied it, covering his mount's left flank.

The boy beside him yelled and fell backward as Hall's opponent's horse swung his head in Mathew's direction. Hall turned in his saddle to see that Mathew was unharmed and, momentarily distracted, very nearly missed blocking the next attack.

The blow caught him high, driving his blade back toward his head and knocking him from his saddle. He landed in a squat and surged to his feet, collecting his wits as the two closest riders circled, one coming at him from either direction.

They might be poorly trained, but they were quick learners, having changed their tactic after seeing their companion's demise.

"Surrender the thief to us," one of them ordered, his voice mechanical and without emotion. "Or die with him."

"I think not," Hall countered, and reached out to grasp the leather thong securing his shield. One quick twist and the lashing gave way, dropping the shield into his grasp.

Let them come now. Two puny men, even on horseback, were hardly a match for Hall O'Donar.

He roared his challenge as they descended upon him and, lifting his shield high for cover, he slashed up at the closest man. His weapon struck home, slicing into muscle and sinew as the rider screamed and fell from his mount. One downward thrust and only two opponents remained, one headed toward him, one hanging back.

Once again, based on what they'd seen, they'd changed their battle tactic.

Hall waited until the last possible second to evade his attacker's charge, bringing his weapon down in a mighty arc as he twirled out of the warrior's path. His sword severed flesh and bone below the man's knee. In response to the mercenary's screams, his mount reared and unseated him, throwing him to the ground at Hall's feet. Even wounded as he was, the soldier swung his sword toward Hall like a man possessed, driving Hall backward a step before he lunged in. From the corner of his eye, he noted the last man starting toward him as he made quick work of the soldier on the ground.

Beside him, Mathew rushed forward, roaring in a pale imitation of Hall's challenge, his voice cracking, as is the bane of many a young man.

Before Hall could order the boy back, he felt the air around him thicken and heard an unusual sound he knew to be metal slicing through the solid air.

The sword in Mathew's hands, so precariously

held, swiped against Hall's arm, slicing through the cloth of his shirt to graze along the skin of his shoulder.

Only a scratch and yet it took him to his knees as the pain of a thousand fires consumed his shoulder and a great roaring filled his ears.

Only a scratch.

Unable to believe his own eyes, Hall looked up from the thin red line of the wound to the boy.

Mathew clasped the sword to his chest and clamped one hand over his ears, a look of horror distorting his features. When the boy turned to run, Hall realized the world around him had slowed, stretching out, as if time itself had turned to deep water.

"Not so brave now, are you, big man?"

Hall swung his head back around to find the last of Torquil's men walking toward him.

"You should have left when we warned you. But, no, you had to involve yerself where you had no business being. And now what do you have to show for yer mischief, eh?"

Like the rest of his body, Hall's lips refused to work. He could produce no sound other than a weak grunt.

"I'll tell you what you've got. You've got yerself killed, that's what. Perhaps in yer next life, you'll have learned to mind yer own business and do as yer told."

Unable to move, Hall prepared himself for what

was to come as the warrior drew back his sword, waiting for the sound of metal striking bone to send him to his reward in Valhalla.

Instead, a whining *zing* filled his ears, like some giant summer midge headed in his direction. When he managed to lift his gaze, his attacker teetered over him, eyes vacant. A single trail of blood trickled down between his eyes from a spot on his forehead where a large metal point protruded.

The lifeless body toppled over backward, leaving Hall a clear view of the trail beyond. What he saw set his heart wildly pounding.

The beautiful Valkyrie charging toward him could mean only one of two things: Either the sword that struck him had been tipped with poison and he was hallucinating or, more likely, he was already dead and the Valkyrie rode to carry him to his just reward in Valhalla.

Nine

BOLLOCKS!"

Brie had spent the better part of the last week fantasizing about how events might play out when she finally caught up with Halldor O'Donar.

This little scene had been nowhere in any of those fantasies. Halldor on his knees like some helpless puppy, waiting for that great grinning bastard who loomed over him to lop his head off.

Not on her watch.

She and her bow had made easy enough work of that one. But Halldor remained on his knees, slumped to the ground.

No, no, no! If he thought he could simply up and die on her, after she'd gone to all this trouble to find him, he'd better just think again. She was having none of that.

Brie jumped from her horse the instant she reached him and shoved the body of the man she'd shot to one side before she kneeled to capture Halldor's cheeks in her hands.

"O'Donar? Can you hear me?"

He blinked repeatedly, as if trying to focus his vision, and grunted something she couldn't understand.

"Where are you wounded?" she demanded, running her hands over his broad chest and down his arms.

From the looks of his condition, she didn't have time for a guessing game, but the only thing she could find was one small scratch high on his arm where his tunic had been sliced open.

"Answer me, O'Donar! What have they done to you? Where are you hurt?"

No blood on his clothing, no blood on the ground. Well, none of *his* blood on the ground, though she couldn't say as much for his opponents.

She grabbed his shoulders and shook until he swung his head back and forth, yet still his eyes continued their slow, confused blinking.

"Not Valkyrie," he slurred, his voice sounding raw.

"Valkyrie? Me?" She shook her head, capturing his face with her hands again cupping his cheeks. "Hardly. It's naught but Brie MacCulloch who sits before you now. Have you forgotten?"

What in the name of the Seven had those bastards done to him? Her great, strong warrior, reduced to a grunting half-wit.

"No," he whispered, closing his eyes. "Not Brie."

Whether he rejected the idea of her coming to his

aid or simply didn't recognize her, she couldn't say. She almost hoped it was the latter.

"Look at me," she ordered, giving him another gentle shake. "Do you no ken who I am? Surely you canna have forgotten Bridget MacCulloch so soon."

This time when his eyes opened, recognition shone in them. "A brainless question, that," he muttered on a deep sigh. "Help me to my feet."

He laid an arm over her shoulder and she struggled to help him stand. How could she have forgotten what a big man he was? She towered over most men, yet next to this one, she felt almost dainty.

Together, they managed to get to a large tree where he leaned against the trunk, breathing heavily as if he'd run a great distance.

She was more than a little winded herself.

"What's happened to you, to leave you so weak? I canna find a wound of any consequence upon yer body."

"It's of no matter," he responded, scanning the area around them. "Did you see which way the lads went?"

"Lads? I saw none but the men on the ground as I approached. Them and that grinning fool who thought to take yer head."

"Ah, yes." He glanced toward the fallen warrior as something of a smile curved his lips. "Then it would be your arrow that brought him down. It would seem that I am in your debt, my lady."

Staring at him, she realized with a shock that his beard was gone, his face clean-shaven and ruddy with cold. And that smile! With no whiskers to conceal it, the expression transformed him in a way that made her breath catch oddly in her chest.

"You owe me nothing," she managed at last, clearing her throat to cover her confusion while she looked away to gather her wits. "Consider it my payment for yer help at Tordenet. We're even now."

He grunted and she glanced back up at him, to find him trying to push away from the tree.

"Stay where you are for a bit. Get yer legs well under you. And while yer about it, perhaps you can answer my questions. What lads were you speaking of, and what has happened to you?"

He remained where he was, his cheeks drained white from his exertion. "I found Mathew. Seems he's joined company with another young man. One of rather ill repute, I fear. And as to what's happened to me . . ." He glanced to the small cut on his shoulder, pulling aside the cloth of his tunic to inspect the wound. "The Sword of the Ancients has happened to me."

"Mathew did this to you? He attacked you?" She could not bring herself to imagine sweet, gentle Mathew harming Halldor—or anyone else for that matter.

"I don't believe it was his intention. I think he meant to help me fight these men, but the sword was more than he could control."

Brie leaned into Hall, brushing aside his hand so that she could better see the wound for herself. It was small, but it appeared red and swollen, as if infection had already set in.

"We need to do something with this. I dinna think I've seen a wound go bad so quickly. And never in one so insignificant as this."

Halldor leaned back against the tree, allowing his eyes to close for a moment. "A wound from the Sword of the Ancients is hardly insignificant. It's fatal. It's betony and yarrow I need now. Agrimony and vervain. Perhaps even a pinch or two of joy-of-the ground."

"Herbs?" Brie choked out, Halldor's calm pronouncement ringing in her ears.

He had to be wrong. She wouldn't accept his having been struck with a fatal blow, not even from a weapon as mysterious as the Sword of the Ancients.

There had to be something she could do to slow the progress of whatever evil the sword had left upon his body.

"Honey smeared over the opening would do more good than yer weeds. If only we weren't caught in the dead of winter, I might find an active hive."

"If we weren't caught in the dead of winter, I'd have my herbs."

Wishing for the impossible wasn't going to do a bit of good, so she'd have to make do with what she carried in her provisions. She might not have honey, but she did have the next best thing.

Brie hurried over to her horse and dug through her pack of supplies to find the flask she sought. Returning to Hall's side, she pulled out the stopper and poured a bit of the contents onto his wound.

His eyes flew open and he jerked away from her, sniffing the air. "Mead? I'd be better off to have that inside my body rather than poured upon it. At least drinking it might afford me some relief."

"Honey ale," she corrected, turning her concentration to his shoulder.

With her tongue pressed against her teeth, she made a *tsk*ing noise, and pressed a tentative finger to the wound. The opening seemed to sizzle as if she'd poured the ale into a hot pan.

One thing was clear to her.

"This is beyond my abilities." She waited for his sarcastic response, but none came. Apparently he agreed. "We need to get you back to Castle MacGahan."

"Eventually," he said, pushing away from the tree to stand on his own two feet for the first time. "But first we need to see if our young friend left anything behind. Ah, I see he's abandoned his fine, fine steed."

Hall's strength might be returning but his good sense had taken its leave. Brie shook her head as Halldor slowly made his way across the opening to the worst example of horseflesh she'd ever seen. Not even old Cook would be seen on such a pitiful excuse for a horse.

Halldor unlaced the bag tied to the saddle and

poked around inside, turning a worried frown in her direction as she reached his side.

"The sword and the scrolls have escaped our grasp, but not the jewels. All the jewels are here, save for the one I already carry."

That was excellent news, but to look at the big man next to her, she'd never have guessed it. "I'd think you'd be happy to retrieve at least part of what you set out to find."

"You don't understand," he said. "The jewels serve as a guard upon the sword and the scrolls. A barrier to control their power, like guards around a prison. Without the jewels, there's no telling what mischief their evil can cause."

Explanation enough for his frown.

He reached for the palfrey's reins and headed toward his own mount, stumbling halfway there.

Brie was at his side in an instant, dipping her shoulder once again under his arm, ignoring him when he tried to push her away.

"There's no dishonor in accepting assistance from an ally."

A trace of his earlier smile reappeared when he looked down at her, bringing with it the odd tightening in her chest.

"Wise words, little one," he said at last. "I'll try to remember them. I'd be grateful for your assistance so that we might be on our way."

"Good." This new, reasonable O'Donar was quite the surprise. "Yer sure you can ride?"

"I can ride. We've wasted more than enough time here."

They had indeed. She needed to get him home, where someone could deal with his baffling injury.

He swung up into his saddle with only one short pause and urged his horse onto the trail, heading west.

"Hold on," Brie called as she finished tying the lead for Mathew's horse behind hers and mounted. "Where do you think yer going? MacGahan lies in the other direction."

"Mathew is on foot. If we put ourselves to it and scour the woods, we can catch up with him. Maybe even before nightfall."

The old O'Donar had returned. Stubborn, stubborn man.

Brie grabbed his reins as she reached his side, pulling them from his hands. That, as much as anything, convinced her that his strength had not really returned. And if that tiny cut on his shoulder could rob a man such as Halldor O'Donar of his strength, she could only imagine what else it might do to him if they didn't seek the help of a healer. His prediction of *fatal* could well be accurate.

"There are men from MacGahan on the trail as we speak, headed to this very spot. We'll no doubt cross their path as we return."

"We aren't going to—"

"Do you remember saying to me that I should try, for once, to do as I was told without a blighted argument? Well, I'd give that same advice to you now. Yer in no shape to win such an argument. Not with me or anyone else." Brie tugged on the reins she held to emphasize her point. "Besides, what good would it do you to reach Mathew and the weapon if you've got no strength to take it from him? We need to get you back home. To get you to a healer."

She knew she'd won when his shoulders slumped and he stared into the distance.

"As you say," he sighed. "I cannot fight you on this. But I suspect there's none that can heal what ails me."

Brie handed back his reins and pulled her horse up next to his, refusing to accept what he said. By the Seven, she would not give up on him so easily.

THEY RODE IN the wrong direction.

It hung in Hall's craw, gnawing at his guts like a diseased worm. He'd been so close. He could have taken the sword from boy but he'd chosen to protect him first, planning to reason with him after. His failure lay bitter in his mouth.

"Bah!"

"What's that you say?"

Bridget pulled her horse closer to his and reached out a hand to brush his forehead with her fingertips. He ducked away, too slow in his movements to effectively avoid her touch.

He needed to think clearly and her touch had the uncomfortable effect of muddling his thoughts.

"Move away from me if you like, but it does yer argument no good. I can see the fever in the color of your face."

As if he needed her to tell him he had a fever. The burn spread out from his arm to consume his whole body, like a dry forest under siege of wildfire.

"We should have stayed on the sword's trail," he muttered, knowing she would hear and take the bait. Anything to distract her from her constant hovering. He could deal with her irritation; it was this tender worry that drove him to distraction.

"There's no point in yer wasting yer breath on it, O'Donar. That discussion ended miles back down the road."

"I'd reopen it, then. I'm feeling better now."

A truth, more or less. Though he had little hope of recovery, he did feel much stronger than he had immediately after his injury.

"Oh, of course you are." As if sarcasm hadn't hung heavily enough in her tone, her accompanying snort clearly carried her opinion. "If yer so much better, then answer me this. Why is it that yer clearly burning with the fever? The way you felt to my touch, we'll no even need to build ourselves a fire this night. We'll just heat our meal by holding it close to yer skin."

The chuckle rumbled up from deep in his chest and out into the open, beyond his ability to stop it. Damn, but the woman lightened his spirit, even when she was angry.

"You think any of this is funny? This is *not* funny. It's damned deadly serious."

Perhaps most of all when she was angry.

"You're correct. Our situation is no laughing matter." He allowed a moment to pass before he circled back to the conversation she wouldn't like. "But neither can we continue to ignore that which is most important. We must have the sword and the scrolls. We cannot allow them to fall into the wrong hands. And while we bicker, they travel farther away from us with each step we take."

She shook her head, stubbornly refusing to look over at him. "No. I'll hear none of it. Any moment now, we'll cross paths with Patrick and Jamesy and all the others. We'll tell them what happened and they can go after the sword. We've a more important challenge ahead of us. You put yer mind to yer healing."

The men from Castle MacGahan were not nearly so close as Bridget hoped. He'd been listening for them to no avail for quite some time. Them and the other party of riders Torquil had sent out.

"By the time they could reach the sword, it might well be too late." He breathed deeply before forcing himself to confess his darkest distress. "How can I make you understand, Bridget? I need to go after it myself. It was within my reach and I let it escape me. How am I to go forward, knowing that?"

Beside him, Bridget jerked on her reins, stopping her horse to turn a powerful glare in his direction.

"You go forward exactly as I have. Do you think yer the only one to carry regrets on yer shoulders? I not only allowed the sword to slip through my fingers, I missed the opportunity to kill the Beast who owns it. Twice."

"That's different." She'd had no way of knowing what the sword—or Torquil, for that matter—was capable of. And when she'd tried to kill him, she'd very nearly ended up dead herself.

"*Different?* And exactly how is my failure any different from yers?" she ranted, holding up a hand to silence him before he could answer, anger flashing in her eyes. "No. Dinna you even bother to answer that. I'll hear no more from that bucket of cold slop you men are determined to serve me."

She'd completely misunderstood him, but there was no reining her in now.

"Here's the way I see our predicament, O'Donar. We could turn around and follow the sword and wait for you to die along the way. But since I'm no willing to drag yer sorry dead arse back to Castle MacGahan, that's no going to happen. So that leaves us with only two viable choices. We can continue in this direction and hope to find help before you keel over, or I can go after the sword and you can continue on without me. You choose."

Let her go back to confront Mathew and the inevitable reinforcements Torquil would send to reclaim the weapon? Never. The fact that she was right made his options no less bitter to swallow.

"Presented as such, I can see I have no choice at all."

"And about damned time you realized that, too."

With a jerk to her reins, Bridget set her animal in motion and he followed suit. His only hope lay in a small band of men supposedly heading in their direction.

He tilted his head, straining to hear far into the distance, praying that if he did hear riders it would be the men from MacGahan, and not those Torquil had sent.

There was no band of riders within his hearing, but something else lay ahead of them. A familiar tinkling sound he recognized immediately.

By Hela! Even approaching his end, he couldn't escape the damned Fae.

Ten

"AARGH!"

Torquil covered his eyes and stumbled away from the fireplace, gasping for air. There were few things he disliked more than being in a mortal's psyche at the moment of death. It was a disorienting jolt like no other.

"So close," he moaned, sagging into the nearest chair.

His sword had been there in the clearing, almost within his reach. He'd seen it with his own two eyes. Rather, he'd seen it through the guardsman's eyes.

The scrolls must have been there, too. If not for the big warrior, he would have had them all.

There was something familiar about the big man, as if he'd seen him before. No doubt he and Torquil had crossed paths at some point before Fenrir had taken full control of this body's consciousness.

What had happened to his foolish guardsman, anyway? He'd watched through the man's eyes as his companions had been cut down. He'd seen the big warrior drop to his knees and the youth wielding his sword run away. He'd felt his guardsman's gleeful anticipation as the fool prepared to take the big man's head.

And then, without warning, a blinding flash of light and intense pain, followed by the all-consuming darkness of death, had driven him from the man's mind.

Foolish, careless mortal. He had allowed himself to be so consumed by his own plans, he'd forgotten to watch for what others might be planning.

Torquil sighed, rubbing his fingers against his eyes to clear his vision. He had long known these pathetic beings were incompetent. It was for that reason he had sent more than one hunting party.

As soon as this weak body he inhabited recovered from the experience, he would seek out one of the others. It was the only way for him to direct their progress in securing the treasures. Without them, and the jewels to control them, his freedom, his very existence, was in danger.

Eleven

"S OMEONE'S COMING!"

Relief jolted through Brie's chest as she stared down the path. At last they'd found someone, even though it wasn't her brother's party, as she'd hoped. She leaned forward in her saddle, straining to see who approached them. "Is that . . . ?"

"It's the Tinklers," Halldor answered flatly, sounding resigned.

Even better, to her way of thinking. She understood that many people looked down on the Tinklers and considered them little better than thieves and whores, but she'd assumed Halldor was more open-minded and less judgmental than that. It bothered her more than she would have expected to realize that she might have been so mistaken about his character.

The Tinklers had been good to her. And they seemed to know more about the oddities of her world than anyone she'd ever met. So in spite of Halldor's bad attitude, if anyone would be able to help him, Brie had not one doubt that it would be Editha Faas.

"Hurry," she ordered, urging her mount to a trot to more quickly close the distance between them.

"Welcome back to us!" William Faas called, drawing his wagon to a stop only seconds before his wife, Editha, hopped to the ground.

The Tinkler ran past Brie as if she didn't exist.

"Come down from there and show me what's happened to you," she ordered as she stopped beside Halldor's horse.

Brie turned to study her companion more closely. Had something in the way he carried himself on the horse given away his distress? There was nothing she could see, but in all honesty she didn't really care how the woman knew Halldor had been injured. She cared only about curing what ailed him.

"It's only a small wound," she offered as Halldor climbed down off his horse. "But it's gone to infection wickedly fast."

Halldor dropped the fur he wore at his feet and kneeled in front of the Tinkler woman so that she could examine the wound for herself.

Editha's expression spoke of things Brie suspected she didn't want to hear.

"*Wicked* is an apt description," Editha murmured, poking at the wound while Halldor gritted his teeth. "I've seen its like only once before, and I know yer circumstances are not the same. What manner of thing has done this to you?"

When Halldor didn't answer quickly enough, Brie spoke up. "The weapon is called the Sword of the Ancients. But it passes my understanding how it could affect him so badly, since its blade barely grazed his skin."

A tiny scratch of a cut. A wound that should have all but healed itself by now.

Editha looked up, a momentary flash of surprise on her face before she masked the emotion. "Is this true?" she asked Halldor. "The Sword of the Ancients?"

He nodded, his gaze fixed upon the Tinkler's.

"How is it possible for the sword to have . . ." Editha's voice trailed off as both she and Halldor continued to stare at one another. "I see. I should have known. How, then, is it that yer still alive?"

"You should have known what?" Brie asked. "What's going on here?"

Both of them ignored her.

"I suspect it has to do with the jewels I carry."

Brie moved closer in an effort to hear the conversation, her patience wearing thin with the quiet back-and-forth. The Tinkler needed to do something for Halldor and she needed to do it quickly.

"Can you no help him, Editha? Surely you have a poultice or a salve to heal a wound such as this."

The Tinklers were known far and wide for the herbs and tinctures they supplied to which no others had access. It couldn't be possible that they didn't have something to help Halldor. Brie simply wouldn't accept that.

"It is an ancient *seid*, a very old dark magic, that

afflicts our warrior friend. Its power is too strong by far for my healing skills." Editha slowly shook her head. "The best I can hope to do is to delay the inevitable. He needs a far more powerful healer than I. One born to the talent. And he needs her soon, by the looks of the wound."

"There is one who might help him at MacQuarrie Keep." William spoke from behind Brie, having approached silently.

"No." Editha responded with finality. "He canna go there for help. She's no yet ready for such a step. Besides, her destiny is already written. I think only Orabilis can help him now."

At last, they were saying something Brie understood. "The witch of Rowan Cottage? Should I take him there?"

"No!" Halldor shook his head like a wounded bull about to charge. "Bridget cannot be allowed anywhere near Tordenet again. You know it's a death sentence for her if she falls into Torquil's hands."

For once, Brie agreed with Halldor. Anywhere near Tordenet was the last place she'd choose to go until she had recovered the sword. Then she'd be ready to take her revenge on the monster who had murdered her father. Unfortunately, it sounded as if the choice was not hers to make.

"Torquil and his intent for me are of little importance. If that's the only place to seek healing for O'Donar, then that's where we'll go."

"No," Halldor said again, attempting to rise to his feet, but Editha held him where he was with one delicate hand to his wounded shoulder.

"In that case, I'll do what I can to help him get there. Bring me water and bandages," the Tinkler ordered, and her husband hurried back toward their wagon. "And you, Halldor O'Donar, I'd have those jewels of which you spoke."

"Wait!" Brie could hardly believe her ears. According to Halldor, the jewels were as necessary to their quest as the sword itself. He'd told her the jewels must be reunited with the sword to rein in its power. Giving them to the Tinklers was out of the question. "There must be some other payment you'd accept."

"Bah! Dinna you be so foolish, lassie." Editha's eyebrows knit together into a straight, dark, disapproving line. "I've no desire for payment. I need the gems to bind the evil within his wound."

"Oh."

Brie's face flamed with her embarrassment as she silently berated herself for sinking to all the closed-minded judgment she'd heaped at Halldor's feet such a short time ago. She was every bit as bad as he was. Worse, in fact, because she'd convinced herself that she had no prejudices, and yet, at the very first opportunity, she had jumped to the wrong conclusion about the people who had risked so much to help her when she needed their help.

More proof, as if she required it, that her father had been right. Her lack of patience and hasty judgment made *her* her own worst enemy.

"Bridget!"

Brie's head snapped up, her attention refocused on the scene before her.

"I need you out here with us, lass, no drawn deep inside yer own thoughts. Listen to me well. Should the bandage need redressing before you reach Rowan Cottage, there'll be none but you to do it, aye? You must pay attention to the proper way."

Brie nodded and sank to her knees next to the Tinkler. Though why the woman seemed to think dressing a wound was so complicated was beyond her understanding. A bandage was a bandage.

"Watch carefully," Editha instructed, pointing to the ground in front of her, where a long strip of folded linen lay with the jewels tucked in between the layers of the cloth.

"You'll line the stones up, just so," she said, working through the linen to straighten the stones next to one another like little soldiers standing at attention. "You'll want to make sure you dinna touch them with yer bare hands. You must ensure that the five of them are kept close together at all times with the linen drawn over them. To do otherwise could give Fenrir a clear view of everything around the jewels."

"Fenrir?"

"The Beast that inhabits Torquil's body. An ancient being of immense evil."

A shudder crawled down Brie's spine and she drew back a little, uncomfortable with her nearness to the stones. She'd known they were powerful, but she'd had no idea just how powerful they actually were. Neither had she understood how direct their connection to the Beast could be.

"You'll want to make sure the center stone is directly over the wound," Editha continued. "Come. Watch."

As Brie leaned in close, she could feel the heat rolling off Halldor's fevered skin. The wound had puckered, the skin red and heated. Small gray bubbles formed along the line of the opening, tumbling out over one another like ants escaping a hill, battling for their release from the confines of his skin.

Editha laid the cloth over the wound and Halldor sucked air into his lungs as if he fought off some great pain.

Unable to stop herself, Brie reached for his hand, holding on as his grip tightened around her fingers.

"And you tie it, just so. You see? Twice around and tie it again. You can do this, yes? Yes." Editha answered her own question, nodding to herself as she rose to her feet and brushed her hands off on the long folds of her brightly colored skirt.

Halldor squeezed Brie's hand and then released his hold, pushing himself up to stand and offering a hand to assist Brie. Already the normal skin tone had returned to his face and he seemed steadier on his feet.

"Excellent work, my lady Tinkler." He bowed his

head respectfully before turning to catch up his horse's reins. "I feel well enough to return to our hunt for—"

"Three days at most," Editha cut in. "Time to reach Rowan Cottage if you hurry, but nothing more."

"Reclaiming the sword is more important than what might happen to me."

"No!" Brie's cry overshadowed the Tinkler's.

"You are wrong, Halldor O'Donar." Editha pointed a finger in his direction, her voice taking on a musical quality Brie hadn't heard before. "You must live. Perhaps you forget that you are indebted to me—and not even death frees you from a debt owed the Fae."

The Fae? Brie had no time to consider Editha's startling revelation or Halldor's apparent lack of surprise at the Tinkler's words.

He ran his free hand down over his mouth and chin as if he'd forgotten his beard was no longer there. "Even if I go along as you say, the protections set at Rowan Cottage will prevent my entry. We both know that."

"Bridget will gain your entry," Editha responded. "Trust in her."

The Tinkler was correct—Halldor should trust her. By the Seven, nothing would keep her from getting him the help he needed. Not Torquil, not this creature Fenrir, and certainly not the big, stubborn warrior standing beside her.

Twelve

THE DIFFERENCE IN how his shoulder felt since the Tinkler had bandaged him was amazing. Hall could still feel the evil seething just under the skin, but not as pronounced as it had been before. His strength had returned, though he accepted this to be a temporary state of well-being. The evil would win out as the Tinkler had warned, of that he had no doubt.

None of Asgard's bloodline could hope to survive an encounter with the business end of the Sword of the Ancients.

He would do his best to reach Rowan Cottage as Editha Faas had instructed. Considering his debt to her, his honor demanded it. But knowing as he now did that Orabilis was not a witch but a powerful Faerie healer, he had little hope of making it through her defenses to obtain her help. No matter what Bridget said, if Orabilis had designed those defenses to keep out the descendents of Asgard, there was no way he was getting past.

A sideward glance brought Bridget's profile into

view. She rode tall in her saddle, back straight, eyes focused into the distance. A whole range of adjectives flooded his mind every time he looked at the woman.

Strong. Determined. Proud. Beautiful.

A ridiculous thought, that last one. Her beauty was of no matter to him. Even if he weren't doomed by his encounter with the Sword of the Ancients, no woman in the whole of this world would be interested in tying her fate to a man like him. A *being* like him. He was bound in service to an ancient god, his whole life at the mercy of Thor's every whim.

Bridget brushed a stray curl from her face and a spear of regret stabbed through Hall's heart.

Funny, how traveling the world in defense of Mortals who called on Thor for help had never rankled before. Maybe it was only his own mortality that made it feel like such a burden now.

"What?" she asked, turning to catch him staring at her.

"Nothing." She arched an eyebrow and he was forced to come up with a better response. "Fine, then. I was only wondering how much longer you might last before we have to stop for the night."

"How much longer *I* might last?" She snorted her derision. "My stamina is hardly in question, now, is it? Yer the one with the patched-up arm. Better I should be asking *you* how much longer *you* might last."

Prickly-spirited, as always. It was one of the adjectives he'd somehow left off his earlier list, along with *impatient* and *annoying*. The woman had a temper that made him grind his teeth.

She would be one of the things he'd truly miss when he left this world.

"You think that's funny, do you?" she asked, her brows drawing into a frown as she glared at him. "I fail to see anything the least bit amusing about our situation. It's no bad enough that we've two days of hard travel ahead of us, into territory where neither of us is welcome. Now yer sitting there with that silly grin upon yer face. And look at this, would you . . . it's starting to rain! On top of everything else. Fine reward that is, and me trying for nothing more than to see you safe." She wiped a hand over her face and pulled up the hood of her cloak with one last annoyed look in his direction.

As if the rain were his fault.

Hall stared into the solid gray wall of precipitation moving toward them, knowing that, in fact, the rain *was* his fault. He'd allowed his emotions to run wild, doing nothing to cloak them. Nothing to prevent the all-too-obvious result of his depression

He'd never realized that masking the way he felt required so much energy. Energy he simply didn't have to spare right now. But mask it he must.

With an effort on his part that stole from him his ability to do anything else, the pounding rain slowed to a light, annoying mist. By the time they reached a spot where he felt they could camp for the night, the rains had completely stopped.

He brushed away the assistance Bridget offered and slid down from his saddle, praying his legs would hold him.

"Leave the horses and I'll see to them after I've taken care of a fire." Her words were more a command than an offer, leaving him no alternative but to argue with her.

"I'm not on my deathbed yet. I can still take care of our animals."

Bridget glared at him, her mouth set in a hard, straight line as if she had something she wanted to say but held it back. Finally, after a long moment, she shrugged and turned away, leaving him to lead both their horses to drink.

It was as if, no matter what he did, he managed to anger her. Never in all his days had he dealt with a more complicated, more strong-willed, more annoying woman than Bridget MacCulloch.

He had also never before crossed paths with a woman he found more appealing.

Had the Norns not conspired against him long before his birth to eliminate any chance for a future of happiness, Bridget, with her bravery and her willingness to confront every situation head-on, would have been exactly the woman he would have looked for to share that future with him.

THE FIRE BLAZED steadily and Bridget had already begun to lay out their evening meal by the time Halldor finished readying their animals for the night. It had taken him twice as long as it should have, and he wore his exhaustion like a heavy cloak when he approached the fire.

"Best we enjoy the luxury of this warmth tonight," he offered as he sank down to sit across from where she stood. "Another day's travel will bring us too close to Torquil's domain for us to risk drawing his attention with such a large fire."

If only he had shared that handy bit of information earlier, she might have had time to bring down some fresh meat for them tonight. A rabbit, perhaps. But no, he'd waited until well after dark before he bothered to—

She clamped down on her internal rant, common sense rearing its unfamiliar head. She needed to curb her unreasonable anger over every little thing Halldor did. It wasn't his responsibility to point out the obvious. *She* should have thought of it herself.

Fear curled in her stomach as she wondered, if she'd overlooked something as minor as this, what more important things might she miss?

As if she'd opened a door and recognized the person standing there, she realized that fear was the source of all that impotent anger churning inside her. Fear that she'd fail in her task to save him, just as she'd failed in her task to avenge her father's death.

It wasn't anything Halldor had done that set her off, but rather the fact that he seemed so calm about everything in the face of her own fear. He worried about nothing and she about everything. Even now he was only trying to make small talk, and if she had any good sense left at all, she should do the same.

"I hope the Tinklers remembered all we asked them to tell Patrick about the men who are following Mathew."

Halldor picked up a stick and poked at the fire, saying nothing. He didn't need to. His expression quite clearly announced his feelings on the subject.

Brie couldn't let his silence go unchallenged. "What? Surely you canna believe they'd withhold such information." Knowledge of what the men from Castle MacGahan faced could mean the difference between success and failure.

His jaw tightened as if he fought some internal debate. She'd seen the same expression on her brother's face too many times not to recognize it.

"*Do* you believe they'd withhold it? You do! You actually doubt the Tinklers' willingness to help."

He tossed away the stick and looked up at her, shaking his head. "You have it wrong. I've no doubt in the Tinklers' willingness to share our message with Patrick's party, *if* they see them. It's the likelihood their paths will cross I find worrisome. Patrick knows as well as I that Mathew heads for Skye to sell the scrolls. Cross-country is the fastest way there, not along the trails the Tinklers follow. Our friends will likely miss Mathew altogether, and instead will be walking into Torquil's men blind."

So he did worry! The realization was like cold

water to Brie's face. One more example of her rush-
ing headlong into a mistaken assumption, exactly as
her father had so often warned her to guard against.
At least this worry was one she didn't share.

"No, yer wrong about that. You chose the less-
traveled path, but Patrick willna do the same. He's
a fine warrior, make no mistake. But he thinks in
a straight line. My da said it was too many years
of being his brother's second in command that left
him seeing only right or wrong, black or white. And
those who follow him will not question his decisions
or his course. Trust me on this. They'll stick to the
trails."

Brie tore off a piece of bread and handed it over
to Halldor. He accepted the offering wordlessly and
took a big bite, staring into the fire as he chewed.

"Your reasoning is sound," he said at last, looking
up to meet her gaze. "I do not give my trust easily. But by your actions, Shield Maiden, you have
earned it. As you say, I will put that worry from my
mind."

He trusted her. Just like that. No conditions or
exceptions. None of the *"If only you were . . ."* any
of the hundreds of things her father and Jamesy
always said she must improve upon before she met
their standards.

No. Halldor had looked at her actions and found
her worthy simply as she was.

It humbled her. It weakened her knees.

Or perhaps that particular sensation was due to

his touch as he accepted the cheese she handed him. Was it her imagination that his fingers lingered over hers longer than necessary? Or that his eyes seemed more intensely alive with the light of the fire dancing in them?

Her gaze locked on his as he pulled her hand toward his mouth to accept the morsel of food. His lips grazed against her fingers and the memory of his stolen kiss flooded her mind, warming her and sending tremors dancing into parts of her body she rarely remembered she had.

She leaned in toward him as his lips parted, expecting at any moment he would pull her closer as he had done once before, wrapping his hand in her hair to bring her mouth against his to once again—

"Your oats appear to be burning."

"What?" She jerked upright and stumbled backward, only to have her hand caught by his before she fell.

"Your oats. They are burning."

"My oats," she repeated, at last realizing he spoke of the meal she was preparing. "Damn and double damn!" she hissed, hurrying to pull the little pot off the fire.

Her oats weren't the only thing that was burning, and the wide grin on his face assured her that he knew it as well as she did.

Damn and double damn indeed.

Thirteen

W HAT ABOUT HERE? Does *this* place meet with yer approval?" Brie struggled to keep the irritation out of her voice but failed to reach that goal.

"Defensible enough," Halldor murmured, lifting his head to scan the small glen. "Water for the animals. Shelter back under those rocks. Aye, it will do."

It had damned well better do. He'd rejected the last two spots she'd chosen, and now she'd be lucky to finish setting up their camp before they had no light left at all.

Their second full day on the trail had gone by without incident and Brie wanted to keep it that way. No arguments tonight, she reminded herself. No making a fool of herself like last night, when she'd allowed her imagination to get the best of her.

She managed to hold her tongue as she dismounted and offered a shoulder to assist Halldor off his horse. When his feet hit the ground, he leaned on her more heavily than she'd expected. More heavily than he had the last time they'd stopped.

"How do you fare?" she asked as she helped him to sit under the overhang of rock, protected at last from the unrelenting drizzle of rain.

He leaned his head back against the stone wall supporting him, eyes shut, and grunted his non-committal response. It had been a long day of hard riding, and every mile of it showed in his weary demeanor. Dark smudges stained the skin under his eyes in a way she was sure they hadn't just an hour or two earlier.

Brie hurried through the tasks at hand, expecting at any moment that he'd insist on helping.

He didn't. A glance to where he sat confirmed that he hadn't moved a single muscle.

That, more than anything, heightened her concern for his condition. A hand to his forehead told her all she needed to know. The fever was back with a vengeance.

"Editha promised three days before the Magic overtook you again, and it's only been two. Something's gone wrong."

"Three at most," Halldor muttered, his eyes still closed. "Promised nothing."

Maybe there hadn't been an explicit promise, but Brie counted on the Tinkler's word. Three days, the woman had said. What else had she said? Something about redressing the wound.

"I need some light."

Brie scrambled to gather whatever she could find

that was dry enough. She piled the tinder together and gently coaxed a small flame.

"No fire," Halldor reminded her. "We agreed. It's not safe here."

"A small fire," she countered. "And though you might have made that assumption, I agreed to nothing."

Not that it mattered to her now. She needed to have a look at his wound, and that wasn't something she could do in the dark.

"Can't draw attention. Not safe for you this close to Tordenet."

"It's not safe for either of us this close to the castle," she responded, kneeling at his side to pull away the heavy fur and expose his arm. "But here we are and here we must make the best of it. By the Seven!"

The bandage had slipped down off the wound, lodging around his bicep. A foul black ooze trailed down his arm, bubbling out of the wound. Brie had never seen its like, not even in the most neglected of battle injuries.

"Well. Here's our problem."

The first thing Editha had asked for when she'd seen the wound was water. Brie grabbed the small pot from her provisions and hurried to the stream's bank to scoop it full. Once she nestled it directly into the fire, it wouldn't take long to heat.

"That needs cleaning," she stated, as much for her own benefit as for his.

If only she'd thought to bring along a spare shift, but she hadn't. A warrior traveled light for speed, with no need for changes of clothing.

Grasping the bottom of the shift she wore, she tore off a strip from the edge and dropped it into the now boiling water. Carefully, she fished it out and wrung as much water from it as she could before turning to wipe the sticky black ooze from Halldor's arm.

Though he made no word of protest, his hissing gasp was sign enough of his suffering. She pulled the flask of honey ale from her pack and placed it to his lips.

"Drink."

He did as she instructed and a renewed thread of fear curled around her heart. This meek compliance was not a good sign.

Remembering Editha's warning about the jewels, Brie made sure to keep the stones wrapped tightly together in the linen as she reset the bandage and tied it around Halldor's arm. To make sure it didn't slip again, she knotted the second turn up and over his shoulder.

He seemed to relax almost immediately after she finished.

"There you go, O'Donar. Good as new."

"Hall," he murmured, his eyes fluttering open to focus on her. "I'd have you call me Hall. It's the name given me by my friend and brother, Chase Noble. If yours is to be the last face I see in this world, I'd have it be the face of a friend."

"Dinna you say such," she said with all the ferocity she felt. "I'll no let anything happen to you out here. I'll get you to Rowan Cottage as I promised, and the witch will heal you. Yer no going to die."

"All the same," he countered, "I'd have you use that name when you speak of me."

"*To* you," she corrected. "If it makes you happy, I'll use that name when I speak *to* you."

Speaking *of* him would imply he was gone, and just the thought of that made it hard to catch her breath.

"Say it." He clamped his fingers around her wrist, pulling her closer, his eyes bright with the fever, holding her gaze. "I'd hear it from you now."

"Hall," she whispered, and then once more, louder. "Hall."

His hand dropped from her wrist and he smiled. The expression that had once before sent tingles of excitement rippling through her had exactly the same effect this time.

What a fool she was, allowing herself to get all bothered over the crazed rantings of a fevered man. It wasn't as though he'd chosen to be here with her now. He traveled with her out of necessity.

And yet . . . the kiss he'd stolen in the Tinkler camp burned on her lips as if he'd placed it there only minutes before.

She lightly pressed her fingers to his cheek. Only to check his temperature, she assured herself. Certainly not because the smile lingering on his lips compelled her to make such contact.

No sign of the fever remained on his cool, whisker-stubbled skin.

"Is there anything I can get you? Anything you want?"

His eyes opened slowly to her question, revealing two mesmerizing blue pools filled with a heat that had nothing to do with the recently departed fever.

"Yes," he answered, his hand rising up to rest over hers against his cheek. "I'm hungry."

So was she, but her hunger had nothing to do with food.

WITH THE JEWELS properly placed to hold back the evil in his wound, Hall's strength returned in a rush. And with it came a new companion. Desire, hot and heavy, flooded his loins.

Having Brie hovering so close to him, her palm cupping his cheek, all he could think of was kissing her. Tasting those perfect lips until they were swollen under his touch. Feeling her body close to his, her skin next to his.

No good at all could come of this. He'd be lucky to live out the week, and even if he did, what had he to offer any woman?

Despite all reason, he felt himself powerless to stop the wheel from turning. The tapestry had been woven and it was beyond his power to change what was to be.

With a hand to the back of her head, he slowly pulled her toward him, waiting for some sign of resistance in her expression.

None came.

Her mouth opened as if she might speak, but she made no sound. He leaned into her, pressing his lips to hers.

No hard, fast, spur-of-the-moment kiss like their last one. No, this time he meant it to be slow and gentle. This time he meant them both to enjoy it.

His tongue explored the soft contours of her mouth, and her body molded against his. His spirit soared with her eager response. He wrapped his arms around her and, without breaking their kiss, rolled her onto her back, careful to support himself on his good arm to keep from crushing her under his full weight.

She moaned and twined her arms around his neck, tangling her fingers in his hair and rubbing them against his scalp.

By the Norns, but her touch drove him wild!

He broke the kiss to trail his lips down the length of her neck as his fingers fumbled to part the cloth at her bodice. Caressed by the cold air, her soft skin erupted in small bumps, and she shivered.

Need consumed him. He wanted this woman in his arms more than he could ever remember wanting anyone before.

When he settled his mouth over one perfectly budded breast, she sucked in her breath and he looked up to find her staring at him, her eyes reflecting the desire he felt coursing through his body.

Outside, thunder rumbled and lightning crackled in a nonstop performance, casting a brilliant glow across the velvety night sky.

After a lifetime spent in service to others, this one thing, this one time, he would do just for himself.

With his knee, he nudged her heavy skirt upward until he could run his hand along the bare, smooth skin of her thigh. Up, higher, to the silky softness of her stomach, where the muscles clenched reflexively under his touch.

Grasping her hips, he settled himself between her knees, where she welcomed him by locking her leg over his.

So close. He was so close to where he wanted to be, buried deep inside her warmth. His body ached to take her fast and hard, but he fought the temptation. This was a moment to be savored, not to be rushed.

He pressed against her, his erection so hard he felt as if his skin might burst. When she lifted her hips against him, he had to force himself to wait. Enter her now and he would be lost. It had been too long, and he wanted her too badly.

A moment to regain his control.

A moment to ensure her passion spiked as high as his own.

He shifted his weight to one side and trailed his hand down to her waist and around to the juncture between her legs.

So hot, so welcoming, her hips lifted and she moaned with pleasure as he slipped one finger inside her.

With one finger inside and his thumb covering the hard little nub, he had but to flex his hand and her moan turned to a breathless whimper, her hips lifting rhythmically to meet the movement of his hand.

Two fingers. Two fingers pressing deep inside, readying her body to accept him. Massaging, slow at first, building in tempo until her body convulsed, her throbbing muscles pulsating around his fingers.

He held her through her climax, his lips covering hers until she gasped for breath.

She was ready for the next step.

With his hands at the small of her back, he lifted her hips and positioned himself against her.

She tangled her fingers in his hair and pulled his mouth to hers, opening for him, her tongue fencing with his in a magnificent dance.

It was now. She would be his.

He'd just begun the exquisitely slow slide into her welcoming sheath when an unearthly scream shattered his moment of bliss.

Not quite human, not quite beast, the sound pierced the night, echoing louder than the rumble of the crashing storm outside.

Hall leapt to his feet, grabbed his sword in one hand and his fur in the other. The sword he raised in front of him. The fur he tossed over the fire, smothering the flames and dousing every last bit of light.

"What was that?" Bridget asked in a whisper, lifting herself up on her elbows.

He didn't answer, tilting his head to one side in an effort to catch the smallest ripple of vibration for miles. In the silence of the suddenly stilled storm, only one sound reached his ears—the steady beat of massive wings passing through the air, racing away from them.

Fourteen

PAIN FROM THE depths of Niflheim wracked his body, radiating along the length of his arm.

Fenrir slid from the window ledge into his tower to land on his bare feet. Earlier in the evening, he'd taken the form of the great owl to investigate the odd vibrations he'd sensed from the far corner of his lands.

Half an hour into his flight, he'd spotted it, a strange red glow pulsating up from the ground, flowing out into the night. He'd known that whatever emitted that light was a danger to him, because the five oozing sores around his heart had pulsated in conjunction with the glow. Whatever had caused the wound to Torquil's body was somewhere down there in the night.

He'd been closing in on the source when a sudden, savage storm exploded the sky around him.

He could find no respite, no safe escape. The lightning caught him, charring his feathers and searing his skin. In his agony, his concentration wavered, and with it, his form. He plummeted helplessly toward the land below, struggling desperately to recover his hold on the transformation Magic.

In his original form, the form in which he had been created, such a near crisis would never have occurred. But his own form was long gone, destroyed by the Elves of Niflheim when they imprisoned his spirit in those accursed scrolls of theirs.

His merging with the laird of the MacDowylt was nearing completion, and his senses accepted the body he had borrowed as if it were his own. And this body, this weak, helpless body, had plummeted from the skies like a boulder when he was attacked.

And it was an attack. No mere storm, no mere coincidence, could have formed so quickly or so viciously to drive him away.

"I must have my scrolls," he roared to the heavens, clutching his injured arm.

Without them, he was trapped as a lesser being, unable to enhance this body to prevent such a thing as had happened tonight.

Without them, he was separated from the vast power of his Magic.

Without them, he risked another imprisonment within the Magic of the symbols scrawled on their faces.

The pain in his arm pulsed with every beat of the pitifully small heart in his chest. He turned his attention to study the wound. A burn, jagged and scarring, raced the length of his arm from shoulder to elbow. The sickly sweet stench of charred flesh rose up from the gaping rip in his skin, churning his stomach.

Silently, he sent an order to the captain of his guard to bring a healer to him. He hurt as only a feeble Mortal body could hurt. Great heaving waves of pain assaulted his physical being. Never before, never in his true form, had he experienced torment like this. The need to relieve the agony was so great that he reached for the jug of spirits on the shelf above the fireplace. Whisky might dull his senses, if only for a short time.

He tipped back the container, allowing the liquid to flow down his throat, burning the tender flesh as it gurgled toward his stomach.

Even before this calamity struck, his evening had been one frustration after another.

None of the remaining men he'd sent in pursuit of his treasure had managed to locate the thief yet. His attempts to control the boy through his dreams were thwarted by the power of the sword. And when he'd attempted to view the culprit's location through the jewels, his view had been blocked as if the stones were swathed in layers of protective covering, the five of them united in their effort to reject him.

He prayed that the jewels hadn't been separated from the scrolls. That sort of a foolish move would leave the powers of the scrolls, *his* powers, available for anyone to claim, a completely unacceptable outcome.

It was his concern over the jewels that had sent him winging into the night.

Whisky in hand now, he stared out into the star-sparkled heavens. After spending an eternity imprisoned by the jewels' power, he recognized the feel of them, and tonight he was sure he'd felt them somewhere in the vast dark of the night, heading in his direction.

Perhaps it was only the dilution of his powers he suffered as he melded with this form, but uncertainty clouded his thoughts. The sudden storm, so strange and unusual for this time of year, had assailed him as if engaging in battle.

Mere chance?

He downed another long draught of the heady drink before turning his back on the window.

He didn't believe in chance.

Something was out there. A threat greater than he had faced in many years.

Though he wouldn't be flying again anytime soon, he would be vigilant. He would find a way to search for whatever had given off those peculiar vibrations. To search for whatever life force had lit the night with its eerie red glow.

And when he found it, his justice would be swift and merciless to whoever dared approach him with such a burdensome gift.

Fifteen

EVERYTHING BRIE HAD ever imagined about what the future held in store for her had changed completely over the course of this strange and wonderful evening. For the first time in her life, she could envision herself with a man at her side as she rode into the hereafter.

One very specific man, upon whose broad chest she rested her head. Halldor O'Donar.

Hall. *Her* Hall.

The warmth of happiness cocooned her and she ran a hand across the hard expanse of chest that served as her pillow. His hand covered hers, offering the reassurance of a light squeeze.

What might have happened between them had they not been interrupted by that horrible scream would remain fodder for her fantasies for the moment. The need to remain vigilant for whatever had lurked outside in the dark outweighed their desire to lose themselves in the fog of sensual pleasure.

What she couldn't even begin to conceive of,

even in her own admittedly overactive imagination, was what kind of beast could possibly have issued that hideous shriek. Never in her life had she heard such an unearthly sound.

After checking their campsite, Hall had returned with a growled "No fire."

Under the circumstances, she agreed.

Beneath her ear, his heart pounded strong and sure. Thankfully, adjusting the bandage over his wound had made a remarkable difference in his strength. She prayed, to whatever gods would listen, that he would remain his strong warrior self until they reached Orabilis.

Her strong warrior.

She'd never dared to think of any man as hers before. But she'd never met anyone like Hall. He, unlike every other man she'd ever known, accepted her as his equal. It seemed only natural they should be together. He was so much like her—a warrior with nothing but his honor, and no place to call his own.

"Will you remain here?" Her question echoed off the rocks above them, jarringly loud in the silence. She lowered her voice to barely more than a whisper to continue. "When all this is over, I mean."

It seemed a logical question. His brother, Chase, had married Christiana MacDowylt, so without question he would remain at Castle MacGahan.

But would Hall do the same?

"At Castle MacGahan, you mean? Such a prospect paints a most pleasant picture to a man such as I." He stroked his fingers softly through her hair for several minutes before he spoke again. "But such is not woven as my fate."

Surely he didn't still believe she'd allow him to die out here.

"Your fate is not what you fear. I intend to see you safely to Rowan Cottage, where the witch *will* heal you. I so swear it. You have no call to doubt that outcome or to expect the worst will happen."

A chuckle rumbled under her ear. "I have not one doubt about your good intentions, Shield Maiden. But even should you be successful, once our task is finished and our enemy defeated, I have no choice but to return to my home."

She wished for light so that she might see his face as he spoke. So much meaning was lost in the words floating in the dark void where they lay.

"Where is home for you?"

"I live along the northern coast of the Isle of Mists," he answered, his voice little more than a whisper as well. "Ireland, you'd call it. Home of my grandmother's people."

He meant to return to Ireland? And leave a whole entire ocean separating them? That would never do. Whatever laird he served would simply have to make do without her big warrior.

"You ken there's a place for you here, aye? You dinna have to go back. Forget about those you served there. We need you here."

She needed him here.

"My days are not my own. My life's path is not my own to choose. I am committed to go when and where I'm needed, when and where I'm sent, no matter where I might want to be. I don't have the luxury of forgetting those for whom I am responsible. Though I'd venture a guess, as often as I'm gone, they might feel forgotten. Nonetheless, they are my people and I have an obligation to see to their welfare."

"Yer people?" She lifted her head and turned toward him, straining to see his face. In the dark, she could barely make out his shape, let alone his features or expression.

"Yes. With my grandmother gone, Haven Castle and all her people have become my responsibility. I must oversee their welfare and safety, as well as the welfare and safety of those I'm sent to help. It is the destiny I was born to. My path in life. And I cannot change it, no matter that I might want to."

Brie struggled for her next breath, feeling as though her heart had stopped beating.

He was a laird. With a castle and responsibilities. A man born to substance and wealth.

And she? She was no one. She owned nothing but a few paltry household goods she could carry upon the back of a horse. She was certainly not the dowried lady a man such as Hall would one day wed.

All the ridiculous fantasies she'd allowed herself to indulge in as she lay in his arms disappeared like smoke on a blustery day. She'd never been much of a dreamer and she certainly was no fool. A landed man like him would never want someone like her for more than a quick night's tumble.

And Bridget MacCulloch, daughter of the House MacUlagh, descended from the Ancient Seven, tumbled for no man. Especially not a man who could so easily break her heart.

If she allowed him that power over her.

She rolled to her knees and placed her palm against his forehead, fighting to keep her roiling emotions in check.

"Fever's completely gone. I think it's best we get some sleep. We'll want an early start."

She crawled away from him and built a physical barrier between them by piling up the bags of provisions they traveled with.

If only she could build an emotional barrier as easily.

"Bridget?" He sounded confused, and she hardened her heart against the hurt in his voice.

"Go to sleep, Hall. Morning will be here soon enough, and we've a long way to travel to reach Orabilis on the morrow."

She'd done herself proud. Only calm and determination rang in her voice. Not even the tiniest hint of the hurt eating away at her soul had escaped.

She would have to keep it so. It was her only hope against losing her heart and her soul.

Sixteen

KEEP UP WITH me, Hall. You can do this. We've no much farther to go now."

Hall nodded his acceptance of Bridget's encouragement, hoping he wouldn't let her down. Fearing he already had.

She'd been distant since last night, when he'd confessed to her that his life was not his own to control. As he'd suspected, no woman, not even Bridget, wanted a man who was always gone, battling some new enemy, leaving her to a life of loneliness.

Not that it mattered now. He'd be lucky to live through the day, so worrying over how often Thor dispatched him to see to the welfare of one of his believers was of little consequence.

All he could do now was put her out of his mind and focus his efforts to stay alive. In the long run it was better this way, the way he had always known his life was meant to be.

What life he had left, anyway.

He couldn't hold on much longer. Between keeping the rain at bay and the vile Magic eating its way through his body, he'd about reached the limit of his strength. Pain radiated out from the wound and up into his neck. For the past several minutes, he couldn't quite get that side of his face to work as it should. His eye drooped shut, no matter how hard he struggled to keep it open. His shoulder felt as if lightning bolts sawed back and forth within the wound, and that was with the bandage-wrapped jewels firmly in place.

Day three, the maximum extent of time the Faerie had allotted him.

He lifted his hand up toward the west, his shaky palm facing him. Four fingers' distance remained between the sun and the horizon. On this last day Editha had given him to reach Rowan Cottage, maybe an hour of daylight remained, and he was fading fast.

The way he felt now, he wouldn't last to see another sunset.

He tied a knot in the end of his reins, slipped them down over his head, and fitted them under his arms. When he lost consciousness, that precaution might at least keep him in the saddle. If he fell to the ground, he doubted Bridget's ability to get him back on the horse, though he didn't doubt her willingness to try.

The woman was stubborn to a fault. It was one of the traits he'd come to admire most in her. That and her temper.

"It willna be long now. We're close," Bridget called over her shoulder, continuing the repetitive encouragement she'd adopted over the past hour. "Oh, bother it all, the rains are back."

So they were. He had no choice but to let something go, and it was taking everything he had left just to remain upright on his horse.

"Sorry," he managed to mumble, but doubted she'd heard him. He wasn't even sure he'd heard it himself.

He regretted all the people he'd be letting down. Regretted how angry Bridget would be that she hadn't been able to get him to Rowan Cottage in time. Most of all, he regretted that he wouldn't get to witness it. Nothing he'd ever seen was quite as beautiful as Bridget MacCulloch in full rage, her eyes sparkling with the fire of her emotions, her cheeks pink with the heat of her anger, her tongue honed to its sharpest point as she argued her case.

He would miss that.

The only thing he could think of that was more beautiful than Bridget in full fury was Bridget lying beneath him, her eyes unfocused with a need he was prepared to meet.

He didn't want to leave that behind. Perhaps he could hang on just a bit longer . . . but no. Even as the thought flared, all control drained from his arms and his back began to buckle.

He pitched forward as if in slow motion, to bury his face in the wet hair on his mount's neck.

BEHIND HER. THE sound of hoofbeats slowed to a stop and Brie huffed out an irritated breath. They'd stopped too often today already. If Hall didn't get a move on, it was going to take until well after dark to reach Rowan Cottage. They were running out of time.

"How many times do I have to tell you to keep up with me? Yer no helping in the least, when you constantly . . ."

Her tirade faded to a stop as she turned. "No, no, no, no, no," she cried, hopping down from her mount to race to his side. "Hall? Hall! Answer me, damn you!"

He lay sprawled facedown on his horse's neck, motionless.

Had the bandage slipped again? That must be it. She wouldn't accept anything else. She'd simply redress the bandage, snugging the jewels over the wound again, and he'd be good as new in no time.

Hoisting herself up onto his horse behind him, she struggled to pull away the heavy wet fur he wore. The momentary satisfaction of success evaporated as she checked the bandage and found it securely in place.

This was far more serious than the bandage slipping.

"Day three," she whispered, resting her head against his back.

It wasn't fair. Day three hadn't yet come to an end.

Gradually, she became aware of a faint sound beneath her ear. A steady, if not strong, heartbeat.

Hall still lived, and that was enough for her. She wouldn't give up, either.

"Hold it together, Brie MacCulloch," she ordered aloud.

If there'd ever been a time she needed her wits about her, this was that time.

She directed his horse next to hers and gathered up the lead of her mount.

They still had time to reach Orabilis. They had to.

"We will arrive at Rowan Cottage by nightfall. I've sworn it and it will be so. And you, my big warrior . . ." She ran a hand down Hall's back before lifting the fur back up to protect him from the cold rain. "You must do yer part in this, too. If you know what's good for you, you'll keep right on breathing, do you hear me? Elsewise, you'll have me to answer to."

Seventeen

THE WESTERN SKY flamed with the last traces of red and pink light as the trees surrounding Orabilis's home came into view.

Brie didn't dare yell out to try to attract the old woman's attention. Though they were many miles from Tordenet, with the Beast's powers, they were much too close for comfort.

Step by step, she waited on full alert to confront whatever Hall had expected would keep him from crossing onto the property around Rowan Cottage. She directed his big horse to within a few feet of the front door before dismounting to survey her surroundings.

Nothing at all unusual happened. No beasts or invisible barriers of any kind.

If Hall were conscious, she'd give him a piece of her mind for all the useless worry he'd caused her.

"Later," she whispered as she approached the door. There would be plenty of time to chastise him for having worried her later.

Please let there be plenty of time later.

She lifted her fist to knock, but the door glided open and Orabilis stepped out into the evening to greet her.

"Well, well, if it isn't the last daughter of the House MacUlagh. Yer back so soon, Princess. To what do I owe this grand honor?"

Brie's face heated, remembering her first meeting with the old woman, and how she'd embarrassed herself by listing her birthright and ancestry as if it might give her some added authority.

Orabilis had been less than impressed with her pedigree. It was more important who *you* are, the old witch had informed her, than who yer family had been in generations so long gone that few even remembered they'd ever existed.

The witch, it seemed, was as wise as she was aged. Brie hoped now that her generosity would rival that wisdom.

"I need yer help. My . . . my companion has been injured and the Tinklers tell us yer the only one who can help him."

"The Tinklers told you that, did they? Well, let's have a look at him, then. If the Tinklers chose to send him to me, he just might be worth saving." Orabilis tottered over to the big horse and squinted up toward Hall. "Wake up!" she yelled, slapping a hand to his leg.

"He's no asleep," Brie said, straining to keep the desperation she felt out of her voice. "He's dying, damn it all. Can you no see that? He's losing the battle with the poisonous Magic that infects his wound."

"Magic, eh?" Orabilis scratched at her chin, studying her patient. "Magic too strong for the Tinklers means we've got our work cut out for us. We'll need to start by getting this big one down from his perch."

"We can do it," Brie answered, sounding much more confident than she felt.

Climbing back up on Hall's horse behind him, she worked the reins up and over his head before sliding back down to the ground.

"There. I'd think that if we give him a good tug, between the two of us, we can catch him as he slides down. Can you do that, do you think? Help me to catch him before he hits the ground?"

Eyeing the old woman, Brie felt some doubt as to the possibility of success for her plan, but Orabilis nodded enthusiastically and positioned herself next to Brie.

"Here we go," Brie encouraged while she put her back into pulling Hall toward her. "It's working! It's . . . oof!"

As Hall's body gained momentum toward them, Orabilis stepped back and away, leaving Brie to shoulder the full brunt of his weight. As strong as she was, she wasn't strong enough for that.

She fell to her back, him spread-eagle on top of her. The only thing that saved her from a painful landing was Orabilis's hands at her shoulders, slowing her fall a bit, guiding her to the ground. Thank the Seven the old woman hadn't completely deserted her.

"Good of you to help," Brie managed to squeak when she'd caught her breath. "Yer stronger than you look."

And a good thing it was, too. Without Orabilis to slow her descent, Brie suspected she might have been seriously injured. As it was, she was simply pinned to the ground under Hall's weight, barely able to catch her breath.

Orabilis stepped back, hands on her hips. "I suppose I am strong at that. But then, I'd have to be, living out here alone as I do, now, wouldn't I?"

"If you could just help roll him off of me," Brie grunted.

"Sorry, lassie. I canna see that happening. But perhaps I've something inside that might give us some assistance," Orabilis answered, turning to hobble back inside her little cottage.

At least Brie assumed the old woman returned to her cottage. With Hall on top of her, her view of everything other than a few degrees to her left was blocked.

So here she lay, unable to move, struggling for breath, deserted by the only creature within miles who could help.

"Bollocks," she muttered, and tried in vain to pull her arm to freedom.

Hall's face lay next to hers, his shallow breath

hitting her cheek in short little puffs. At least he still lived.

She quickly realized that he lay so close, if she turned her head at all, her lips brushed against his. She did so, then tried it a second time, just to make sure she wasn't imagining it.

"Ahem. Am I interrupting the two of you in some sport?"

"No!" Brie's shout of surprise sounded more like a flattened huff of air. "I was only checking to see if the fever had taken him again." Why she felt the need to explain was beyond her.

"And has it?" Orabilis asked as she squatted down next to them.

Brie regretted that she hadn't actually been thinking of fever when her lips had touched his. Her lie forced her to turn her face back toward his to rest her lips against his once more. Heat flooded her body, assuring her that one of them was excessively warm.

"Yes," she responded breathlessly. "There is a fever."

Orabilis chuckled as if someone had told her a wonderful joke, leaving Brie with the awful suspicion that *she* was the punch line in whatever the old woman found so amusing.

"Turn yer head away, lassie," Orabilis instructed, and thrust her hand between them, up next to Hall's nose.

With so little warning, Brie wasn't quite fast enough.

An acrid, bitter odor crawled into her nostrils and rushed straight to her oxygen-deprived lungs. She panted, unable to fully catch her breath under Hall's weight. The need to gasp for air or to cough out the stinging fumes overwhelmed her.

"What is that?" she choked out after a moment.

"Strong, is it no? A potent wee tincture of my own making. Good for waking a body from almost anything. Any moment now, yer big warrior here will be able to help us get him inside under his own power."

"And off me," Brie grunted.

As Orabilis had predicted, Hall groaned and began to stir.

"Where?" His voice rasped as if his tongue were too thick for him to form words.

"Dinna you try to speak, good sir," Orabilis said as she tugged at his arm. "Save what little strength you have for getting on yer feet."

"Who?" He tried again while pushing up to his knees.

"A stubborn one, you are." Orabilis chuckled, her eyebrows waggling like fuzzy caterpillars. "I see you've found a match for yer own willfulness, have you no, lassie?"

Brie ignored the question and got to her feet, snugging her shoulder under Hall's arm to help support him. She could only hope his mind was too fuzzy to have registered the old witch's question.

Found herself a match indeed. Not hardly. Though a night ago, she'd allowed herself to believe the same thing.

"How?" Hall muttered, attempting to pull away as if he thought he could do this on his own.

"Easy, now," Orabilis cautioned as she shoved the cottage door open with one hip and guided them all inside. "Into the chair with him. Over here, near the fire. I need to see what I've got to work with."

The old woman grunted as they eased their burden down and then stepped away, hands on her hips as if admiring her accomplishment.

"You said he'd been poisoned by Magic. What exactly has done this to him?"

Brie straightened, her back protesting sharply at the last several minutes of mistreatment she'd given it. "The Sword of the Ancients. It barely touched him, but Editha Faas said its Magic is most powerful. And, judging by what it's done to Hall, I have to agree with her."

"Sword of the Ancients, eh?" Orabilis chewed on the corner of her lip, her sharp eyes boring a hole in Hall. "If that's the case, how did you pass through my ring of rowans, my good man?"

Hall shook his head back and forth like a man waking from a long dream. "Tried to ask you that."

"So you did. That's a mystery we'll worry ourselves over later. Yer here now, are you no? Might as well get out of that tunic and give me a look at that injury of yers so we can see if Editha Faas kenned what she was talking about when she sent you here. You should be feeling a little stronger by now. Are you?"

"Mistress Faas isn't likely to make an error on something such as this. No Fae would." Hall pulled the tunic up and over his head and let it drop beside him.

Brie tightened her hands into fists as Orabilis laid a gnarled finger upon his wounded shoulder. The old woman traced the curve of his muscle to the edge of the bandage and Brie could almost swear she felt the touch of his heated skin upon her own hand.

The light of the fire glistened off Hall's chest and Brie's heart beat a little harder, forcing her to breathe deeply to calm it down.

Too bad he wasn't what she'd thought him to be. Too bad she wasn't what he'd want in a wife. Too bad, all of it, because he was exactly what she would—

"Bridget!"

Brie's head snapped around to face Orabilis, realizing as she did that she'd missed whatever her hostess had said earlier. She'd been completely lost in staring at the beauty of Hall's bare chest, remembering how it felt to be held by those strong arms.

"I said I need more light in here. Run out to the shed and bring in peat staves for the fire." The old woman spoke slowly, deliberately, as if her words were meant for a dullard.

Brie deserved as much.

"Right away."

She cast a quick glance in Hall's direction as she headed for the door. In spite of his condition, a smile lifted one corner of his mouth.

A mortifying certainty swirled in the pit of her stomach and heated her face. She'd been so obvious in her lusting after his body that, even at death's door, he, too, had known she'd been lost in staring at him.

If there was a greater name than *fool* for a fool, she had more than earned it this day.

BRIDGET HAD DONE it. Just as she'd vowed she would. Somehow, this wild-spirited warrior had managed to get him to Rowan Cottage before the Magic of the sword had taken him.

What an amazing woman she was.

He tried for a smile as she headed past him, hoping she realized how grateful he was for all she'd done for him. But her gaze skated past him as if she couldn't bear the intimacy of their eyes connecting.

Little surprise there. He was hardly worth her time. One way or another, he'd be out of her life soon enough—a fact she'd apparently accepted.

Hall turned his attention to Orabilis. His only hope for survival tottered around, looking as if she were on her last legs. Witch or Faerie, it made no difference to him. They needed to act quickly.

"It's betony and yarrow I need now—" he began, but the old woman interrupted.

"Dinna you be telling me how to go about healing, boy. I was working with herbs long before you were born."

"I wouldn't be so sure of that." In fact, he quite doubted it. To say he was older than he looked would be a great understatement. Though if she were indeed Faerie, her looks would have no bearing on her true age. The Fae wore appearances as Mortals wore clothing.

"Well, I'm sure of it. I ken what you are. I felt it when I touched you. And dinna you bother to argue with me. You'll want to save yer strength for answering my questions. The potion I used willna last overlong. What I do want to hear from you is where you got yer hands on the amulet that hangs around yer neck. The one that allowed you through my defenses."

So it was his talisman that had granted him entry to Rowan Cottage. His hand rose to clasp the wooden goat. It was one of his most prized possessions, and where it came from was none of her business.

"It was a naming gift from my friend and brother, Chase Noble," he answered, the words pouring out of his mouth in spite of his intent not to tell her.

What the hell had she given him?

Orabilis nodded, a satisfied expression settling on her wrinkled face. "Honesty is a good trait to find in a man, even if it's not necessarily his first inclination. Very well, then. Since you received my little billy there as a naming gift, by what name are you called?"

"Hall O'Donar." When her eyebrow raised, he felt her disbelief like a slap to his face. "It is as my brother named me. I was called Halldor before the gifting," he explained.

Again her face creased into a satisfied smile. "So it's Thor's Rock gracing my humble home. I should have guessed. You hail from the Thunder people in the Lands of Mist, do you?"

"I do." Though he rarely spoke of his family roots with anyone, he would never deny them. Not that he had the ability to speak anything other than the whole truth, thanks to whatever Orabilis had given him.

"In that case, I'd say my little billy had nothing to do with yer being here. All in all, good enough," she muttered, crossing to a shelf on her wall to retrieve several pots. "Herbs," she announced, returning to the fire to dump their contents into a bubbling cauldron hanging there. "Of my choosing, no yers."

Some of the aromas he recognized but others were strangely foreign to him.

"A wound such as yers requires other than the usual healing herbs, wouldn't you say, lad?"

He nodded his agreement. The sword had been created specifically to kill those from his world, so he wasn't at all sure that even one as powerful as Orabilis was reputed to be could find a way to save him from the ancient Magic at work in his blood.

"There's a way, never you doubt that, lad." All traces of humor faded from her face as she held a hand over his bandage. "There's always a way. I can only guess that whatever is wrapped in this linen is responsible for yer reaching my door with a breath of life left in you. And there's only one thing I can think of strong enough for that. Would I be right in my assumption?"

"The jewels," he confirmed.

It had taken more effort to speak this time than it had before. The old Faerie had been correct about the potion she'd used wearing off soon.

"When I remove them, you'll likely drift away quickly. Never fear, lad, I'll bring you back from the middle lands. But before we begin, let's get you into the back room while we still can. I've no desire to be hauling yer great body around without yer assistance."

Hall rose slowly to his feet, surprised at how difficult it was and how weak his legs felt beneath him. As he followed Orabilis, he tottered as much as she did.

She opened a door and pointed to a tidy little bed. Obediently, he crossed to it and lay down. His mind heavy with apprehension, he waited as her gnarled fingers began to work at the bandage on his shoulder.

"I have them. Shall I put them on the fire now?"

Bridget's voice floated to him on a rush of cold air, settling around him like a favored blanket as the bandage on his arm was lifted away.

You've returned, he attempted to say, but the

sound that came out of his mouth was little more than a garbled, gurgling noise.

He fought the thick, black ooze settling over his mind, using what strength he had left to reach out his hand as he forced his eyes open once more to focus on Bridget standing in the doorway.

She dropped the armload of peat she carried right there in the doorway and hurried to his bedside, catching up his hand and reaching out to caress his cheek.

It felt good to have her here with him. To have her touch upon his face. If this was to be his last interaction in this world, he could think of no one he wanted more than this woman at his side.

"WHAT HAVE YOU done to him? Why did you remove the jewels?"

Brie's breath seemed to be blocked somewhere in her throat, as if there were no longer room for the air to pass into her lungs.

Hall's fingers loosened in her grip but she couldn't make herself let go of him. Maybe, somehow, she could pass her strength to him. Pass her will to keep going on to him.

"Here." Orabilis handed over a bowl and cloth. "Clean that wound while I gather what I need for the poultice. Mind you, try not to get those nasty bits of the ooze on yer own skin."

"Will it harm me as it has him?" Not that it would

stop her from helping him. She only wanted to know what to expect.

"No," Orabilis answered, a sour, wrinkled expression on her face. "But it has a fair nasty smell that people like you would find difficult to wash away."

Reluctantly, Brie laid Hall's hand on his chest, then dipped the cloth into the warm water.

People like her? What was that supposed to mean? She would have asked, but the old woman had already wobbled off into the other room.

Brie turned her attention to the task at hand. She cleaned the black oozing secretion from Hall's shoulder to reveal a deep, jagged opening underneath. The wound had swollen, puckering and tearing the opening, which had once been only a tiny slice of a cut.

"The wound looks to be badly infected," she called out.

From the other room, the old woman's mirthless cackle reached Brie's ears.

"That's no infection yer seeing there, lass, but pure evil Magic. The only Magic that can bring about the demise of one such as he."

One such as he.

Another comment she'd have to ask Orabilis about when all of this was over. Their number was growing by the minute, as was Brie's suspicion that Orabilis knew as much about Hall as she did about her.

The old woman returned, carrying a large mortar and pestle and a wicked-looking iron rasp. She tossed a couple of the peat staves into the little fire and sat down on the hearth to unwrap the jewels.

"No! You must keep them covered. Editha told us if we bared them, Fenrir would be able to see through them!"

"You've no cause to worry over Fenrir. Not even one such as he has power within the protection of the Rowans. We're safe here."

Brie tried to console herself with the old woman's words and use them to put Torquil out of her mind. The only thing that mattered to her right now lay in the bed at her side, his face as pale as death.

Orabilis ground each of the jewels against the metal rasp, catching small bits of the stones in the mortar. Then she went back to the main room and returned with a cup of the herbs she'd been boiling. She added them to the mortar and mixed it all together into a thick paste.

Brie stroked her fingers over Hall's stubbled cheek and sent up a quick prayer to the Seven that they might watch over him as he traveled through the middle world. Though he could never be hers, the thought of his death was more than she could stand.

"Can you save him?"

It was the one question she most feared asking. But now the words were out there, lying bare and naked in the air between them.

"I will do my best."

It was not at all the reassurance she had hoped to hear.

"A shame it is you dinna recover the Elven Scrolls of Niflheim when you liberated the jewels. A peek into their wisdom would tell us exactly how to heal our good warrior."

With a grunt, Orabilis pushed up from the floor and crossed to the bed, carrying a bowl filled with what looked like a mash of dark purple-green goo.

One arch of Orabilis's bushy eyebrow, and Brie vacated the little stool next to the bed so that the crone could sit down. Orabilis slathered the paste in a thick layer over Hall's wound and then bound his shoulder with a clean linen bandage.

"There," she pronounced as she stood up.

"Now what do we do?" Brie asked, willing and ready for any action Orabilis demanded.

"Now we wait. Without the guidance of the scrolls, there's nothing else we can do."

Eighteen

OF ALL THE unpleasant activities Brie could imagine, none was more torturous than waiting.

Patience is a virtue, her father had often said. But both of them knew it wasn't one of *her* virtues. Sitting, doing nothing, grated on her every nerve and brought out the worst in her attitude.

After a night of sitting helplessly at Hall's side, waiting for any little sign of recovery, Brie was ready to snap.

There had to be some constructive way she could help. Something she could do that would be more helpful to Hall than simply sitting here worrying over him.

She needed a task to occupy her hands. Her mind worked better when her hands were busy. And now that she thought about it, she knew exactly what that task should be.

Hall's pack lay in the corner where she'd put it. It took only a few minutes of snooping through his things to find what she sought.

After filling a small bowl with warm water, she

returned to Hall's bedside, armed with her tools—a bar of soap from the shelf above the bed and the small silver razor she'd found in his pack.

Shaving a man's face wasn't something she had personal experience with, but she'd seen it done often enough. Both her father and her brother had cursed their way through the ordeal.

If they could do it, with only their wavery reflection in a shield or pot as a guide, there was little doubt she could do it, too. And likely much better.

She dipped the soap into the warm water and rolled it in her hands, releasing the soothing aromas of lavender and balm. After smoothing the soap over Hall's stubbly cheeks, she lifted the razor and gently stroked down his face. The trail left behind invited her touch. His skin was smooth and soft under her finger, like a page from one of the books the laird's wife, Dani, valued so highly.

Brie returned to her self-appointed task, swiping the razor down Hall's face again, allowing her mind to run free now that her hands were occupied.

One day, perhaps, she'd make the time to learn how to put the letters she already knew together so that she could read words. Just like the laird's wife. Maybe her brother Jamesy was right and she would find reading a useful skill in the long run. It would have been helpful to have been able to read when she'd first found the scrolls in Torquil's solar.

Chances were that whoever Hall did end up wedding would, like Lady Dani, spend her spare time engaged in the art of reading. Brie could almost picture herself tucked into a bright corner of some solar, an unrolled scroll propped in her lap, children on the floor at her feet. . . .

Wait.

Her hand slowed to a stop, and she lifted the razor from Hall's face while she waited for the universe to catch up with her. Something in that little fantasy she'd just concocted tickled at the back of her mind.

The scrolls!

What was it Orabilis had said about the scrolls?

A peek into their wisdom would tell us exactly how to heal our good warrior.

That was it! *That* was what she could do to help him. If it was the scrolls Orabilis needed in order to save Hall, then, by the Seven, it was the scrolls she'd have.

There was nothing to be gained in waiting for her brother and his men to hunt down Mathew MacFalny. Even if they found him, without the jewels, they'd simply return to Castle MacGahan to wait for Hall.

Whereas if *she* were to locate the scrolls, she could bring them directly here to aid Orabilis in healing Hall.

It was settled.

Brie finished shaving Hall, making sure not to rush and risk a cut to his strong jawline. Once his face was cleaned and smooth, she replaced the razor in his pack and made her way outside to find Orabilis, a larger plan taking root in her mind.

Her hostess was in the sheds, feeding her goats.

"When I was here with the Tinklers, you said you knew of my mother's people. When I was very young, my mother told stories of my ancestors marking symbols upon their bodies to protect them in battle. Do you have knowledge of these symbols?"

"I might," the old woman answered, her fingers stroking through her goat's silky coat. "What purpose do you have in asking after such a thing?"

Brie rubbed her hands together, seeking to calm the nerves that tumbled her stomach. A wise woman such as Orabilis would surely see the merit in her plan.

"You said the scrolls would allow you to heal Hall without question. I plan to go get them, but I dinna fool myself into thinking it will be easy. To help ensure my success, I wish to utilize the power of my people's symbols."

She'd set out for battle once before and had failed miserably in her task. The stakes now were higher than any she'd ever considered before. If she succeeded this time, Hall's recovery was guaranteed.

"You dinna need the symbols. Yer power comes from what's inside you, lass, not what's emblazoned on your outside."

"That may be so for most of my people. But no for me." Though it wounded her pride to admit her weaknesses, Brie was sure that only honesty would convince Orabilis to help her. "My mother said the symbols imparted the magic and the wisdom of our ancestors. I'm no strong enough on my own, Orabilis. Though none can best me as an archer, my failings as a warrior are numerous. I'm no a patient woman. I've been known to be rash and overhasty in my choices. My temper gets the better of me, and I falter. In this quest, I mustn't falter. I canna afford to falter."

Orabilis lifted the bag at her feet and scattered its remaining contents into the goat pen before she answered.

"The last time you were here, yer only goal was to avenge yer father's death. Is yer commitment to yer chosen cause such that you so easily change yer purpose in life?"

This was different. Surely the old woman could be made to understand that.

"Revenge is an all-consuming ambition. It soothes the grief and protects you from having to move on with ycr life. It is a goal outside the constraints of time. Though I ken that nothing I can ever do will bring my father back, I will have my revenge in time.

"But now, in this moment, there's something I need to do that is *inside* the constraints of time. I have it within my ability to prevent Hall's death if I act quickly. Saving someone you care for should certainly take priority over revenge, should it no? My need for vengeance can wait."

"And Hall O'Donar is someone you care for?"

Brie considered denying it, but she had little to gain other than trying to shield her pride. But pride was of little use in gaining this woman's alliance.

"He is. Will you help me?"

"Mayhap. Does he feel the same way about you? Do you think he'd choose you over that which is most important to him, as you propose doing?"

Perhaps not. He'd already made it clear he'd leave her behind when Fenrir was no longer a threat.

But what he would do was of no matter to her. She could only control her own actions, not his, just as she could only control her own feelings, not his. And she knew without a doubt how she felt about him.

"What he would choose is of no importance. When you care for someone, you do whatever you can for them. This is what I must do. I ask you again, will you help me?"

Another long pause before the old woman answered had Brie worrying that she would refuse the request.

"Well spoken, Princess. Even the Norns themselves could no have foreseen the last daughter of the House MacUlagh taking a fancy to the Defender of the Thunder's People. Even if I hadna already taken such a liking to you, lass, the opportunity to confound the plans of those condescending old women would be reason enough for my assistance. If it's truly the wish of yer heart, I will help you."

Brie threw her arms around Orabilis, lifting her from her feet to twirl her around. "Thank you! So very much. Thank you." She set the old woman down.

"Dinna be so quick to thank me." Orabilis patted her hair back into place before heading toward the cottage. "The symbols you ask for hold a powerful Magic of their own. They will mark not only your skin but also your destiny. When Magic calls to Magic, Magic responds. The path you choose is no an easy one, especially if yer still determined to see vengeance wreaked upon the MacDowylt. The hunt for revenge might well soothe the grief you feel now. But once the hunt is over, if that's all you have to fill yer heart, you'll be left empty and wanting.

"Here's a wisdom that my people live by: Sometimes in life, you must let go in order to hold on. Before all is said and done, you may well regret this sacrifice yer making."

Nineteen

THE FETID STENCH permeating the little cottage was enough to wake the dead, and still Hall slept.

Though Brie envied him his escape from the sinus-rotting odor, his sleeping through something as awful as this served as proof that what she prepared to do was absolutely necessary.

Orabilis fussed over the little pot by the fireplace, jerking her head back from the fumes when she lifted the lid to stir the thick, dark liquid inside.

Brie fought the temptation to giggle at the expression of disgust on the old woman's face.

"It's a fair vile brew you've concocted there." An understatement if ever she'd made one. *Vile* would be a compliment to the nastiness in that pot.

"It is that," Orabilis agreed, her face still wrinkled in revulsion. "Little wonder yer people were called barbarians. I've always detested the smell of this plant."

It wasn't just the plant. Everything the old witch had put inside that pot smelled horrible, and it had only gotten worse as it had ripened over the past two days.

"As I promised it would be, our stain is ready. If yer sure you still want to go through with this, that is. A commitment such as you intend to make, once it's done, stays done."

Brie glanced to the room where Hall slept. Each night she had sat there next to him, hoping for some sign of improvement. Two days and nights and there had been none, though Orabilis still swore he could awaken at any time.

He lay flat on his back, stiff as the boards that held up his bed. His face had grown even paler than it was when they'd first arrived, except for the two bright red splotches on his cheeks, harbingers of the fever that ravaged his body. Unless the fever broke, he had no chance of survival.

"I'm sure."

She would not stand by and see him die.

"As you wish," Orabilis muttered, ladling out a scoop of the colorful dye into a stone bowl. "So it will be. Strip out of yer shift and climb up on the stool here by the fire, so I can see what I'm doing."

She would have to take her clothes off? In front of the old witch? If she'd stopped for even one single moment to think about what she was doing, she might have reasoned that out for herself. Orabilis couldn't very well paint the symbols of war and protection on her skin without her baring her body to the old woman.

"Come on, come on with you. Quit yer dawdling.

You've nothing to show me that I haven't seen each time I take off my own shift."

The very idea of the old woman standing naked on a stool brought a smile to Bridget's lips and urged her forward.

"Hold yer arms out. Nice and steady. Good. Just like that. Now, dinna you move a muscle."

The old woman dipped the twig she held into the blue concoction and trailed it from Brie's left shoulder down past her breast to a spot just below her belly button, ending in a curled flourish. Chill bumps rose on Brie's skin as the liquid settled to dry. A second dip into the dye and Orabilis painted a mirror image of the first marking, starting this time at Brie's right shoulder.

In what felt to Brie like hours that followed, Orabilis adorned Brie's arms, legs, and back with a series of intricate symbols. When she at last stepped back to assess her work, Brie sagged with relief.

"I felt as though we'd never finish."

Orabilis grinned, flashing her perfect white teeth. "We're no yet done, my fine lassie. We've yer face yet to go. Have a seat so that I can reach you."

As ridiculous as it seemed, after having the whole of her body covered in the symbols, the idea of marking her face set a rush of apprehension churning in her stomach. She shuttered off the desire to escape what was about to happen. This was her choice. Her request. Her path.

What did it matter, anyway? She'd never been vain about her looks. She braided her hair to keep it out of her face, and she wore whatever was close at hand and comfortable. Her appearance didn't matter in the least. It was of no concern what anyone who looked at her would think. She did this for an honorable cause. A necessary cause. It would give her the strength to do what needed doing.

"In ancient times, yer people looked upon these markings as a sign of beauty as well as protection," Orabilis said as she drew the first stroke above Brie's eye.

"It's a small matter," Brie murmured, doing her best to hold back the bewildering tears that blurred her vision.

Thanks to the detail of the symbols on her face and neck, Orabilis took almost as long to finish that as she had to adorn Brie's entire body.

"I'm glad that's done," Orabilis said at last. With a sigh, she laid down her bowl and twig. "I'm fair worn-out. I've a small mirror if you'd like to see what we've accomplished."

"No."

She might know it was there, but seeing it would be a different matter altogether. Seeing it would make it real. And as weirdly emotional as she felt at the moment, *real* was not something she wanted to face.

Orabilis shrugged and toddled over to the corner where their blankets lay in two neat stacks. "In that case we're done here, and I, for one, need some sleep. I assume you'll leave early?"

"At first light," Brie confirmed, reaching for her shift and dropping it down over her head. "I'm going to check on Hall before I turn in."

He slept still, though restlessly, his head turning from side to side as if he tried to escape some torment that plagued his dreams. Fever would do that to a man.

Brie sat down next to him and laid her palm to his forehead. His skin burned under her touch. She dipped a cloth into the bowl of water beside his bed and touched it first to his lips before laying it across his forehead.

"I leave tomorrow morning," she whispered, overcome with the need to share her plans with him. "Orabilis says we need the scrolls to ensure yer recovery. I will find Mathew MacFalny and the scrolls he carries, and I will bring them back."

"Bridget."

Her name left his lips on a whisper so faint, she wasn't sure it wasn't just her imagination.

"I'm here, Hall. Right by yer side."

Whether or not he could hear her, she wanted to reassure him.

"Where is Bridget?" he asked, his eyes fluttering open to stare at her, bereft of any recognition. "I'd have her here with me."

He swiped the cloth from his forehead and she replaced it, laying a hand to his chest. Under her fingers, his heart pounded wildly.

"Lie still and settle yer mind. Bridget will return shortly."

He calmed with that reassurance, closing his eyes once more, though his heart continued to race.

She dipped the cloth into the cool water and gently wiped it over his cheeks and neck, wishing it would have some effect on the heat that wracked his body.

Before she left the room, she bent over him and softly touched her lips to his forehead.

"I willna let you down, Hall O'Donar. I pledge it to you by the lives of the Seven. I will find the scrolls, and I will return to you."

And woe unto any who thought to stand in her way.

Twenty

How long had he been lost and wandering in that strange place?

Freakish shadowy figures populated the landscape Hall had traveled, an alien world unlike any he'd traversed before. Though it might not have been Niflheim itself, it had to have been close. Of that he felt certain.

Hall opened his eyes, searching for any memory of the place in which he found himself. A bedchamber, that much was clear. But *whose* bedchamber was the question.

Memories began to return, slowly at first, in bits and pieces so strange, he doubted their reality. Likely they were figments of his imagination, born out of the madness that had held him in its grip. Excruciating pain. Heat beyond human tolerance as if he'd traversed a land of pure, unrelenting fire.

And through it all, like a cool respite from the torment, Bridget MacCulloch had filled his dreams.

Only it couldn't have been Bridget. The phantom

that had appeared in his delirium had worn nothing more than a thin white shift, her every enticing curve outlined by the flickering fire behind her. Her hand, soft and cool when she'd touched him, bore exotic markings unlike any seen in this world for many centuries.

It would make sense that he'd dream of Bridget, even as his mind distorted her visage. Since dreams were the only place where he could claim her for his own, it was unlikely he'd ever be able to banish her from his dreams.

His mouth felt half its normal size, as if his tongue were swollen and made of paper. He was thirstier than he could ever remember being in the whole of his life. And *that* was a very long time, indeed.

He swung his legs to the side of the bed and sat up, waiting until his head quit spinning before he attempted to stand. It took two tries to make it to his feet and stay there.

This was good. He was standing. Standing, but naked as the day he was born. With a great effort, he pulled the top blanket from the bed, wrapped it around himself, and headed for the open door.

The melodious sound of someone singing reached his ears, the beautiful notes of a woman singing to herself as she worked. A soothing, tinkling, rippling cascade of music floating on the air that took him back to another time and another place. A Faerie glen where his mother had taken him as a child . . .

Orabilis!

He remembered now. Bridget had brought him here for the Faerie healer to work her magic.

Since he was standing on his own two feet, apparently she'd done exactly that, leaving him in the debt of not one but two Faeries.

Two Faeries and one beautiful, stubborn Pictish princess.

As he entered the main room of the little cottage, his grumbling stomach announced him before his words could.

"Oh!" Orabilis turned with a little squeak of surprise and the air shimmered around her, obscuring her for an instant. "Well, look at this. Patience has paid off. It would seem my potions worked after all. Welcome back to the world of Mortals, my young friend."

"Thank you, my lady. I am in your debt." Hall dipped his head in a deferential little bow.

"Indeed you are, Hall O'Donar. Indeed you are. You and yer rather determined companion both."

"My debt to you is my own, not Bridget's." He would not have Bridget held accountable for the Fae's services to him. The last complication Bridget needed in her life was a Faerie seeking repayment for something she didn't owe.

"True. And Bridget's debt to me is hers." Orabilis smiled and held up a bowl freshly dipped from the simmering pot beside her. "I was just about to eat. Stew? Some meat and broth will do wonders for you after all these days without food."

Again his stomach rumbled and he accepted her offering, taking a seat at the heavy wooden table. The first bite was so heavenly delicious he allowed himself a second to enjoy it before pursuing Orabilis's argument.

"What is Bridget's debt to you?"

"Her business, and none of yer own. Now, eat yer stew like a good lad. Bread to go with that? I've some nice cold goat milk, for after yer meal, if you'd like."

She held out a chunk of what appeared to be freshly baked bread and he accepted, forcing himself to wait for his next bite until she was seated across from him with her own bowl.

Of all the conversations he might have expected her to start, the one she chose was not among them.

"What will you do with the Beast once you've captured it?" Orabilis glanced up at him from her bowl, a half smile curling one corner of her mouth. "*If* you succeed in capturing it, that is."

In truth, he hadn't actually given that as much thought as it deserved.

"Return him to his prison in the scrolls, I suppose. Like the Elves who originally put him there intended."

The old woman nodded thoughtfully, as if to herself. "But where will you keep him and his scrolls? Surely you can see now, after the debacle with Torquil, this is a burden not safe in the hands of any Mortal."

He tended to agree with her, but the final decision, ultimately, was not his to make. There were powers beyond him that would decide the Beast's fate.

"When the time comes, I will do what needs to be done. That's the best I can promise."

"Fair enough." Orabilis put down her piece of bread and tapped her fingers on the table as if debating what she wanted to say next. "You do realize Fenrir has the ability to destroy the weave of the world as we know it. The future, as well as the present, lies at risk should you fail. And even if you succeed, *how* you succeed and what you do after carries that same burden of risk."

Why was it the gods never saw fit to save him from the agony of Faerie gibberish? The inscrutable nature of their warnings, their inability to say what they meant in a straightforward manner, always grated upon his nerves.

Still, this particular Faerie had saved his life, so he wouldn't argue with his hostess. He would simply change the subject.

"Is Bridget not taking her meal with us?"

"She is not."

Orabilis flashed her innocent Faerie smile and Hall's stomach knotted with the sure knowledge that something was very wrong.

"Is she out tending to the animals?"

Orabilis's brow wrinkled a bit more than usual as she considered the question. "She is not tending to our animals."

Word games. The Fae simply couldn't help them-selves, perhaps the least attractive of all their annoying habits. They played with language as a child played with toys.

Hall laid down his spoon and the warm bread, taking a moment to consider exactly how to ask the questions that would get her to tell him what he wanted to know. The direct method was usually best when it came to communicating with a Faerie.

"Where is she?"

Orabilis steepled her hands, tapping her fingers together slowly. "I am no sure exactly where she might be by now."

By now. A flaw in her choice of words, which, thankfully, should speed up this blighted process.

"Then tell me this: Where has she gone?"

Because Bridget was, without question, gone. He could feel her absence as a great empty spot in his world. A great empty spot that he didn't like one little bit.

The old Faerie took another bite, savoring the food before answering. "Now, there's a question I can answer. Our determined lass has gone after the scrolls she believed necessary for your survival."

"What?" Hall burst up from the table, sending his chair crashing over backward. "But you didn't need the scrolls. I've recovered just fine without them."

"As I told her you very well might, given time. But it seems she's no a patient lass. She wasn't will-ing to risk my being wrong."

"And you just let her go? By herself?"

Unbelievable! Orabilis had to know how danger-ous it would be for Bridget to leave the protection of Rowan Cottage.

The Faerie shrugged, as if they discussed noth-ing more serious than a misplaced garment. "Young girls these days. Not a drop of patience in the lot of them. They make up their mind and there's sim-ply no talking them out of it. She wanted to go, she went. What's an old woman to do?"

"What's an old—" Hall clamped his mouth shut when he realized he'd been reduced to sputtering. After a deep breath to calm himself he tried again. "Why didn't you stop her?"

Orabilis snorted her disbelief. "Who am I to stop the last daughter of the House MacUlagh, descended from the Ancient Seven who'd ruled the land when not even—"

"Enough!" Hall's own patience, normally quite extensive, was at an end. "I'll hear no more of your nonsense. How long has she been gone?"

"She left here two days ago, armored with her people's symbols of protection and destiny, seeking one she called Mathew. Seeking the Elven Scrolls of Niflheim so that she might ensure your recovery."

Two days' head start?

"By Thor! I'll need food and provisions so that I might leave right away. Traveling quickly enough, I just might catch up with her."

Orabilis motioned toward him with her spoon.

"You'll likely want clothes, too. Just a thought. Yer things are cleaned and folded in the corner of the bedchamber."

With his face as hot as if the fever had never left, Hall turned his back on the Faerie, fighting to keep his anger in check as he left. The sound of her satisfied chuckle followed him until he slammed the bedchamber door.

Quickly, he dressed and returned to the main room to find her packing a large bag for him.

"I'll saddle my horse and return for that shortly." He couldn't abide wasting any more time. "And then I'll be on my way."

"There's no point in yer being in such a hurry. What's to be will be. It's no within yer power to change Bridget's fate." Orabilis tipped her head to one side, her gaze piercing him. "Or is it?"

How could she be so uncaring about the woman who had risked everything to save him? "It's Bridget's safety we speak of. Her life. The dangers stalking her are beyond her abilities."

Again the old woman chuckled. "And what of it? What's happened to your Northman's fatalistic view of life? Where's all yer standard blether about the weave already having been woven and the Norns determining what's to happen to all of us?"

"To hell with the Norns," he growled. "I live outside their tapestry and, believe me in this, I won't allow Bridget to succumb to harm. Not even that which she brings upon herself."

To his surprise, Orabilis laughed out loud. "Oh, lad, it does my heart good to hear you speaking from that half of yer ancestry."

"What do you know of my ancestry?" he asked, suspicion building. She had recognized his name that first night. She had known of his people, and where they came from.

Orabilis continued to gather items and stuff them into the bag, not looking in his direction. "More than you might think. I knew yer mother. She was quite a talented healer in her own right. And every bit as hardheaded as you are."

"And my father, did you know him as well?" If that was the case, then she knew the whole of his secret.

"I did indeed. A disappointing wastrel who proved himself to be much more trouble than his poor mother ever deserved. And definitely more trouble than yer poor mother realized when she ran away with him."

Unable to dispute her description of his father, Hall nodded his acceptance of her words and left the little cottage to retrieve his horse, old feelings of bitterness bubbling within his chest.

His father had deserted his family so long ago, Hall had difficulty in recalling his face. A self-involved coward, he had refused to carry out the tasks required of him to aid Mankind and had forced the burden upon his son.

Only someone with intimate knowledge of Hall's family could have described his father so well. But whether Orabilis knew who—and what—they were was another matter. This was a secret he guarded closely.

With his mount saddled and his sword on his back, Hall led the animal to the front of the cottage, where Orabilis waited to hand to him the bags of provisions she'd prepared.

"You'll want these, too," she said, holding out her hand to reveal the goat carved from rowan wood he'd worn around his neck and a small cloth bag. "Remember to keep the jewels covered once you leave the protection of Rowan Cottage."

"Thank you," he mumbled, embarrassed that he'd lost his temper with the old Faerie who'd saved his life.

She reached out with her gnarled fingers to pat his hand. "Go on yer way confident in the knowledge that it is yer own free will that guides what happens from this point forward, no the aimless weavings of three old women who sit under a tree."

He dropped the necklace over his head and secured the bundle of jewels inside his pack, then tied the pack to his horse. Finally, he turned back to face her.

His fury wasn't with her, and she didn't deserve to be treated as if she'd done something wrong. Especially not after all she'd done for him.

"I apologize for my behavior and for my anger."

"You've no need to apologize to me." Orabilis tightened the ends of the shawl she wore around her shoulders. "But you do need accept that yer anger is but a mask for the true emotion you refuse to acknowledge."

"And what emotion might that be, Faerie? Since you seem to know me so well."

"One of the most powerful emotions of all, my young warrior: fear. I suspect it may be a stranger to you, but you've met it now. It's the beast curling in yer stomach and threatening to crush yer chest. Can you deny the fear you have for Bridget Mac-Culloch's safety?"

He refused to snap at her bait. He also refused to lie. And denying her assertion would be a lie. It *was* fear holding him within its mighty clutches. Fear of what might be happening to Bridget at this very moment, and every moment he delayed.

"I will find her. I *will* see her safe," he said, as much to reassure himself as anything.

"Even if yer actions anger the Norns themselves?"

He would not allow Bridget's destiny to be determined by three old women who spent their days under a tree, weaving the tapestry that ensnared both their worlds.

Foot in his stirrup, he straddled his mount and prepared to leave. No matter what the cost, he would not be deterred from the path he had chosen.

"The Norns may chafe over my actions as they will," he declared.

"Just as the Norns still chafe over Thor's pompous little demigod mating with a Fae, yes?"

Hall dipped his head in a respectful farewell and turned his horse west to carry him outside the ring of rowans surrounding Orabilis's home. Any question he'd had about how much she knew of his family was answered.

His secret was a secret no more.

Twenty-one

THE BOY WAS a day ahead of her. Two at most.

Brie rubbed the ashes from the cold fire pit between her fingers, then stood and dusted off her hands.

Mathew and his companion were clearly idiots. How they could make so little effort to hide their tracks, knowing they were being hunted, was beyond her. No matter their youth, they should have known better.

Unless they didn't understand that they were being hunted.

"In which case yer even bigger fools than I thought," she said.

It felt good to hear a human voice again, even if it was her own. It distracted her from the dark what-ifs haunting the corners of her mind. What if she didn't find the scrolls? What if she did, but was too late to save Hall? What if . . .

"Concentrate on the work at hand, Brie," she encouraged herself. "Dinna dally in the land of what-if. There lie the traps that suck yer will away."

She walked slowly around the campsite, studying the ground for any other signs.

Two sets of footprints, so it was likely that Mathew and Dobbie still traveled together.

She moved farther out from the fire, squatting to examine her latest find.

Hoofprints.

Now there was a different concern. Mathew had left his mount behind when he'd run away. She knew, because she'd held its lead all the way to Rowan Cottage.

She continued to study the ground, finding at last the clue she'd sought: hoofprints over the footprints.

Someone other than her followed the two young men.

The proof marked the ground around her, and made the hair on Brie's neck prickle as if someone watched her from the trees. But that was impossible. She'd just come through those trees and no one had been there.

All the same, she stood and scanned the site one last time, peering into the darkening gloom of the woods, working out her next decision.

She wouldn't be able to make it much farther tonight. The last rays of the sun had already begun to disappear behind the western horizon. This spot certainly wasn't her preference for a place to set up camp. With open ground on all sides, it wasn't easily defensible. No running water nearby. No ready shelter should the rain return.

But it did have one big advantage: Torquil's men had already come and gone. If she continued to ride in the dark she might overtake them, and *that* was not a prospect she found the least bit appealing.

When she met up with them, she'd prefer it be at a time of her own choosing. A time when she'd have the upper hand.

So this spot would have to do for tonight.

She gathered kindling and placed it on one side of the original fire pit. The cold made a fire necessary but, considering how close the men she trailed might be, she'd keep it small. It would be foolish to draw attention to herself.

Once her fire was built, she prepared her meal. Dried meat and hard bread. She rationalized that the lack of water made cooking difficult, but in truth, cooking had never been her strong suit. Her best efforts rarely produced any outcome other than a lumpy porridge on a good day and a burned pot on all others.

Cold food was fine. Though her stomach growled in protest, she swallowed the last bits of her meal and tried not to think of the wonderful soups Orabilis had prepared each day she'd stayed at Rowan Cottage. Perhaps tomorrow she'd keep an eye out for rabbit tracks. Fresh meat would be a welcome change from this dried, salty fare.

Before attempting to sleep, she placed her bow and quiver next to her and pulled out the short sword Orabilis had insisted she take along on her journey. Should she find herself in close combat, it would be a much more effective weapon than the small knives she carried on her person.

Using a heavy stick, she fished a couple of large stones out of the fire pit and fit them under her furs, close to her body. With her woolens pulled tight around her to block the wind, she settled in close to the fire. She forced her eyes closed and hoped sleep would overtake her before her unruly mind had a chance to torment her with worry over all the ways she could fail in her quest.

Four days in the saddle had taken its toll and, in spite of the worries plaguing her, she quickly drifted into a deep, dreamless sleep.

So deep, it felt like only moments had passed when she startled awake, a crushing pain bearing down on her back.

And a sharp blade resting at her throat.

"I thought that might wake even a heavy sleeper like yerself, my lady," a rough voice said from behind her.

She was awake all right, but with the weight of some villain's knee pressing into her back, she couldn't lift her head to identify her attacker.

Slowly, she edged her hand out, but as her fingers raked the edge of her blade, the weapon skittered out of her reach.

Two of them, then. The one holding her down and the one who'd kicked her weapon away.

"No, no, lass. No weapons for you," the second

one said with a chuckle. "The way I figure it, a woman out here all alone, she's either a runaway or a criminal. So which is it?"

"The horse is too fine for a criminal."

A third voice, off to her left.

"She could have stolen it."

A fourth man, on the other side of the fire.

"No. You saw her mounted as well as I did. The tack fits her too well to be stolen. Looks to have been made for her special, right down to the fancy sheath. I'd venture to guess she's running from a new husband."

They'd been watching her all evening. How could she have been so careless as to allow herself to be captured like this?

"Let's have a look at what we've found, aye?"

The weight was lifted off her back and a hand fastened on her collar, dragging her up to her feet. There were indeed four men, spaced around the campsite, warriors from the looks of them. All leering at her like she was a piece of fresh meat up for auction.

"What in the name of the holy mother is that all over her face?"

The man holding her grabbed her chin and turned her face around for his inspection. "She's been marked, Hamish. It's like nothing I've ever seen before."

One of the others approached to peer down at her face. He licked his thumb and scrubbed it back and forth across her forehead while her captor held her still.

"Whatever it is, it's no coming off. Whoever put it there meant for it to stay."

"Must be she belongs to somebody. Mayhaps they'll pay to get their property back, aye? Anyone who went to this kind of trouble to mark it must want it badly."

The four of them laughed at that, as if the idea of ransoming her off was one of the best they'd had.

She stilled, remaining silent as the men surrounding her plotted. Carefully, slowly, she inched her fingers toward the knife hidden at her waist.

"We'll check the villages we pass through while we search for the boy. Mayhap we'll go back to Tordenet wealthier men than we left."

Tordenet?

Her hand froze as she considered her predicament. She hadn't just been careless enough to have been taken prisoner by a band of wandering villains. She'd been taken by Torquil's men.

She rapidly reassessed her situation. Escape from them now would be close to impossible. But since they were looking for the same ones she'd been tracking, biding her time would be no hardship.

Her best course was to let them do the heavy work of locating their prey. By then, surely she'd be able to work out the means to a successful escape.

Twenty-two

SQUATTING ON THE ground, Hall rubbed a bit of dirt between his fingers and tilted his head, straining to catch any sign of the sounds he'd heard earlier. Overhead a distant thunder rumbled, setting a frown of concentration on his face.

This was no time to let his emotions get the better of him. He was too close to finding Bridget.

He rose to his feet and wiped his hands on his plaid before taking a moment to stroke the neck of his massive black horse. They'd ridden through the night with little break for the past three days. Both he and the animal were wearing down.

"Good Beli. Soon enough we'll find her, and then I'll give you your rest, old man."

Hall lifted himself up onto the animal's back and once again tipped his head to listen.

There! The sound he'd heard before was louder in that direction. A rustling, busy sound of men waking. No better time to drop in unannounced than when your prey was still slow-witted from their time in Nott's world.

Urging his mount forward, he followed the sound, feeling more confident of his direction as the noises grew more discernible. Four men, by the sounds.

He briefly considered returning to pick up his original course. Men were of no interest to him, and Bridget would avoid encounters with any other than her intended prey.

If she *could* avoid them.

A darker possibility kept him moving forward, more quietly than before.

The warriors from Tordenet he'd encountered before had traveled in such a number. If these were the other group of Fenrir's soldiers, they searched for the same prey that Bridget sought. Meaning they were as likely to find Bridget as they were to find Mathew and Dobbie.

He quickened his pace, intent upon all the sounds from the camp. Four men conversing as they prepared to break camp. Four men moving about, readying their mounts.

Four men. But five horses.

He stilled, bringing his mount to a halt to allow him to better concentrate on what awaited him ahead. He filtered out the noises of the forest around him and listened.

Five horses and five human hearts beating, just beyond those trees.

Hall guided Beli forward, the horse's training allowing them to silently move close enough that Hall's eyes might confirm the fear his ears had already predicted.

Bridget!

She sat on the ground, her legs drawn up with her forehead resting on her knees. Her arms had been pulled back and bound behind her on either side of a small tree.

If these men had harmed her in any way, they would beg for the mercies of Hela before he was finished flaying the skin from their bones.

Like a berserker in full rage, he charged forward, swinging his sword in an arc over his head. His battle cry pierced the air, echoing throughout the land, louder than any thunder overhead could ever manage.

The men in the clearing scattered. The two already mounted beat a hasty retreat into the woods; he'd worry over their fate once he'd freed Bridget.

One of the men ran toward him, sword drawn, bellowing his own war cry.

Big mistake on his part.

A downward arc of Hall's weapon, and the warrior's head took flight from his body. The torso teetered on lifeless feet for a moment before toppling over forward.

Bridget screamed his name and Hall reined his horse around to find her on her feet, the fourth man's blade at her throat.

By Thor! What had the beasts done to her face?.

IT WAS BEYOND foolish of her to have called out Hall's name. Brie berated herself for having given Hamish the momentary upper hand by acknowledging her recognition. But seeing Hall here, full of life and obviously recovered, had taken her by surprise.

"Is this man the master from whom you escaped?" Hamish hissed the question into her ear as he forced her in front of him like a living shield. "Hold where you are, stranger! If it's yer property yer after, I'm willing to strike a bargain."

"My *property*?" Hall's voice sounded strained as if he strangled on the question. "She is no man's property. Take your hands from her and move away while you still can."

Hamish tightened his hold and the cold metal of his knife pressed against Brie's throat. This wasn't playing out at all as she would have chosen.

"I ken who you are now," Hamish called out. "I remember you, O'Donar. I remember how you ran away the day of the great fire. Ran away with that brother of yers to save yer own cowardly lives. I remained to battle the inferno, and our laird rewarded me well for it. I'm an officer in Tordenet's guard while yer still naught but a penniless mercenary. Hunting some other man's woman for him, are you?"

Hall shook his head, an almost imperceptible movement, his eyes sharp and emotionless, like those of a hawk homed in on his prey. "It was never my life I feared for, soldier. Release the woman. I give no more warnings."

"You think I fear yer sword? With this one as my

collateral?" Hamish laughed, the cold sound sending shivers down Brie's back. "Perhaps you canna see from up upon yer great horse what fate can so easily, so quickly befall the woman."

With a hand wrapped in her hair, Hamish jerked Brie's head back, stretching her neck and forcing her eyes up to the gray, overcast sky. The blade at her throat moved in a delicate arc of motion, leaving in its wake a necklace of burning pain. Not deep enough to do real damage, but inflicting a sting sharp enough to elicit an unconscious gasp.

Across the campsite, Hall lifted his sword toward the heavens and threw back his head, roaring his fury in a deafening cry that reverberated in Brie's ears.

Thunder rumbled overhead, and the ground shifted and buckled as if it trembled before the fury of some angry god's wrath. Lightning crackled across the sky in a pattern such as Brie had never seen.

Once, twice, the lightning flashed from one side of the sky across to the other before one large, jagged bolt arced down like a massive, fiery spear toward the very spot where she and the man who held her stood.

The air around her crackled and the hair on her body stood on end. Next to her, Hamish screamed and released his hold on her. Freed from his hands, Brie flung herself away from him to land flat on her face, her arms covering her head. Instinctively, she curled her body to present the smallest target.

Lightning always goes for the trees, her father had warned her as a child. And here she was, right in the blighted middle of a forest.

She had no time to think or plan, only to cower. As quickly as it had begun, it was over. The stench of burning flesh was sharp and acrid, stinging its way into her nostrils, but she kept her head down and covered, refusing to look up. Silence hung in the little glen until Hall shattered it.

"Bridget!"

His hands fastened on her arms and he lifted her to her feet, crushing her against his chest.

"What happened?" She could hardly force the words past her lips. The storm had come out of nowhere, more potent than any she'd ever experienced.

"Are you unharmed?" he whispered, his breath warm against her forehead. "Have they injured you?"

"They injured nothing except my pride," she answered honestly. She had been careless, and being captured had been her punishment for that carelessness.

She suspected hers hadn't been the only punishment meted out in this glen. It was as if the gods themselves had seen to Hamish's punishment. Though Hall's body blocked her view, she heard no sounds coming from where Torquil's guardsman had stood only moments before.

She could see his headless companion, though.

"Do you always take their heads in battle?" It had been much the same scene before.

"If I can," he acknowledged, his heart pounding like a battle drum beneath her ear. "Ensures I only have to battle them once."

Hall drew back from her, his big hands rising to caress either side of her face, his thumbs gently stroking her cheeks as he stared into her eyes.

"What have they done to you?"

When he spoke, his warm breath tickled the loose hair around her face, distracting her from any thoughts other than of being so close to him.

His finger trailed over her forehead and down her cheek. His arms held her so protectively, his gaze focused so intensely, capturing her own, she could do nothing but breathe in the essence of the man. He filled her senses to the exclusion of everything else.

The tingle of expectation rippled through her body and she leaned in toward him without conscious thought of movement, anticipating his lips once more closing over hers.

He didn't disappoint.

His kiss was exactly as she remembered, exactly as she'd re-created it in her dreams a thousand times. Warm, strong, demanding.

If the gods chose to freeze time at this moment, she could happily spend eternity as she was right now, ensconced in Hall's embrace, his lips fixed upon her own.

She closed her eyes, melting into the sensual haze of the moment, and almost missed his whisper when he placed his hands on her upper arms and pulled back from her.

"Armored with her people's symbols of protection and destiny."

Her eyes flew open when he shook her, shattering into a million pieces the wonderful, fluffy haze that had cocooned her only seconds before.

"I should have realized what the Faerie was telling me. It wasn't these men at all. You did this to yourself. You marked up your face in this manner, didn't you?"

Brie blinked several times, trying to focus her eyes and her thoughts. Marked up her face?

Her face! She'd all but forgotten. Little wonder he drew away from her in revulsion.

There was nothing to be gained in pointing out that in actuality it was Orabilis who'd done the marking. It had been her choice, her decision.

"It was necessary. These are the symbols of—"

"I know well enough what they are," he cut in, his voice harsh with emotion. "More like symbols of impulsive and irresponsible behavior."

Like hell they were! If he thought she was going to stand here and listen to him lecture her for something she'd done in the course of trying to save his sorry ass, he was more than mistaken.

Besides, it wasn't his concern. What she did was

her own business, not his. He had his life to attend to, and she had hers.

"It's of no matter now," she said, pulling her arms from his grip and backing away. "What's done is done. I'm pleased to see the witch's cures worked upon you. And now that yer well, and yer here, we're only wasting time when we speak of any of this. If we're to find the sword and the scrolls, we'd best be on our way."

"We?" Hall's face colored a deep, blotchy red and he actually sputtered as if he'd momentarily forgotten how to speak. "You're going no farther in this hunt. I've worried my last over you. Have you no concept, no realization, of how much danger you've repeatedly put yourself in?"

He sounded enough like her brother to be his twin. And the last thing she needed in her life was two of Jamesy. Did neither of them listen to the words that came out of their mouths?

Did he honestly expect her to believe that she was somehow at more risk in this quest than he? Ridiculous men! All of them thought they were somehow more impervious to danger than she.

"No farther, you say? What would you have of me, then, O wise one? Am I to wait here in this clearing for you to return once you'd completed yer task? It's no been such a safe place so far, now, has it? No safe at all, between getting captured and whatever *that* was."

She flicked her hand toward the smoking, blackened lump lying next to the trees where she'd stood a short time ago and wrapped her arms around herself in an attempt to forestall the shivers that assaulted her. That lump was all that remained of Hamish. Had she not moved as quickly as she had, it might well have been all that was left of her.

"That's not what I meant," Hall began.

"No? You've something safer in mind, have you? Am I to return to the witch, then? Riding through Torquil's territory again, tempting fate once more?"

"Of course not! Don't be ridiculous."

"Ah, then I can only suppose you'd have me go back to Castle MacGahan. Journeying on my own, is it? With who knows how many more of Torquil's men scouring the countryside, looking to find what we should be after ourselves, right this very minute? Am I so much safer doing that than riding along with you?"

They glared at one another across the emotion-charged distance separating them.

"You're impossible," he said at last, turning from her and stalking back toward his horse. "Impossible!"

As perfect a word to describe her situation as if she'd chosen it herself.

Impossible.

As impossible as the dream she realized she still harbored deep in her heart that somehow, in spite of his wealth and her poverty, something might work out between them. She was a fool for not having accepted the truth when she'd first learned that he was a laird, with his own land holdings and responsibilities.

If she'd hoped to overcome the obstacle of their different stations in life, the new one she'd created on her own was the absolute end to any dream she might have clung to for a long, romantic life with Hall O'Donar.

Lairds did not take penniless women as their wives. And they most certainly did not take to wife any woman whose face and body was adorned with the ancient blue markings that were now a part of who she was.

"Impossible," she echoed in a whisper, heading toward her own horse at the edge of the clearing.

She might not be destined for the life she'd dreamed of, but in whatever life she had, she vowed that she would do her best to be bold and in control. Unlike the girl who had left Castle MacGahan with no thought but revenge in her heart, Brie was a new woman now. Determined. Strong.

Destiny might have snatched her dreams away from her, but not even Destiny could force her to live the timid life of an ordinary woman.

Twenty-three

H E SHOULD HAVE taken his brother's advice. He should have trusted his instincts.

Mathew had felt uneasy and suspicious every time Dobbie had suggested they take a different path, but in spite of every warning Hugo had shared about the dangers of trusting people, he'd allowed himself to trust Dobbie anyway. He had *wanted* to trust the boy. Had wanted Dobbie to need his friendship as much as he had needed Dobbie's.

And just look where trusting another person had gotten him. Lost, that's where. Lost and penniless and without any means to accomplish his goals.

Mathew clutched his Dream Guardian to his chest and scanned the campsite once more in the vain hope that Dobbie might have left behind some small belonging.

Nothing.

Dobbie had disappeared sometime in the night, taking everything with him. Everything but the plaid upon which Mathew slept and the sword he clutched in his arms.

At least he still had his Dream Guardian.

What would he do now? What *could* he do?

His dreams of wealth were dashed. Without the scrolls to sell to the MacLeod laird, there was nothing to be gained by continuing his journey to Dunvegan.

He had no horse, no food, no money.

"But all is not lost," he announced defiantly to the forest, a small spark of optimism undaunted.

He still had a head on his shoulders, unlike his brother, Hugo. He still had his wits about him. And he still had this wonderful sword that kept his nightmares at bay and made him all but invincible.

He didn't for one moment doubt its supreme power. It had taken that great warrior to his knees with only the lightest touch.

A wave of guilt swept over him and he struggled to push it away. He had never intended to hurt anyone. It wasn't his fault the big man had gotten too close to him. And once the damage had been done, there was nothing to be gained in staying by the warrior's side. Had the big man survived the wound, there was still the other attacker. Running away had been his only real option. Even Dobbie had agreed upon that.

Not that Dobbie Caskie was any measure of right and wrong. Dobbie, after all, had robbed him blind, disappearing with what few possessions he had left.

"All is not lost," Mathew repeated stubbornly.

He would no longer have the advantage of wealth he'd counted on, but that was no reason to abandon the rest of his plans.

He could still locate the Tinklers and reunite with his cousin, Eleyne. They could return to their home, where, if necessary, he would challenge his uncle for what was rightfully his. With his Dream Guardian at his side, he had no doubt that he would win any challenge, even one against a man as ruthless and powerful as his uncle.

After a stop at the water's edge to wash the sleep from his face, Mathew wrapped his cloak tightly around him and headed out to find the trail he and Dobbie had abandoned after they'd been attacked.

Find the trail and double back north. That was his best bet now. Somewhere along the way, along one of the well-traveled roads, he hoped to cross paths with the Tinklers and Eleync.

Twenty-four

BRIDGET GALLOPED AHEAD of Hall, her bow raised, her long hair flying in the wind.

He drew his horse to a halt to watch. She cut across the flat stretch of open land, building speed as she went. Riding like the wildling she was, she controlled her mount without use of her hands. Like a natural-born warrior, she let loose her arrow and lifted her arms high in the air in an instinctively joyous celebration, as if she knew her shot would meet its mark even before it left her string.

It had.

Tonight they would feast on fresh rabbit.

She slid down from her mount and ran to retrieve her catch. Uninhibited, wild, untamed— the descriptions pounded at Hall's thoughts, each of them more fitting for the woman he watched than the one before.

If he were to design his perfect woman, everything about Bridget was what he would wish for in a life partner.

Too bad his life was destined to be spent alone.

"You see?" she asked as she rode up next to him, her eyes gleaming with the thrill of her catch. "I told you we'd have better than dry bread and oats for our meal this night. Our deal stands. I caught it; you clean it and cook it."

On second thought, perhaps she wasn't perfect. But damn close.

He accepted the carcass without comment and draped it over the back of his saddle. A deal was a deal.

"Impressive marksmanship," he said, acknowledging her extraordinary abilities.

Bridget shrugged off the compliment, but a deep pink colored her cheeks as she guided her horse next to his.

"Is it possible we err in following the others toward Dunvegan, do you think?" she asked.

Hall had considered that very question more than once since they'd first found the tracks he was sure had been left behind by the party from Castle MacGahan.

"I only bring it up because it feels fair odd to me that we've found no sign of Mathew and his young companion for the past day. After following their tracks to the glen where we met, we've since found no sign of them on the trails. No sign of anything but the tracks of our own men."

"You raise a good point," he agreed. "Tomorrow we'll begin again with a fresh eye to refocus our efforts. We'll scour the area until we find some sign of the ones we need to find."

Another half hour of travel and Hall located what he sought, a safe place for them to set up their camp for the night.

"If I'm to clean your little beastie here, we'd best make camp now, before it's too dark for me to deal with him properly."

"A good spot," she murmured appreciatively, pulling ahead of him to investigate his choice. "Our backs to the rocks and running water beyond. I approve."

Just as she had a gift for the bow and arrow, one of his talents lay in his ability to locate a good campsite. After so many years spent living off the land, he'd learned to seek his comfort where he could.

Together they set up camp and tended to their animals, before Hall busied himself with preparing the rabbit.

"While you finish with that, I'm going upstream a bit. I'll be back shortly." Bridget pulled a small bundle from her pack and walked toward the water.

"Stay close." He knew that she didn't really need his reminder, but he felt compelled to give it anyway. "Within hearing distance of my voice."

She laughed over her shoulder, a lilting, happy sound that slid under his best defenses.

"And how far might that be, eh? How am I to ken the distance yer voice will reach? Will you sing for me, Hall, that I might know when I've gone too far?"

If he hadn't enjoyed the sound of her laughter so much, he just might have been offended by such an audacious woman.

"O'Donar men do not sing."

She stopped and turned to look at him, her face clearly showing surprise. "Never? Everyone sings a bit now and then."

He shook his head in denial. "Not without several tankards of very strong ale, and a crowd to drown out the pitiful noise we make."

His reward for his honesty was more of her beautiful laughter as she turned and disappeared beyond the bushes.

With the rabbit cleaned at last and threaded upon the spit, he decided to take it down to the water for a quick rinse. He couldn't abide biting into meat covered with the small hairs left behind by a neglectful cleaning. He might live as a heathen, but that didn't mean he had to be one.

As he made his way beyond the bushes, he caught the faint sound of something equally as lovely as Bridget's laughter. Somewhere upstream, just around the curve and hidden from his view, her voice lilted on the air. Not a melody he recognized, but an ancient one, he felt sure, based on the language in which she sang. Perhaps her song, like the markings on her body, originated with her ancestors.

Like a bee to a blooming flower, he found himself drawn toward the source of the enticing sound.

She kneeled at the water's edge, wearing only her shift in spite of the cold. The last rays of the day glimmered on the fast-flowing water as she dipped her hand down and brought it back up to scrub against her face.

She stood, and sunlight reflecting off the water glowed up around her in shades of pink and silver. Her shift slipped down to reveal the shapely contours of her back, where a blue serpent wound its way around a sword that disappeared below what the shift still covered.

Hall couldn't have turned away if his life depended upon it. Though the markings on her face had faded a bit, those on her back were a bright vivid blue and he could almost swear the lines glowed with movement as the sunlight shone upon them.

Listening to her voice, seeing her standing there, Hall wanted nothing so much as to toss aside the spit he held and rush forward. To take her in his arms and cover her luscious, full lips with his own. He wanted to lay her down on the furs she'd dropped at her feet and bury himself inside her warmth.

He wanted her, body and soul. He wanted her for his very own.

Fool that he was. She was not meant for the likes of him.

He began to back away as quietly as he'd

approached, stopping when her melody abruptly ceased.

"I dinna recall having invited an audience to watch me bathe."

Damn. He was caught.

"Begging your pardon, my lady." Stalling for time to invent some halfway reasonable excuse for his presence, he cleared his throat. Twice.

There was no reasonable excuse.

She drew the neck of her shift up to cover her shoulders but kept her back turned to him, making no attempt to speak into the silence hanging between them.

"I was . . . I was cleaning the rabbit." Like a half-witted sop, he lifted the spit in his hand as if that might explain his standing there fumbling for words, ogling her like some common lecher.

When she didn't respond, he hurried to add to his growing story. "The waters took it from my hands and I had no choice but to follow after. I came this way only to . . . to retrieve our dinner."

The words sounded as false to him as if he'd shouted, *"I'M LYING!"* at the end of his sentence.

He had no doubt they sounded equally false to Bridget. She still made no move to respond, leaving him to wiggle on the spear of truth.

"I'll leave you to your . . . I'm going now."

Making no effort to muffle his departure, he stomped back to camp and fixed the spit over the fire.

When the time came to compile a list of the world's greatest fools, he'd have no competition at all for the top spot on that list. He'd just proven his eligibility.

Prince of All Fools! A perfect title for him.

Spying on Bridget had been bad enough. But having lied to her about it was shameful.

Unwilling to face her after his complete lapse of acceptable behavior, Hall had busied himself at the fire, eyes downcast on his work, when he heard her approaching.

"Is the rabbit done?"

"Not yet. It's barely begun to brown."

He poked at the flames with a stick, wishing the beastie were done. Wishing they'd already eaten and wrapped themselves in their blankets for the night. He could only hope his luck would hold and Bridget wouldn't discover his stupid falsehood.

The coming meal was likely to be the worst—and the longest—of his life.

"Strange . . ." She drew the word out, as if puzzling over some great mystery.

A shiver of apprehension rolled down his back. "What is that you speak of?"

"Well, yer fire there must be blazing hot, given that you had to chase our dinner into the water, and yet the clothing you wear is already dry. A fine trick, that."

"I never entered the water." He considered admitting everything, but only for an instant. Like the fool he was, he chose to compound his error. "The current kept the end of the spit close enough to the shore for me to reach it."

"Really? Now, that is truly unusual. I've never seen a current such as you describe. One that flows along the shore." She paused for a moment. "Upstream."

Not a prince of fools, but a king.

He stared into the flames, knowing he had nowhere to go but to the truth. "I heard you singing. I followed the sound."

"Why would you do that? You need only yer ears to hear, no yer eyes."

Why? Because he couldn't help himself. But that wasn't something he could bring himself to confess to her. Instead he would apologize. Apologize and pledge never to lie to her again.

"I should not have lied to you. I should have . . ." He turned to face her, and all thoughts evaporated from his mind.

She stood at the edge of their campsite, still wearing only her shift. Her thick brown hair, released from its heavy braid, rippled over her shoulders like a silken cloak.

He'd never seen a more beautiful woman. Or one he that wanted more than he wanted this one.

"Why did you kiss me?" she asked. "That day you found me with the Tinklers on the road to Castle MacGahan, when you left me behind to begin this search. Why did you come back and kiss me?"

With four strides he found himself in front of her, close enough to pull her into his arms. He refrained from that unwise action, calling on every bit of willpower he'd ever had, searching her eyes for some clue as to why she asked.

It would be easy enough to brush away her question, but he'd pledged himself to truth with this woman, even if the pledge hadn't been spoken aloud.

"Because I could do nothing else when I saw you standing there. You were days delayed in reaching Castle MacGahan. The need to touch you, to prove to myself you were safe, consumed me."

"So you felt entitled? As if you had the right to kiss me?"

He shook his head. "I felt . . ." How could he make her understand? The blood in his veins warred, demanding he follow the dictates of all his ancestors, both the ancient gods of Asgard and the Fae. "In my family line, the men are not known for their restraint. They take what they want and the consequences be damned."

The actions of his ancestors on both sides were the origin of untold legends and stories, most of which rarely portrayed them as the good guys. And with good reason.

One lovely eyebrow arched in response to his statement. "That's not how it is in my family line. Men would never dare to think they could take what they want, simply because they want it."

Of course they wouldn't. Mortals didn't behave with the same reckless abandon demonstrated by the gods or the Fae. Neither did they condone the ill behavior of those two races.

"With us, it is the women who take what they want." Brie's eyes sparkled dangerously and her hand reached out to rest at the back of his neck. "Be ye warned, my warrior. The women in my line give as good as we get."

Her lips grazed over his, and need, hot and heavy, swelled in his veins. He wrapped his arms around her and clasped her to him.

Shivering in his embrace, she moaned against his lips and he was lost.

With one arm behind her knees and one at her back, he swept her up and carried her to the place where she'd dropped her heavy fur. He kneeled to lay her down upon it, pausing to see whether she meant to continue what she'd started.

One long, slim arm reached up toward him and the sleeve of her shift slipped down, revealing the intricate blue markings curling from her wrists upward toward her shoulder.

He traced one finger along the curving line, noting the trail of chill bumps left in the wake of his touch.

"I'll chase away the cold if you'll allow me," he offered, his voice hoarse with need.

"Allow it?" she asked, her voice equally as hoarse

as his. "I insist upon it." Her fingers wound into his hair and guided him down, his body covering hers.

They'd been here once before. But unlike last time, he was in full control of himself now, his powers fully restored. There would be no storm splitting the skies to interrupt them tonight.

THE LAST TIME she'd willingly lain beneath Hall's body, the evening had ended in her dreams being shattered. This time would be different, she told herself. This time there were no dreams attached to her actions.

She was not tumbling for some great laird who wanted to bed her. No, this time she was boldly taking what *she* wanted. Her need for him was like a nettle in her skin. Coupling with him would either pluck the nettle away, or give her a marker with which to compare every other man she would ever meet. Either way, this was *her* choice. *Her* decision, on *her* terms.

He drew her shift up over her head and tossed it aside, leaving her body open to the cold air and his heated gaze. She lay still as his fingers followed the blue lines Orabilis had drawn upon her body.

The lines he traced seemed to come alive, heating with his touch, and she felt her desire for him writhing inside her, building to the point where she was surprised the lines themselves didn't squirm right off her body.

She refused to be ashamed of the markings; they were a part of her heritage. And though he might not be able to understand why she'd done this, they were as much a part of her now as her nose or her eyes. They *were* her.

Her breath caught when he pulled his tunic over his head, and she reached up to run her hands across his chest. The muscles were hard as stone, but his warm skin was all man.

He lowered himself over her and his head dipped to her neck. The lines where his finger had trailed only a moment before, he now traced with his tongue. Hot, insistent, moving along the paths of the markings, nibbling his way down her neck, along her chest, around her breast.

Again her breath caught, and he chuckled against her skin, the heat of his breath setting her heart pounding so hard he must hear it.

Her muscles trembled as his hand tracked across her belly and down between her legs.

I am in control of what happens here, she reminded herself. *Me. I have chosen this moment.*

One large finger slid inside her and her muscles contracted involuntarily, causing her to lift her hips up off the ground as some primal groan escaped from deep within her.

In control? Who was she fooling? She'd lost any control the minute Hall touched her. No one could control a feeling as intense as this.

He fit himself between her legs, and her feet

hooked behind him as if the two of them had been carved by a master crafter to fit together as one piece.

He gripped her waist with his hands and pressed against her, and again her hips lifted up to meet him.

This time it was no finger entering to stretch her, but a shaft of velvet-covered iron. Slowly, inexorably sliding forward and back, pressing deeper inside her with each small thrust, he stoked the fire of an aching need growing within her.

He filled her, his hands cradling her lower back as her body clenched and tightened around him in sharp, rhythmic little contractions that brought with them a momentary precious relief.

She looked up at his face as he rose over her, his back arched, his head thrown back.

Maybe, just maybe, being in control was little more than seizing the moment and snatching from life what you wanted, as she had done when she'd initiated their lovemaking.

If she could do that, she could do anything. No matter how hard it might be, she would find the strength somewhere deep inside, and she *would* do what was necessary.

Even if that ended up being something as difficult as walking away from the man who would hold her heart forever. He had already made it clear he would be leaving her when their quest was done— but was that still his intent?

To know the answer to that question would require that she swallow her pride and ask it. Orabilis had cautioned her that she must let go to hold on, and that was what she would do. She would let go of her pride to hold on to her chance for happiness.

NOT EVEN THE guarantee of eternity in Valhalla could make him feel as good as he did at this very moment.

Hall kissed the top of Bridget's head and tightened his arms around her. To lie like this, with this woman wrapped in his embrace, was all he needed in life and all he could ever want.

Then his stomach growled loudly.

And food, of course. Give him Bridget and food, and the rest of the world could find its own way without him.

With another kiss to the top of her head, he tossed back his heavy fur and hurriedly dressed before tending to the rather well done rabbit hanging over their fire.

"Meal's ready," he announced with a chuckle.

"Right, then," Bridget muttered.

She reached out from under the fur they'd shared to snag her shift, appearing from the covering only after she'd dropped the garment over her head. Wrapping the fur around herself, she came forward and accepted the piece of meat he held out to her.

Even burned, it was the best rabbit he'd ever tasted. The way he felt right now, he suspected that even straw and dirt might taste good.

"You ken, do you no, that *that*"—Bridget tilted

her head toward the spot where they had laid together—"is no going to happen again."

The meat that had seconds before tasted like a king's banquet took on the texture of the dirt and straw Hall had imagined.

"What are you saying?"

Bridget shrugged. "We're very different people, Hall, each with our own path in life. Could you honestly say to me, here and now, that you'd give up all you know, all you have, to stay here with me?"

He wanted to say yes more than anything he'd ever wanted in his life. He wanted to say the words she obviously wanted to hear from him.

But could he be like his father and think only of his own happiness? Could he abandon all those desperate souls calling upon Thor for help?

No. That simply wasn't who he was.

"As I thought. You dinna have to speak it aloud; the look upon yer face is answer enough." Bridget tossed the bone she held into the fire. "Morning light will come soon enough, and we have our journey cut out for us. Sleep well, Hall."

She crossed to the opposite side of the fire and lay down, pulling the fur tightly around her, her back turned to him.

Sleep well? He doubted he would sleep at all. Not that he wanted to sleep, knowing that his dreams would be filled with nothing but Bridget, as they always were.

He should have counted himself fortunate to

have had those precious moments with her to hold in his memory. But he couldn't. The memory would torment him for the rest of his life.

Not having something you imagined to be what you wanted wasn't nearly so awful as not having something you *knew* was exactly what you wanted.

After this night, Hall knew that Bridget Mac-Culloch was the only thing he wanted. And the one thing he could never have.

Twenty-five

IF SHE CLOSED her eyes and pretended hard enough, Bridget could almost make herself believe she rode this trail alone. But since closing her eyes meant missing valuable signs her quarry might have left behind, she forced herself to keep them open.

It hadn't worked that well, anyway.

Hall's big destrier outpaced her mount and constantly pulled ahead of her, forcing her to face the reality of his riding at her side.

Reality was not the most pleasant companion today. Neither was Hall O'Donar.

They'd barely spoken to one another as they'd broken camp this morning, or for the hours they'd spent following Mathew's trail.

She'd have liked to believe that he carried a lump in his chest to match the one she felt in hers.

The more likely explanation was that he was simply embarrassed for her that she'd expect one bedding would convince him to give up his position and status for the likes of her.

He didn't need to be. She was embarrassed enough for both of them.

Embarrassed, but not sorry she'd pressed the issue. Even if she could find some way to take back the question she'd asked, she wouldn't. Though confirming the truth hurt, it was better to put that ridiculous dream to rest than to continue harboring it in her heart. It freed her to concentrate on the task at hand.

Scanning the ground in front of her, she searched for fresh signs of the boy they followed. "Have you seen any—"

"Shh!" Hall held up his hand, tilting his head to the side in the way he did when he listened to those things she couldn't hear, a small frown wrinkling his brow. "One man, afoot," he murmured. "Heading toward us."

"Toward us?" Brie echoed. "Surely that canna be Mathew. But it could be someone who has seen him."

Hall shook his head, the frown still fixed on his features as he urged his horse to a canter.

Brie matched his speed, pulling her animal to a halt only after they rounded the next hill.

Against all her expectations, ahead of her on the road, walking toward them, was Mathew. The boy spotted them almost immediately and looked around as if trying to choose a path of escape.

"Stay where you are, lad," Hall called out to him. "I've no wish to harm you."

Mathew lifted the great sword he carried in front of him as they approached, holding it at the ready, his gaze fixed upon Hall. "Keep yer distance, the both of you, and allow me free passage. We've all seen what the Dream Guardian can do. I willna hesitate to use her if pressed."

Brie had no intention of letting Hall anywhere near that blade again.

"What rubbish," she muttered, urging her horse to gallop ahead of Hall's so that she might reach Mathew first.

He seemed genuinely surprised when he recognized her. "Bridget! It pleases me greatly to see that you made good yer escape from the laird of Tordenet. No everyone was so lucky, I fear."

"Put down the weapon, Mathew." She was in no mood for pleasantries, not with him threatening Hall as he did. "Put it down right now. Dinna make me pull out my bow and beat you about the head with it."

Hall arrived as she uttered her threat, his glare reflecting his anger.

"I have no idea what this Dream Guardian blether is, but I need that sword you're holding, boy. And the scrolls you took. We've no time to waste."

Mathew pulled the sword close to his body, tip still pointing toward the sky. "I named her Dream Guardian because, with her at my side, the red-eyed beast canna enter my dreams. You canna have her. She is mine."

"Red-eyed beast, eh?" Hall exchanged a look with Brie before dismounting and approaching them. "That would be Fenrir. I think you've seen his work. He's a beast of considerable power, and a terrible scourge to release upon this world. The death and destruction he'll bring will put entire armies to shame. I wouldn't want that burden of guilt to lie upon my conscience."

"Nor would I," Mathew agreed.

As they spoke, Brie shifted her stance, edging herself between Hall and Mathew. All it would take would be one small accident to re-create the precarious situation she'd worked so hard to remedy.

"It was this Beast Fenrir who murdered Hugo," Hall said.

Terror clouded Mathew's eyes and he clutched the sword to his chest.

"And by your actions at this moment," Hall continued, "you are responsible for Fenrir remaining in this world. By your actions, *you* will be responsible for the atrocities he will commit in the name of evil. Atrocities much worse than the fate that Hugo met."

Mathew's face paled and he stumbled back a couple of paces. "What you say is not possible. It canna be my fault. I've done nothing. I've harmed no one."

Hall shrugged, his expression void of all emotion. "So you may believe. But you withhold what I need. Without the sword and the scrolls, I cannot defeat Fenrir. Without the sword and the scrolls, the Beast will be free to carry out whatever evil he wants, and we will all be lost. For that, you will be to blame."

"I will not be to blame." Mathew dropped the sword to the ground and retreated another pace. "Take the sword. Do with it as you will. But I canna give you the scrolls. They are gone."

Brie placed her foot squarely across the blade of the sword, just in case Mathew changed his mind.

"Gone?" Hall growled. "Gone where? What have you done with them?"

Mathew suddenly crumpled to the ground to sit, his head in his hands. "Dobbie Caskie. When I awoke this morning, he was gone with everything I had excepting the sword."

Hall set his hands on his hips, staring down the road. "Then we must find young Dobbie. Would I be correct in supposing that having lost your possessions is what sent you backtracking?"

Mathew nodded. "I had no horse, no jewels or scrolls to sell, no food, nothing. No way to continue on with what I planned to do."

In the face of the boy's desolation, Brie couldn't stop herself from asking, "And what was that, Mathew? What was yer plan?"

"After I found Hugo—" Mathew paused, eyes closed, to take a shuddering breath before he spoke again. "After I found what was left of Hugo in the laird's solar at Tordenet, I realized it had fallen to me to provide for Eleyne. I took what treasures I'd found, planning to sell them so that I might collect my cousin and return her to our home, with the power of a fortune in my pocket as protection against our having left in the first place."

"Surely you dinna require silver to return to yer own family." The idea was preposterous to Brie. Family was family no matter what. Even her uncle, obsessed as he was with finding her a husband, would never require silver from her to return home.

"No to return, but to return *safely*. My uncle is no a forgiving man. Nor a charitable one."

"We'll have to deal with all that later," Hall interrupted brusquely. "Finding Dobbie and the scrolls is our priority now. Where did you last see him?"

Hall leaned over to reach toward the sword, but Brie stopped him with a hand to his chest.

"Do you really think that's wise? Best we keep the blade away from you, aye?" She looked up at him. "I'm thinking I should carry it, no you. Just in case."

"As you wish. For now," he agreed, and turned to remount his horse before sticking out a hand toward Mathew. "Well, come on, boy. What are you waiting for? We've a thief to catch and our time is running low."

"Yer no going to leave me here?"

"Dinna be such a dullard," Brie scoffed, reaching down to pick up the sword. "What do you take us for? We would never abandon you out here."

Mathew rushed past her toward Hall, as if he

feared they might change their minds, but any words the two exchanged as the boy climbed up onto the big horse were lost to Brie when her hand closed around the sword's hilt.

The hilt molded to her hand as if it had been made for her, heating her palm. A great *whoosh* of roaring air filled her ears like a mighty storm wind blowing through the forest. It carried with it the voices of unseen hordes whispering messages into her mind that she couldn't quite decipher.

She dropped the sword and the noise abruptly subsided, leaving a strange emptiness.

"Is there a problem?" Hall asked.

Again she reached for the weapon, and again the rush assaulted her ears. This time, prepared for it, she ignored the distraction. "No problem but a clumsy hold on a heavy blade."

Crossing to her horse, she slid the weapon into the sheath on her saddle before mounting the animal.

Her hand still tingled from contact with the sword, but she could determine no other ill effects. After what she'd seen the blade do to Hall, she considered herself lucky.

When she lifted her gaze, she found Hall and Mathew staring at her.

"What's all this dallying about? We dinna have time to waste. On with the both of you!"

THOUGH HE'D SEEN no sign of tracks, Hall had been hearing riders for the last half hour. Four . . . no, five of them, moving slowly, all spread out. Perfect formation for a search party.

The MacGahan men, or more of Torquil's? There was only one way to know for sure.

He'd delayed sharing the information as long as possible.

"Make yourselves ready. Just around the next curve of the trail, we'll be overtaking some riders."

Bridget visibly jerked in her saddle, as if her mind had wandered far afield. To her credit, she recovered instantly and pulled her bow from her back to fit an arrow into it.

"Dobbie, do you think?" she asked, her gaze fixed on the spot ahead where the path disappeared around the side of a large hill.

"No. Too many of them and all on horseback. Five riders as best I can tell. Could well be more of Torquil's men."

Sharing his saddle, Mathew tensed. "Turn back. If it's Torquil's men ahead, we should turn back now. I have no desire to cross their paths again."

"Calm down, Mathew." Bridget had dropped her bow to her side but kept the arrow nocked in place. "It could be anybody."

"We'll know soon enough."

As they rounded the hill the men he'd heard came into sight, along with a large ragged dog that loped toward them, tongue hanging out of his mouth as if he wore a wide grin.

"Jamesy!" Bridget leaned forward in her saddle

and kicked her horse, sending the animal into a full gallop as she waved one arm in the air. "Jamesy!"

"I take it those are no Torquil's men." Relief was evident in Mathew's voice.

"They are not," Hall confirmed, urging his own mount to a trot.

"You seem well recovered, O'Donar," Jamesy greeted him, though his look was anything but welcoming. "And still encouraging my sister to pursue this dangerous path, I see."

Hall bristled at the accusation he heard in Jamesy's tone, but he held back any comment. He'd likely feel the same if the roles were reversed, and a sister of his traveled with some stranger on a perilous cause. His best course of action was to maintain as much distance as possible from this argument.

"You think he could stop me from doing what I choose?" Bridget, on the other hand, appeared to be in no mood to hold back. "You tried as much when you left me behind at Castle MacGahan. How successful were you at that, brother?"

Unlike his sister, Jamesy seemed in full control of his temper. He turned his emotionless stare from his sister to Hall. "My apologies, O'Donar. It would appear all our hands are tied when it comes to Brie risking her safety to do as she pleases."

"No apologies necessary, MacCulloch. I'd be the first to agree this is no safe place for your sister." Not that he could think of a better alternative right now. Staying with them was much safer than venturing off on her own. "But I have little to say about what she does."

"You have nothing to say about what I do, and no right to say it," she asserted, pushing her wild hair back from her face.

"And what in the name of the Seven have you done to yer face?" Jamesy pulled his horse next to his sister's and pushed back the hair covering her cheeks. "Oh, la, dinna tell me you gave yerself over to the auld stories. What fool allowed you to do this?" He turned a sharp eye toward Hall.

"No one *allowed* me to do anything. I did this of my own free will, choosing to honor the truth of our ancestors." With a toss of her head, Bridget turned her mount, pulling away from the group to wait alone.

"They were but stories, Bridget," her brother called after her. "Stories told to a small child to quiet her down for the night. And now look what you've done to yerself."

"I dinna believe I've ever heard these stories, of beautiful women who decorate themselves as they might decorate their tapestries." Jamesy's friend Finn drew his horse closer, peering at Bridget. "But I would like to hear more of them."

"Our mother's stories," Jamesy explained, shaking his head in disgust. "Children's fantasies about our ancient ancestors, who painted their bodies with magical symbols to protect them in battle and frighten their enemies."

"They're not fantasies," Bridget called, leaving little doubt she had heard every word even if she didn't choose to respond to her brother.

Finn arched an eyebrow, turning his gaze from Bridget to Jamesy and back to her again. "The *whole* of their bodies? Now, that *does* sound like a story worth investigating."

"I wouldn't recommend that course of action," Hall heard himself saying.

So much for maintaining his distance.

Finn laughed, his eyes lighting with amusement, and he dipped his head in mock apology. "As you say, O'Donar. All things considered, it's perhaps best all round that I leave this subject entirely alone."

"Is this yer missing minstrel?" Patrick MacDowylt brought them all back to the reason they were here. "Does this mean you've reclaimed the items we need?"

"Only the sword," Hall answered. "It would appear that Dobbie Caskie made off with the scrolls. We're headed now to the site where Mathew saw him last so that we might pick up his trail."

"Dobbie Caskie! I had hoped one day to cross paths with that young man again." Eric MacNicol's lips curved in a humorless smile. "The lad claimed he was headed to family on Skye, back when I took Jeanne to deal with Eymer's remains. If he's still prowling these trails with the same claim—"

"Then like as not he's part of a gang of thieves," Patrick jumped in. "And that would mean they've an encampment or a house or someplace out here where they hole up."

"And that would mean we can find them," Hall finished.

Patrick's conclusions confirmed his own suspicions regarding Dobbie Caskie. He just needed a trail to follow.

"Why are we wasting time on the scrolls? We have the sword," Bridget interrupted as she joined them again. "Why not simply cut our losses and go after Torquil now?"

Hall answered, "We need the scrolls if we're to capture the Beast."

"Then our path is settled. We follow you," Patrick said. "We find this Dobbie Caskie and his friends, and we take back our scrolls so that we can get on with what's most important—securing the future."

Twenty-six

WAITING, WAITING — IT WAS as if her whole life had come down to waiting! Brie pulled her fur up over her head and huddled against the wind blowing off the loch beyond the trees.

Just before noon they'd picked up Dobbie's tracks and within another hour or so they'd arrived in this place. And here they sat, hours later, powerless to move against the men who held the treasure they sought.

Without having met Caskie, Brie already detested the wee thief with every bit of her being.

"I dinna suppose there's a back way into the floating fortress?" Mathew sat across from her, close enough that she could just make out his form in the dark.

"They don't float," Hall corrected. "The crannog is set upon poles to hold it above the water. And no, there is no back way in, else we wouldn't be sitting here in the cold dark, waiting for them to make a move. The only way in is to cross the water."

Light wavered eerily from the center of the loch,

taunting them. With only a sliver of moon, and that well hidden behind a thick layer of clouds, it was impossible to see exactly where the light came from. It was as if a magical sprite danced out there in the black just beyond their reach.

In spite of the way it looked now, she knew well enough that there was nothing at all magical about the house on stilts sitting out in the water. The sun hadn't yet set when they'd arrived here, and they'd all seen it well enough. But without a boat to reach the man-made island, seeing it was all they could do.

"If it were summer, we might try to swim over," Eric muttered.

"And if I were only the eldest MacCormack son, I'd be home in my warm bed, fast asleep," Finn retorted with a chuckle. "Alas, I'm sixth in line to a holding that would do well to support one, and here we all sit, freezing our arses off, with no fire and no way across those waters."

"And snow beginning to fall." Brie held out a hand to make sure she'd been right as a few groans pierced the dark. "Don't forget to add that to our list of complaints."

Maybe if it got cold enough, the lake would freeze and they'd be able to walk out and knock on the gate to demand entrance.

Something wet and cold touched her cheek and she jumped, realizing as she did that it was only Finn's huge wolfhound nuzzling up next to her. The big animal's soft brown eyes seemed to beg, and she lifted her fur to allow him to edge in close. He lay down with his big head on her lap before she pulled the fur back up to cover them both. The extra body heat more than made up for his dirty smell.

"Quiet yer blethering, all of you," Patrick ordered, his voice moving away from them in the dark. "I'll take the first watch. You've only a few hours left to get some rest. We'll want to be sharp when they begin to stir and head for the shore."

"*If* they head for shore," someone muttered in the dark.

If was right. With proper stores, the thieves might remain in their compound for days.

Brie huddled down into her fur and put her arms around the big dog, who seemed quite agreeable to cuddling. With his warmth next to her, she couldn't help but think of another large body she'd so recently held even closer.

Memories of her night with Hall tumbled one over the other, leaving her aching for his touch and wishing it was he who shared her bed.

But only Dog wanted to be her sleeping companion this night. Hall had remained withdrawn and aloof ever since they'd joined up with the men from Castle MacGahan, ignoring her completely.

She scratched the big dog's ear and he breathed a heavy sigh of contentment. When all this was over, she just might get a dog of her own. A dog would return her affection and her loyalty. A dog wouldn't ignore her.

Unlike one particular man she could name. And after all she'd done to help him, this was how he repaid her.

Yes, she was definitely getting herself a dog. One who hated men as much as she did.

HALL KEPT HIS gaze fixed on the woman across the clearing. Unlike his fully Mortal companions, he was able to see, despite the lack of light.

Though Brie had shown herself to be a resilient warrior and a skilled tracker, it was apparent that she'd paid no attention at all to any lessons on how to choose a place to bed down.

Lying in the open, she caught the full effect of the winds blowing across the big loch. Even without the whiffs of snow that assaulted them throughout the night, the wind itself blew cuttingly cold across the water.

Bridget had rolled herself into a ball, curved around the massive dog that belonged to her brother's friend. Shielded by her body from the breezes blowing off the loch, no doubt the animal was quite comfortable lying there in his spot.

Hall's spot.

It should be him lying next to Bridget, not that ragged animal. It should be him holding her in his arms, protecting her from the biting cold. It should be him—

But none of that was possible. She was not his to hold.

Hall dragged his palms over his face, scrubbing his eyes. He'd given up that right when he'd rejected her last night. But that didn't mean he couldn't do something to ease her discomfort.

Though he had no right to hold her, that wouldn't deter him from protecting her.

He waited until the sounds in the camp assured him that everyone slept before he made his move.

Quietly, he crept across the campsite to position himself only feet from Bridget, using his own bulk to shield her from the wind. The big dog at her side lifted his head, peeking out from under the furs where he huddled, but made no sound.

"As well you shouldn't," Hall muttered under his breath.

The lucky beast would benefit from his move as well.

Hunched against the biting breeze, Hall tightened his fur, confident in his ability to serve as an effective windbreak, if nothing else.

Just before the first glimmer of light painted the sky, he quietly moved back to his original spot. His muscles protested after hours of cramped exposure to the wind, but the effort had been well worth it.

He'd barely slipped into a comfortable position before Patrick entered the circle, bending to shake Eric's shoulder first before approaching him.

"There's movement out in the crannog," Patrick said, his voice a husky whisper. "Keep yer noise to a minimum so we dinna alert them to our presence."

Hall tossed off his fur and made his way toward the shore for a better view.

He'd best remember to send thanks up to his *Hamingja*, because the luck riding at his side today appeared to be all good. Dobbie Caskie himself waited at the open gate as an older man lowered a small, rounded boat into the water.

"No more worthless scribbles," the man ordered with a slap to the back of the boy's head. "It's food and silver yer to bring back. You ken yer orders this time? Food and silver."

Dobbie nodded, rubbing his head before he dipped an oar into the water.

"It's him, for sure," Eric whispered as he kneeled at Hall's side. "One of my fondest wishes is to cross paths with this wee lying turd again."

"I'll be the first to admit the lad has done naught to endear himself to us," Hall returned. "But it could be he has a story of his own to tell."

Eric snorted. "There's never an excuse for stealing from those who extend you a helping hand. Especially not when yer theft endangers their lives as he endangered Jeanne's when he stole our horse and provisions."

Hall shrugged, remembering the circumstances of his first meeting with Eric and the woman who was now his wife. The warrior had good reason for his ire and in his position, he'd like as not react in the same way.

"No, no excuse," he agreed. "But perhaps a reason."

Crouching low, Hall began to make his way
through the brush to position himself along the
bank to intercept the boy once he brought the small
boat ashore. He heard the others join him, but he
kept his eyes fixed on the approaching craft.

They all waited, watching as the boy drew the
boat up onto the bank and hopped out, his stride
long to avoid the cold water. He wedged the small
boat into the bushes and tied its rope to a sapling
before they made any move.

At a whispered command from Finn, the big
dog pushed past Hall and out into the open ground
around the shoreline.

"Oho," Dobbie called, obviously surprised to see
the animal. "Where did you come from?"

Tentatively he reached out one hand toward the
big animal and the dog licked him, his tail wagging
as if he'd discovered a long-lost friend.

Dobbie dropped to one knee, burying his hands
in the dog's fur to scratch his head. When he stood,
he shook his head and turned his back on the dog.

"Sorry, boy. I've nothing at all to give you, no
even a morsel. Off with you, then."

Dobbie started forward toward an area where the
underbrush was trampled down, obviously a well-
used trail for the crannog's inhabitants. Only lack
of experience kept the boy from recognizing that

the big dog now stood guard, blocking the pathway between him and his only means of escape.

Hall rose to his feet and the others followed.

"Dobbie Caskie!" he called out. "Stop where you are with your hands in the air."

The boy froze for just an instant, his expression that of a hunted animal before he turned to run, only to find his way blocked by the snarling dog.

Dobbie turned back to them, looking resigned to whatever fate awaited him.

"I only want the scrolls you took," Hall said as he approached the boy. "We have no wish to harm you."

"Speak for yerself," Eric growled, coming up to join him. "Remember me, do you? Me and the generous lady who shared our food, only to have you steal her horse and all our provisions?"

Dobbie backed up a step, unable to move farther away thanks to the big dog directly behind him.

"Maybe I recall you," he said, his eyes shifting from one to the other of the men confronting him. "Maybe no. I meet many people along the trails."

"Well, lad, you met yerself the wrong one this time," Eric threatened, cracking his knuckles for effect.

Dobbie shook his head and lifted his chin. "Do you think to frighten me? I'm no afraid of the likes of you. I been beat regularly by men twice yer size." The boy lifted his fists as if to invite a fight. "Be warned, I've learned to give as good as I get."

A memory of the last time Hall had heard those words flashed through his mind, and he glanced up to find Brie staring directly at him. From the color rising in her cheeks when her gaze met his, he had no need to wonder whether she remembered too.

Hall stepped forward and the boy flinched, but kept his fists lifted.

"I don't want to fight you, Dobbie Caskie. I only want the scrolls you took from Mathew. You can keep whatever else you've taken."

"Not my horse," Eric added. "I want my horse back, too."

"The scrolls and Eric's horse," Hall echoed.

Dobbie shook his head, shivering in the thin plaid he wore wrapped around his shoulders. "Can you pay? Elsewise, they willna return yer rolls of symbols. They'd as soon use them as tinder for their fire. As for yer horse, it's long gone, I'm afraid. Sold to the laird of the MacKenzies. If you want it that bad, you'll need to speak to him about its return."

Hall had no intention of haggling over what had been stolen. "There will be no bargaining. You're going to get in your boat and row yourself back out to your crannog—"

"No!" Eric interrupted. "You ken as well as I do, once he's there, we canna touch him. They'll simply wait until we tire of the hunt and go away."

"As I was saying, you'll row yourself back out there," Hall repeated as if there had been no interruption. "And you'll take this message to the leader of the men inside: Return the scrolls to me within the hour, or everyone in the crannog dies. I am not open to negotiation or bargaining of any kind. Do you understand?"

Dobbie nodded and turned to run, clearly anxious to be on his way, but the big animal behind him halted his escape.

"Finn!" Hall turned to locate the warrior who traveled with the beast. "Allow the boy passage."

"Dog! To my side," Finn called.

Tail once again wagging like a playful puppy, the big animal trotted past Dobbie and Hall to sit down next to Finn.

Dobbie raced to retrieve his boat and hopped inside as if he expected the men to change their minds at any moment. He rowed much faster as he headed back to the crannog than he had on his way to the shore.

"I hope you've got yerself one hell of a plan," Patrick muttered. "Because that one's no likely to ever set foot on this shore again of his own free will."

Hall had a plan, right enough.

"We wait," he counseled, straining to hear what reception awaited the boy. "You can't always trust the way a thing looks."

Dobbie pulled himself up into the open gate and lifted his boat inside when he reached the crannog, shutting the gate behind him with a resounding *thud*.

The sounds of laughter assaulted Hall's sensitive

ears, as if the whole compound found his message hugely amusing. It was exactly what he'd expected. Men who'd spent too long thinking of themselves as safe often forgot their own vulnerabilities.

"Mathew," he called to the minstrel. "Bring me my shield."

No sense getting caught unprepared, should the inhabitants of the crannog have bows at their disposal.

Inside the fence, a crude ladder slammed up against the side of the building and one lone man climbed up onto the roof. With a deliberate show of contempt, he turned his back and lifted his plaid, baring his arse to the men on the shore to the accompaniment of laughter drifting across the water.

A gesture the Scots had long favored, though it was beyond Hall's understanding why they'd choose to present such a tempting target. Perhaps it was time a Northman showed them the error of their ways.

"Bridget?"

She waited behind the others, her brother doing his best to block her view of the crude display out on the water.

"Aye?"

"Do you think you could place an arrow temptingly close to our provocative friend there?"

Having seen evidence of her skill when she'd saved his life, he felt more than confident in the next step of his plan.

"Of course I can," she responded without hesitation.

She disappeared for a few moments, returning with her bow and arrows in hand, making her way to his side.

"Shall I aim for his hairy pink arse?" she asked, a wide grin on her face.

"No need for that. Setting it directly beside him into the thatched roof will do well enough for the warning we want to send."

Bridget lifted her bow, nocked her arrow, and let fly. The arrow whistled through the air. The men in the crannog saw it coming, and the man on the roof leapt down before it arrived to poke neatly into the thatch beside the spot where he'd stood moments before.

"Well done," Hall murmured quietly.

A broad smile split her face and she dipped her head in acknowledgment of the compliment.

"I could have put it up his arse, if you'd asked," she said with a shrug, though her smile remained in place.

"I have no doubt about your ability to have done exactly that," he assured her while turning to motion Mathew to his side. "Kindle a campfire, lad. Big enough that our friends out there cannot possibly miss the flames."

As if Bridget had read his mind, she dropped her bow to rip a strip of cloth from the tail of her shift.

"We're sending them a warmer greeting next

time, are we no?" she asked as she wrapped the cloth around an arrow.

"Two, in fact. Can you put the first one completely over the crannog to land harmlessly in the water?"

Her grin broadened and she touched her arrow to the flame, sending the arrow skyward as the fire began to eat its way through the cloth.

Hall cupped his hands to his mouth and yelled, "Last warning. The next one will be on your roof. And all the ones that follow."

Bridget readied her next arrow, but he stopped her before she set it on fire.

"Wait. These men are thieves, not fighters. Bravery is not a trait high upon their list."

Within minutes, the gate swung open and Dobbie reappeared. He dropped his little boat into the water and begin paddling in their direction. When he reached the shore, he climbed from the boat and pulled the scrolls out from under the plaid he wore over his shoulder.

"MacAngus says that you should take your damned scrolls and go as far away from here as you can. He asks only that you leave us in peace."

Hall took the scrolls from the boy, unrolling one to verify it was what they sought.

The power of the markings on the parchment slithered over his skin and up his arm, crawling toward the almost-healed wound on his shoulder like lice on a rat.

There was no doubt that these were the Elven Scrolls of Niflheim.

"You may tell MacAngus that we will plague him no longer." Hall rolled the parchment back up and tucked it away, nodding toward the boy. "And as for you, Dobbie Caskie, don't let me catch you bedeviling any of my friends in the future. You'd be best off making your way to those relatives you claim to have on Skye, and keeping your head down. Otherwise, I can promise you, I'll be back. And I won't be in such a forgiving mood the next time I pass this way."

Something told him everyone in the crannog would likely reconsider his thieving ways.

At least for a day or two.

Twenty-seven

Ir's SETTLED, THEN." Patrick MacDowylt pulled his pack from his horse and tossed it to the ground. "At first light, we head for Castle MacGahan to collect reinforcements before continuing on to Tordenet."

"It's not settled at all," Hall responded, a scowl darkening his face. "Time is an issue. The longer we wait, the stronger Fenrir grows. I say we go directly there. Our success depends upon the items we carry, and how effectively we employ them, not upon the number of men in our force."

Brie agreed with Hall but didn't voice her opinion. Knowing this group of men as she did, she was aware that her voice could well be more detriment than help. Besides, bringing attention to herself would only lead to—

"We have to return to the castle first, in any event," Jamesy said. "To make sure Brie and Mathew are safely behind the walls before we lead the attack on Tordenet."

Exactly what Brie had expected. But she had no plans to accept her brother's decree without a fight.

"You've no need to go to Castle MacGahan on my behalf. I'm going to Tordenet with you," she said calmly.

"Like hell you are. Yer no going anyplace close to that castle or the Beast within." Jamesy shook his head, his frown grown to match the best Hall had ever worn. "I've heard the stories of how close I came to losing my sister as well as my father to the Beast that lives there. Yer staying at Castle MacGahan, where I have no need to fash myself over yer safety. I have no appetite for losing the whole of my family to the MacDowylt."

"Revenge for our father's death is my right." Brie kept her voice low. She wouldn't be prodded into an angry confrontation over this. She might actually be getting the hang of this patience thing. "With you or without you, I intend to see Torquil MacDowylt's debt to our family paid."

Torquil's and the Beast's that lived inside him. They'd both pay.

Hall, thankfully, kept his peace in this particular battle, turning back to Patrick to press his contention that they would have better luck with a smaller party of men.

"There's nothing to be gained in wasting time or risking additional lives. Chase told me the Mac-Dowylt castle is rife with hidden passages. Our number could easily slip inside and find Fenrir without involving his entire army. Or risking ours."

"There are passages aplenty as Chase described, but that's no the tactic Malcolm has chosen to pursue. He himself was captured sneaking in through the passage leading from the shore into the castle grounds. This time he has decreed we approach with our army and enter through the front gates." Patrick was adamant.

"Your brother's choice is wrongheaded," Hall insisted. "We risk too many lives with a direct confrontation. And the longer we wait—"

"My brother, wrongheaded or no, is our laird, and his word is our law," Patrick interrupted.

Brie walked away to lead her horse through the trees and down to the water for a drink. There was nothing to be gained by playing audience to their continuing disagreement.

In the end they would do as Patrick insisted, even though Hall was likely right that they'd have more success with fewer men. Patrick followed his older brother's lead, just as she was expected to follow her older brother's lead.

Only Bridget MacCulloch was no Patrick Mac-Dowylt.

With the sword whispering encouragement in her ear, there was no way she would allow anyone else to wield it against Torquil. It was her duty. Her right. Fate had given her a second chance at the man who'd murdered her father, and she had no intention of passing up this opportunity to redeem herself.

She had the sword in her possession and that was all she needed to accomplish her goal. Hall's scrolls were of no importance to her. He intended to capture the Beast and confine it once more to its prison in the scrolls.

She had no interest in taking any prisoners. Whether it had been Torquil MacDowylt on his own who had ordered her father hanged, or the Beast that had driven the action, she intended to kill them both.

Hearing a noise behind her, she glanced back to find Hall leading his mount to the water.

"Will it be Tordenet or Castle MacGahan?" she asked, knowing full well what answer he would give.

"MacGahan," he answered, irritation thick in his voice. "I've been overridden by the lot of them. Shortsighted, small minds."

"I think you had the right of it," she murmured, not daring to look at him. "For whatever my opinion is worth to you."

"Your opinion is of high value to me. Higher than you know."

His words gathered around her heart, warm and comforting in a way she'd never expected. If only— But no. There was no *if only* with this man. She'd already tried that.

She met his gaze, stark and serious. He lifted a hand toward her, but allowed it to drop to his side when the sounds of others coming through the underbrush reached their ears.

Damn the others for choosing that moment to join them. She wanted to thank Hall for not backing her brother's insistence on leaving her behind. She wanted to thank him for trusting her skills in the confrontation with Dobbie and the bandits this morning. She'd even begun to consider the possibility of including him in the plan brewing in the back of her mind.

With the others approaching, that wasn't possible now.

She'd just have to hope that he'd still hold her opinion in equally high value tomorrow morning.

With her animal settled for the night, she tossed her pack down by the fire alongside the others and began to mix the pieces of dried meat and fruits with the porridge for their evening meal while Jamesy's friend Alex built their fire.

Keeping her thoughts to herself while she stirred the boiling oats, Brie listened to her brother and Patrick discuss their plans and their expectations for reaching Castle MacGahan tomorrow if they started early and rode into the night.

By utilizing the same strategy, rising early and riding late, she could reach her destination in only two days.

"I see you still haven't learned to cook a decent

bowl of porridge," her brother joked as he took his first bite.

She smiled and nodded, keeping her temper in check. If this were the last encounter she would have with Jamesy, she wouldn't go to her reward knowing it had ended in a fight.

Besides, Jamesy had the right of it. She didn't like cooking and it showed in the food she prepared. She'd jumped at the chance to be responsible for the meal preparation tonight for only one reason.

No one ever paid attention to where the cook repacked the supplies, and she would need to apportion out her own share of their provisions for her journey.

Finn's big, shaggy animal nudged at her leg and she fished a few bites of dried meat from the bag next to her. Dog could be a problem when she tried to slip away, unless he was already used to taking food from her. If necessary, she'd bribe him to silence with a few more tidbits.

When they'd all finished eating, Alex offered to clean up but Brie brushed aside his offer of help, in order to prepare things as she needed them done.

Once she'd finished, she sat on her blanket next to the fire where Jamesy had laid it out for her, only feet from where the others would sleep.

This wouldn't work at all. These men were all warriors and not likely to sleep through her rising, rolling up her blankets and slipping away in the middle of the night.

Looking across the fire, she caught Hall staring in her direction and she glanced away. Sometimes it almost felt as if they shared thoughts, and she couldn't afford to risk any suspicion tonight.

But the moment of connection with him made her remember his actions of the night before, when they'd waited for Dobbie Caskie at the loch.

Foolishly, she'd chosen a spot to sleep where the winds swept off the water and buffeted her mercilessly, ruining any chance for a decent night's sleep. When the sharp sting of the wind had suddenly ceased, she'd peeked out from under her furs to find Hall had moved close by, blocking the wind with his body.

One more thing for which she owed him her thanks. The list just kept growing. And now she could add another item to it. His actions of last night gave her an idea of how to solve her current problem.

Putting her arms around herself, she exaggerated a shiver and rose to her feet. "I am not sleeping in a draft again tonight," she grumbled as she gathered up her blankets and pack. "This will do," she announced, and dropped her things beyond the fire's circle of light, separated from her companions by a big rock.

"You'll regret that choice in a few hours," her brother cautioned. "It's warmer by the fire—and besides, I hardly feel the wind at all."

"Maybe not where your bedding lies," she

responded, curling into her furs. "But I felt it. I like this spot much better."

When the only sounds in the camp were those made by sleeping men, Brie quietly gathered her things and made her way to her horse. She loosened his tether and led him into the forest, walking him for at least half an hour before risking the noise of taking to her saddle.

She wouldn't look back, wouldn't consider the concern the men she'd left behind would feel in the morning. By their actions, they had chosen her path for her.

Except for Hall. She did feel a moment of regret at not having said good-bye. But of all of them, he, more than any other, would understand.

At least, she hoped he would.

Twenty-eight

H E SHOULD HAVE guessed she'd do something as stubbornly foolish as this. But he hadn't, so which of them was truly the more foolish?

Hall stood beside the smoldering remains of their campfire, staring at the empty spot where Bridget had slept the night before.

When she'd moved her bedding so far from everyone else, he'd convinced himself it was just to find a warmer spot.

When she'd offered to cook, that should have been clue enough. She hadn't the natural ability to boil water without burning it.

And taking her brother's criticism of her efforts in stride without a single angry retort?

Beyond foolish for him to have missed all the signs.

He should have known she would do exactly this. It had all been laid out before him as if it were a bedtime story, and he had closed his ears, closed his mind, and ignored every piece of evidence.

His normal suspicions, his ability to reason, even his good sense, had all lacked their usual clarity since Bridget had entered his life.

When he found her, and he *would* find her, he planned to give her such a talking-to she'd think twice before ever trying something like this again.

"Get yer gear packed and let's be on our way," Patrick called out as he headed toward the horses. "We'll need to push hard to reach the MacGahan this night."

"Bridget's gone."

His announcement sounded flat and lifeless—surprising, considering the panic bubbling in his chest. He could have waited to let them discover it for themselves, but the sooner they all knew, the sooner he could be on his way to find her.

"I'm sure she's only strayed a bit. Down to the water, mayhap," Jamesy said, crossing the camp to stare down at her empty spot as if he expected that she would suddenly reappear.

"She's gone," Hall repeated, lifting his pack and heading for his own horse. "Bridget, her horse, and her packs. All gone."

There was no time to spare. He knew from experience that, unburdened by hunting for tracks as she had been the last time he went after her, she would be hard to catch. The woman could ride like the wind. He'd seen her do it.

"Where could she . . ." The words died in Jamesy's mouth.

Her brother, as well as every other person in their camp, had to know where she was bound.

"Did you see her leave? Why dinna you try to stop her?"

An idiot question, that. If Hall had seen her leave, he wouldn't have *tried* to stop her. He *would* have stopped her.

Or gone along with her.

"I found her place empty when I awoke."

"I canna believe this. This is yer fault, O'Donar." Jamesy, eyes flashing, turned and stalked toward him. "You could have spoken up in favor of Brie returning to Castle MacGahan. She might have listened to you, since she seems to agree with everything you say. Instead, you held yer peace and encouraged her to this action with yer silence. Whatever befalls her is on yer hands, and it's me you'll answer to for it."

"You didn't strike me as a fool, MacCulloch." Hall continued to saddle up his horse as the young man approached. They had no time for this senseless bickering. "But if you think anything I could have said would have stopped your sister from doing what she wanted to do, a fool is exactly what you are. You would have been better off had you not insisted on her staying behind. At least then we'd have the ability to protect her. Bridget is a strong-minded woman, with a will of her own."

"What do you ken of my sister?" Jamesy demanded, puffing out his chest.

"Best you stand down, Jamesy," his friend Alex advised, placing a hand to his shoulder and pulling him back. "Now is the time to deal with the situation at hand, not to fight over what might have been or to attempt to assign blame."

"Your friend gives you good advice." Especially considering the peril Bridget rode toward. "We should focus our efforts on catching up to her before she reaches Tordenet. She may have the sword in her possession, but she left the scrolls behind. Without them, she has no chance of survival."

Patrick mounted his animal and extended a hand to Mathew, pulling the boy up behind him. "Be off with you, then, all of you. Find her. I'll take Mathew to Castle MacGahan and meet you at the gates of Tordenet with reinforcements."

With kicks to his animal's sides, Patrick was gone, and silence reigned in the little clearing until no sound of hoofbeats could be heard.

The five of them were headed north before anyone spoke again.

"How would the scrolls save her?" Jamesy sounded calmer now, though worry was evident in his expression. "I've seen my sister use her weapons. Many's the time I've practiced with her. Between her bow and the sword, Bridget is a formidable opponent. So why do you say she canna survive without the scrolls?"

Formidable wasn't good enough in a fight with a beast the likes of Fenrir.

"The treasures we carry work as a single unit to defeat the Beast. The sword drives the Beast from Torquil's body. The scrolls capture the essence of the Beast and contain it. The jewels serve to hold everything in check, like a lock."

"Trying to think as my sister might"—a sheepish expression crept over Jamesy's face—"which I should have tried before now, she has no interest in capturing yer Beast. She plans to kill it."

Hall knew well enough how Bridget thought. He'd already considered the scenario her brother described, and it was that knowledge that worried him most and drove him to ride harder now.

"The Beast knows all too well the danger of the sword. As a result, it can only be destroyed while it is contained within the scrolls. If it is driven from Torquil's body without the scrolls being close enough to capture it, it will simply enter and inhabit the nearest living host."

Jamesy's expression of horror indicated the moment he understood the danger to Bridget.

"Yer telling me that the Beast will claim Brie."

"Body and soul," Hall confirmed. Neither of which he was willing to cede to Fenrir.

Twenty-nine

BRIE AWOKE LONG before the sun made its appearance. Not that she'd slept all that well to begin with. She was too close to Tordenet to risk a fire of any size, and the night had been especially cold.

In spite of the nerves churning her stomach, she needed to eat to prepare herself for the long day ahead. Today she would face the greatest challenge of her life, and this time she would not fail.

Before nightfall had forced her to seek shelter, she'd spotted the tower spires that heralded the approach to Tordenet. They'd been little more than tiny lines against the sky, but she'd known them for what they were. As she drew closer today, they would gleam white in the sun.

Not in welcome, but in warning.

She reached out from under her heavy furs to drag her pack in next to her. Digging inside it, she found the dried meat she hunted. Tough and salty, it did little to settle her stomach, but she ate it anyway for nourishment. She couldn't afford to falter due to weakness.

Today she would ride north, keeping under cover of the woods while she skirted the castle walls, until she reached the sea. From there she would follow the shoreline to the castle and make her way inside.

She refused to worry about locating the passageway that Hall and Patrick had mentioned. If it was there, she would find it.

She had to.

It was her only chance to get inside.

Her only chance to surprise the mighty laird and mete out the punishment he and his Beast deserved.

Next to her the sword sparkled, as if a stray shaft of light had reflected off the weapon's blade.

Her imagination must be playing tricks on her. There was no light to reflect. No moon, no fire, and no sun yet brightening the sky.

Curiosity piqued, she reached for the sword, surprised at how warm the metal felt to her touch. Distracted by the odd warmth, she inadvertently let her finger glance along the edge of the sharp blade.

She jerked her hand away and quickly brought her stinging finger up to her mouth. The coppery tang of blood coated her tongue and she fought back a momentary panic.

How could she have been so careless? To have her second chance at taking her vengeance cut short by such a small and insignificant wound was simply wrong. A perverted prank on the part of some bored god.

She waited for the pain she'd seen Hall endure.

Waited for the debilitating weakness that had brought him to his knees. Waited, her unwavering gaze fixed on the sword, until once again she could have sworn a streak of light glimmered down the length of the metal.

She might have thought she was seeing things as a result of the wound, if not for the fact that she'd seen the first glimmer before she'd touched the blade. And after the wound . . . nothing out of the ordinary. Just the sting of a simple cut as anyone might expect. Not one single bit of the suffering Hall had endured.

How could that be possible? What was it that protected her from the effects of the sword but hadn't protected him?

A little stab of longing pricked at her heart as she pictured Hall in her thoughts. She saw him as she wanted to remember him best, his face clean-shaven, his beautiful lips drawn up in the smile that never failed to squeeze her heart.

More than anything she'd ever wanted, she wished that he was with her now, as if his presence might somehow make her braver.

"I'm brave enough," she whispered into the dark, denying that which her heart called out for. "As brave as I need to be. I've no need of him or any other man to make me into the woman I'm supposed to be."

One day, if she repeated the assertion often enough, she might actually believe it. Until then, she would have to be vigilant in keeping him from her thoughts.

To do otherwise was simply too painful.

Her finger had ceased to bleed, and still nothing out of the ordinary had happened. Apparently the gods had more to occupy their time today than messing with her pathetic little life.

The first glimmer of gray pushed up into the eastern sky; it was time to get going.

She closed her pack and pushed herself up to stand, her muscles protesting a night of cramped inactivity in the cold. She had a long day ahead of her, and the last thing she needed was to get caught due to wasting time daydreaming.

Thirty

BRIDGET HAD BEEN here. In this very spot.

Hall squatted on the ground, balancing himself on one knee while he ran his fingers over the almost imperceptible depression in the soft earth.

She'd slept here. He was sure of it. And not too long ago, at that.

"We might well have already missed her." Jamesy stared out toward the towers in the distance, ragged worry haunting his eyes. "What if we're too late? What if she's already inside? What if the Beast has found her and she's already . . ." He clamped his lips together as if saying anything more would be too painful.

"We're not too late," Hall reassured him, rising to his feet. "We're only an hour or two behind her at most. I can't imagine the secret entrance into the castle will be easily located. It is, after all, *secret*. Have faith in that, Jamesy. Have faith that we'll reach her in time. We still have an opportunity to find her before she makes her way inside."

Hall had faith that he would find her. He would not fail in this.

"I've no wish to distract from the importance of the rescue at hand but, as close as we are to the castle, should we no consider coming to some decision about what we plan to do?" Eric's gaze was fixed upon Tordenet as well. "Once we're spotted, as we likely will be when we move in closer, we'll no have the luxury of waiting for Patrick and his reinforcements."

"We don't need reinforcements." Hall had tried to tell them this all along. "Not with the tools we carry."

"Bridget carries the sword," Jamesy pointed out. "Without the weapon, the scrolls are of little use."

She had it now, but that would change as soon as Hall found her. There was no way he'd allow her to get close enough to the Beast to use the sword.

"You've naught to worry about on that count. I'll have the weapon in my own hands before we confront Fenrir," he assured. "But you must remember, each of the treasures plays an equally important part in what we attempt to do. The scrolls cannot contain the Beast until it's forced from its host by the sword. Wielding the sword does no good if we can't get to the Beast to confront him. That's where the jewels come in."

Hall pulled a small bag from his things and spilled out the contents into the palm of his hand. Sunlight sparkled off the polished facets of five distinctly different jewels, except along one rough edge where Orabilis had ground the gems with a rasp.

He handed one jewel to each of his companions, retaining the ruby for himself.

"It feels almost as if it vibrates against my skin," Finn said, holding the emerald up between two fingers.

"The jewel is searching for its companions. Together they will create a barrier against evil Magic. Our task is to erect that barrier around Tordenet."

"How do we . . . wait." Finn drew the jewel close to examine it. "I dinna feel anything from it now."

The others nodded their agreement.

"That's because the jewels have connected with one another. Each of us will approach Tordenet from a different side. As we close in around the castle walls, the barrier formed by the jewels will prevent Fenrir from accessing all but the most rudimentary Magic. That loss of access should drive him from the castle and into our trap."

"And we'll tighten the noose once he's outside the walls of Tordenet." Eric stuck the jewel he carried into his sporran. "To trap him and drive the Beast into the scrolls you carry."

"Exactly," Hall confirmed.

"What of Bridget?" Jamesy asked.

"I'll find her. I feel sure she's headed to the shore side of the castle, which is where I plan to go now. As there are no gates along that wall, it will be the safest place for her to remain. With the jewel I carry turned over to her possession when I collect the sword, the barrier can remain intact, allowing me to go after Fenrir."

"You are confident in this plan?" Eric waited only for Hall's affirming nod. "In that case, I, too, am confident."

Jamesy sighed heavily, as if struggling with some great internal debate. "I suppose we have little choice in the matter. We can but take up our positions to wait for Fenrir's departure from Tordenet, and pray that you find Bridget and the sword in time."

Hall remounted his horse and set out, Jamesy's words ringing in his ears. He, too, had been praying for that outcome since the moment he'd found Bridget missing from their camp.

Thirty-one

How HARD COULD it possibly be to find one secret entrance?

Brie crouched against the rock outcropping, studying what she could see of Tordenet's long protective wall. Though she'd spent several days at the castle when she'd been here before, she'd never seen it from this angle.

Now she wished she'd taken the opportunity to walk back here. It would have made life so much easier. But wishing for the impossible only wasted time. Her challenge at hand was to figure out how she was going to get inside.

Between the rocky coast where she hid and the castle wall there lay a wide expanse of open ground. She could hardly expect to make her way across that area unseen if Torquil had posted guards on the wall walk. And surely, he had. It was the first thing she would have done if she were walled inside that fortress.

Squinting up into the sunlight, she tried to catch sight of any movement along the top of the wall walk, but it was useless. Either no one was there or the outer wall was simply too high for her to see movement beyond.

For the second time since she'd started her surveillance, water lapped up onto her feet and she scrambled to higher ground, cursing the icy cold that clung to her.

There were a few crevices large enough for her to wedge herself into, but the tide was on the rise and she had no idea how high the water might end up. Having wet feet in this weather was bad enough. The thought of a full-body dunk in those waters was enough to send her inching farther up the rocky ledge.

She could see no other course but to wait for night to fall before she crossed to the wall. How she would locate the hidden entrance without light, she didn't know, but she had no other reasonable choice. Any attempt to cross now would make her an easy target and end her quest before she'd even begun.

The last thing she could afford was to be captured with the Sword of the Ancients in her possession. What a gift that would be to Torquil.

It would be better now to work her way back through the rocks along the shore and into the trees beyond, where she'd left her horse. Remaining here with the wind and the frozen spray beating at her body was hardly the sensible thing to do.

With her boots freezing over, thanks to the dousing they'd taken, the trip back to her horse was slow going. She lost her footing more than once before she traded the rocky cover for the protection of shrubs and brush and, finally, the trees.

She had a long, cold wait ahead of her this day, with little means of warming herself. She would gladly have given all she owned for even a small fire.

An involuntary snort of laughter escaped her, startling her horse. She glanced over to where her animal waited for her, his ears pricked up in alert apprehension.

"Easy," she said under her breath. She doubted the sound had carried to the castle walls, but she had no desire to test her theory.

She needed to use more caution in the noise she made. Turning back, she leaned against one of the trees, peering out to study the castle wall and wait.

In spite of her discomfort, the idea of giving all she owned for anything, let alone a fire, still amused her. She owned so few items that if she bundled them all together in one place and set fire to the lot of them, she'd likely still be cold out here.

Possessions had never had any importance to her. She'd never cared one bit for the things that others coveted. Her bow and her horse were all that had ever mattered.

She suspected the idea of owning things was only on her mind now because of Hall. Because of the time she'd spent in wondering if her life might have turned out differently if she had wealth. If she owned *things*, perhaps then he would have wanted her enough to—

No! She balled up a fist and pounded it against the cold bark of the tree. Wandering down this path accomplished nothing. He had proven himself her friend, and that was all she could expect from him. He'd been honest with her from the first about what he would do.

Wishing and wanting only made her weak.

Her mind could be put to much better use trying to discover a way to find the hidden opening once she reached the castle wall.

What would Hall do if he were here? If she couldn't stop thinking *about* him, maybe she could try thinking *like* him. If he were here, he might—

A big hand slipped over her mouth and tightened, forcing her back against an equally big body.

HE'D FOUND HER!

An overwhelming emotion that Hall refused to name filled his chest. It washed over him in a great wave, leaving his legs weak and trembling. Torn between a desire to crush Bridget in his arms and the urge to yell at her for her stupidity in having run off without him, he chose to resist both temptations.

He couldn't afford to startle her and risk a scream that might alert the whole castle, so he opted for the only action that seemed reasonable.

Her horse sensed his presence before she did, and he stilled when she turned to murmur comfort to the animal. Nothing to be gained in giving her a fright if she mistook him for one of Fenrir's men.

Moving stealthily forward, he made his way through the trees to a point where he was close enough to reach out and slip his hand over her mouth to prevent the scream he feared. Or at the very least, stifle one should it come.

In his vision of the way this would go, he would announce himself as he pulled her back toward him, once he had her close enough that he wouldn't need to raise his voice. It was a sound plan.

Unfortunately, as he should have considered in dealing with this particular woman, her reaction wasn't at all what he anticipated.

Bridget wasn't a screamer. She was a fighter.

Her teeth clamped down hard on one of his fingers. At the same time, her free arm swung up toward his head, leaving him barely enough time to stop the wicked-looking blade she aimed directly at his face.

"By Odin," he snarled, shoving her away from him. "What's wrong with you?"

"Wrong with *me*?" she hissed, stabbing her index finger into his chest. "What kind of an addle-brained thing was that to do, you great fool? Grabbing me from behind and scaring the life right out of me! Yer lucky I didn't gut you right then and there."

"My apologies for alarming you. It was not my intent. As a matter of fact, it was alarming you that I had hoped to avoid by my actions."

Bridget still glared at him, but the finger poking his chest stopped. When she turned from him she muttered something that sounded very much like *witless turdling,* but he chose to let the insult go unchallenged.

In hindsight, he could see that Bridget was right. Not about the gutting, of course; he was never in any danger of that. But he did recognize how his actions had been so easily misinterpreted.

He wouldn't fight with her now. They had too much to do. He'd found her, safe and sound, and that was what really mattered. If all went well, they'd have more than enough time for arguing later. He looked forward to it, in fact.

"I see you've come alone. What are you doing here, anyway?" she asked, crossing her arms in front of her as if to completely shut him out.

"This," he answered, and pulled the ruby along with a thin leather strap from his bag. "This is what I'm doing."

While she watched without comment, he tied the strap around the middle of the jewel and then wrapped it around the other direction end to end before tying it again. After ensuring his makeshift necklace was securely knotted, he held it out and dropped it down over her head.

"What's this for?" she asked, followed by a little gasp of recognition. "It's one of the jewels we recovered. Why are you giving it to me?"

"For protection." Though it wouldn't work for

long, should the essence of the Beast attack, it might give her enough time to escape. "And I'm not alone. Eric, your brother, his friends, all of them are positioned around Tordenet right now, each of them carrying one of the jewels."

"Little good the jewels will do them if we canna get inside to confront the Beast. And with only the five of you, yer no likely to meet with success in storming the front gates. So why aren't they here with you, waiting for dark to hunt for the hidden entrance?"

"Because we don't need to go inside. Fenrir will come out to us."

Bridget looked skeptical. "I find that hard to believe. It would be a far wiser strategy to remain behind the walls of Tordenet. And the Beast, foul as he is, strikes me as being at least as smart as I am."

"Likely much smarter." Fenrir had a millennia of experience that Bridget didn't have. "But every living creature has a vulnerability of some kind. An enemy has but to find that weakness and exploit it. In Fenrir's case, he can't bear to be separated from the flow of his Magic. It is as life and breath to him. It drives him in all he does."

Though it was clear Bridget still doubted him, she was at least listening. "Assuming I accept yer story as truth, how would we manage to exploit this vulnerability you claim he has?"

"We've already begun. With the jewel you wear and its four companions, we've formed a ring around

Tordenet. A ring that effectively blocks the flow of Magic into the castle. Fenrir will have no choice but to leave the protection of the castle walls, seeking that which he must have. And when he does, I'll be waiting for him outside the front gates with the Sword of the Ancients in my hands and the Elven Scrolls of Niflheim at the ready."

Bridget's gaze shifted to her horse and back, a quick little movement that signaled her thoughts as clearly as if she'd spoken them aloud.

Sure enough, the Sword of the Ancients hung from her saddle, its hilt peeking out of the sheath that sheltered the weapon.

"I canna allow you to do that, Hall. For one thing, yer no safe anywhere near that damned sword. We saw all too well what it can do to you. And I ken from experience that it's no the same danger to me."

"I'll handle it with caution." How stupid did she think he was? That he'd carelessly risk another encounter with that deadly blade?

"For another thing," she continued, shifting her feet as she glanced quickly to her horse and back again, "wielding this blade is my right. Justice is my right to serve upon Torquil MacDowylt and the Beast. I will not let this opportunity slip through my fingers. No even for you."

"I understand your feelings." Hall glanced toward Bridget's horse, estimating which of them could reach the animal first. "And you already know that I respect your abilities as a warrior. But . . ."

She simply wouldn't understand why he couldn't allow her to carry on with her quest for revenge. She might well have few equals on the field of battle, but none of that mattered to him right now. All that mattered was that he would not allow her to risk her life.

"There's always a *but*, aye?" Bridget smiled, inching closer to the spot where he stood. The spot between her and her mount. When she reached his side, she reached out to caress his cheek with her cold palm, her expression unreadable. "You disappoint me, Hall. In spite of everything, when it comes down to it, yer no so very different from Jamesy or my uncle. You all picture me spending my days before some man's hearth, cooking his meals, raising his children."

"Never," he denied truthfully. The idea of her as some other man's wife was intolerable to him. Instead of telling her that, he grinned. "Your food would be the death of this imaginary man long before you had any children."

She didn't return his grin, refusing to be swayed by his humor. "You see me as vulnerable."

"You're wrong, Bridget. I see you as irreplaceable," he whispered.

As she broke to run past him, he lifted her from her feet and swung her over his shoulder, carrying her as he had so long ago on that night he'd first met her. The night he'd first saved her from Torquil and the Beast inside the MacDowylt laird.

"Put me down!" she ordered, her feet kicking wildly as she pounded her fists against his back. "You've no right to do this!"

He had every right. She just didn't accept it.

With one hand securely on the sword's hilt, he allowed her feet to drop to the ground. The weapon was in his possession now, and no matter what she tried, he had no intention of relinquishing it to her again.

"You canna do this. It is my responsibility, my calling, to put an end to this monster."

He held her back with one hand, almost without thought, his attention fully fixed upon the weapon in his grasp and the buzzing that filled his ears. Like the approach of angry bees disturbed from their nest, the sound grew, building in intensity and applying pressure inside his ears. At the same time, his fingers began to pulse with a stinging burn as if he'd wrapped his hand around those same bees.

As if from far in the distance, Bridget asked, "Hall? What's wrong with you? What's happening?"

Between the noise in his head and the paralyzing pain crawling up his arm and into his chest, he couldn't begin to find the words to answer.

As if a giant fist tightened around him, his lungs labored to suck in the air he needed for his next breath. A cacophony of clanking, cracking dissonance pounded at him, building to a deafening crescendo designed to burst his eardrums.

It was the sword, rebelling against him, fighting

him for dominance, and the sword was clearly winning. He was powerless to do anything to stop it.

"Hall!"

Even hearing the desperation in Bridget's voice, he could do nothing. She grasped his hand, peeling his fingers one by one from his deathlike grip on the hilt of the weapon.

When the sword hit the ground with a dull *thud* he shuddered and bent forward, gasping, filling his lungs with air as desperately as a drowning man might.

"I told you, did I no? I warned you to stay away from it. Sit," she encouraged, one arm around his shoulders. "Rest for a moment to recover yerself."

With his legs refusing to support him, it was easy to follow her suggestion. He dropped to the ground, legs crossed, his head in his hands, until he heard Bridget moving away from him. He looked up in time to see her reaching down to recover the blade from the forest floor.

"No!"

She straightened, holding the sword in front of her, and the air between them shimmered as if the sword itself were a light source of immense power.

"I am the one to wield the sword," she said calmly. "I, and I alone. You must accept this."

He wanted to deny it, to jump to his feet and sweep the weapon from her grasp. But there was no denying what he saw with his own two eyes.

The light that shimmered in the air coalesced

around Bridget. The markings on her face, which had begun to fade, glowed a bright luminescent blue. Like candles behind the stained glass in a cathedral he'd seen on a trip to York, the light flickered and danced just behind her skin.

He couldn't deny what he recognized as truth.

"It's the markings you wear. The weapon has chosen you as the one Pure Soul of an Ancient Warrior. You're right. You alone can wield the victorious blow with the sword."

"I tried to tell you. It is my destiny," she said quietly, replacing the sword in the saddle sheath before approaching him with her hand outstretched. "Are you better now?"

He nodded, still struggling to accept what he couldn't control as he rose to his feet. "I am."

"Does this alter your plans?"

Mightily. If he were to have his way, he'd call everything off and demand that they ride for safety as quickly as possible. The problem with that solution was that with Fenrir loose in the world, there would be no safety to be found anywhere.

"It only changes which of us will be waiting outside the gates when the Beast leaves the castle. You'll need these." He walked quickly to his horse and removed the scrolls from his pack to hand to Bridget, who'd followed behind him. "You've but to touch Torquil with the blade to drive the Beast from his body. Once you've done that, it will have no choice but to return to the scrolls. We'll secure them with the jewels, and our task will be accomplished. No one needs to get hurt if we're all mindful of the parts we need to play."

She nodded, taking the scrolls in one hand as she walked toward her own mount. She stopped a few paces before she reached the animal to turn back to him. "I willna fail in my calling this time. I will do what I should have done when I first laid eyes on the sword. By the Seven, I swear it."

"Use caution, little one." Hall couldn't keep himself from touching her one more time, tucking a stray lock of hair behind her ear. "Remember that you're not out there alone. We're all in this together. Once Fenrir breaks from the confinement of the castle, you must wait. Don't follow after him until the five of us regroup with you. We all must be there together to keep the circle tight around him."

"I understand." She smiled sadly, lifting a hand to his cheek before rising up on her toes to place her lips softly against his.

He crushed her to him, soaking in the moment as if it were his last.

She broke the kiss, her hands cupping his face, her eyes suspiciously bright. They didn't speak as he lifted her to her saddle and she started off, him following along for a few steps.

"Keep to the cover of the trees," he called out as she rode away.

As he watched her disappear into the forest, a misty cloud blurred his vision for the first time since his childhood.

A fine mess the Norns had woven for his lifepath this time. Not only could he not claim Bridget for his own, now he couldn't even protect her as he wanted. He had done what little he could, leaving the ruby in her possession. It could end up being all that stood between her and Fenrir if their plan should go awry.

So much for the free will Orabilis and her kind espoused. The moment was out of his control. What would be, would be—the Norns had woven the threads of their lives long before he or Bridget had been born. They could only accept what the Norns had chosen for them as the path of their days.

Hall repeated every platitude he'd ever heard, in an attempt to ease the worry that wouldn't be eased.

Events of this day would go according to plan. He would climb on his horse and head for the castle gates, exactly as . . .

His thoughts faltered to a stop as he noticed an oddity in the bush where Bridget's horse had been tethered. In one spot, the branches of the hardy evergreen hung strangely askew.

He reached his hand inside the bush, fearing what he'd find there yet knowing what it would be before his fingers raked over the ancient sheepskin.

The scrolls, deliberately shoved into the branches to hide them. She'd never had any intention of following his plan.

She still intended to kill Torquil MacDowylt. And unless he acted quickly, she'd pay for her deception with her life. She'd pay for her deception with her soul.

"To hell with the Norns," he growled, hoping against hope that Orabilis had been telling him the truth about the role his own free will could play.

Even if the old Faerie had been wrong, what did he have to fear at this point? What could the Norns do to him anyway? Snip his thread, ending the path his life traveled down?

If his current path included Bridget's death, he had no desire to continue along that path anyway.

"Send your worst, old women," he called out, snatching up the scrolls and running to his horse.

He *would* protect Bridget, and there was nothing any creature in any corner of this world or the next could do to stop him.

Thirty-two

CLOTHED IN THE body of Torquil MacDowylt, Fenrir stalked across the bailey toward the barracks. He had grown used to this body, thinking of it as a second skin. But today it felt uncomfortable and foreign, like a wrong-size hand-me-down.

As if the Universe were trying to warn him of impending danger, his disquiet had been growing over the course of the last few days, and more than ever he mourned the loss of his own form.

All would be well once he had the scrolls and the sword back under lock and key. The anxiety plaguing him stemmed as much from his lack of control over the situation as anything else. After weeks with no results, he was tired of waiting.

It was time to send out another party of men.

Halfway to his destination, the air around him began to shimmer and his chest constricted with each breath he took. The five oozing sores around his heart throbbed as one, sending pain radiating out to his arms and legs.

Damned fragile Mortal body. Always some new way to harm it looming close at hand.

The air began to compress around him, packing in against his eardrums until he was forced to open his mouth wide to relieve the pressure.

What could this be? A storm coming? A new disease? Some new plant to which this body was sensitive? It could be almost anything, but it felt like no Mortal threat he'd previously encountered.

It felt almost like . . .

His foot slid to a stop on the gravel and he stilled, stretching out his senses in all directions to study the vibrations around him.

Impossible!

He'd checked in on each of his search parties this morning and none of them had so much as spotted the thief, let alone retrieved the scrolls and returned with them.

And yet he would swear the scrolls were nearby. He lifted his head and sniffed the air.

He smelled them. By all that was unholy, he could feel them.

The scrolls were here.

"Man the gate!" he ordered in a roar, reversing his course back toward the keep.

If he could feel their presence this strongly, there was no time to waste.

Breaking into a run, he burst through the big doors of his keep and headed straight for the tower, where his power was strongest. From the window he leaned out to scan the courtyard and the wall beyond. He could see nothing out of the ordinary, but the feeling persisted, growing in strength.

The scrolls were nearby. Calling him. Taunting him.

Never again would he allow any creature to imprison him within the scrolls. It had taken too long for him to find the one who had set him free, and he wouldn't give up that freedom easily.

He could transform into the big bird, but his last foray in that form had left him with a jagged, puffy red scar marring the skin from his shoulder to his elbow. A strong reminder of the vulnerability inherent in the bodies of this world's creatures.

No, he didn't like the idea of risking that again. He needed to be away from this place. A clean escape. Now.

Moving to the center of the room, he willed the change that had saved this body once before. As a smoky mist, he had risen above the fire that had threatened to consume him when he'd taken control from the MacDowylt laird. That same form would transport him, unnoticed, from this place to another, safer location.

Calling on the Magic to fill him, he waited, his body vibrating with an expectant hum, as if in anticipation of the imminent arrival of a favored lover. He waited for the familiar power to wash over him, to fill his senses. He waited until his patience abandoned him.

What was this travesty? He had never been bereft of his Magic, except during his confinement within the scrolls. Only the jewels had the power to limit his access in this way.

His stomach churned with a rising panic.

Not only were the scrolls waiting somewhere nearby for him, so, too, were the jewels.

Whoever, whatever, had gathered his treasures now thought to close in on him. To use the tools of his confinement to cast him back into that hell which had held him prisoner for so many centuries.

He would *not* be captured here. Not like this.

But how could he leave? Without access to his Magic, his only alternative was to seek escape as any Mortal might.

He would claim the fastest horse in his stables and break free from the trap that threatened to spring closed around him at any moment.

Once he was outside the net created by the jewels, he would again have access to his Magic. And then he would travel to safety, far, far away from this place.

Thirty-three

BRIDGET DREW HER horse into position just inside the tree line ringing Tordenet Castle. From this distance she was well hidden but still had a view of the gates and the field where the Tinklers had camped. This had to be very near the spot Hall had described as where she should wait.

Hall.

Her heart hurt just thinking of him.

As much as she hungered for his touch, she prayed that after today, she'd never have to see him again. Every time she saw him, every time she touched him, walking away and leaving him behind became harder and more painful than it had been the time before. She wasn't sure how many more gracious exits she had left in her before she'd break down and beg him to reconsider his rejection of her.

And wouldn't that make for a pretty show? Her blubbering like some lost bairn, setting herself up for another round of disappointment.

Whatever destiny had in store for her after today, she only prayed it would cease to torment her with the delectable temptation of the man she would never be able to call her own.

She also prayed she'd hidden the damned scrolls well enough that he wouldn't find them. Because if he did, he would come bursting out of those woods like a madman and ruin her plan.

Though she accepted that he didn't love her as she loved him, she knew well enough that his need to *rescue* her would override his good sense. She'd seen it happen before.

Waiting, as usual, was hideously difficult, made more so this time by Brie's concern that Hall would arrive at any moment, waving the scrolls at her like some demented creature, determined to capture the enemy she wanted dead.

Though it would take the Sword of the Ancients to kill the Beast, the body belonged to a man, and she intended to bring down that body with a bow. Once he was disabled, it should be easy enough to deal with Fenrir. After all, the blade had barely touched Hall and he'd nearly died.

Though it had no effect at all on her.

She'd begun to suspect that the sword had chosen her because of the ancient markings she wore. Orabilis had warned her of something like that, Magic being drawn to Magic. Perhaps this was exactly the situation that Orabilis had envisioned when she warned that Brie might regret her sacrifice in the end.

Her stomach churned as she considered what was to come, making her regret the few bits of food she had managed to force down hours before.

If only the damned Beast would hurry up and show himself! According to Hall's claim about the jewels, Fenrir should have burst out of the gates by now in a mad dash to claim his Magic.

Unless Hall was wrong. Unless the jewels had absolutely no effect on the Beast's Magic, and he was completely unaware of their presence. Or worse yet, maybe he was very much aware of their presence and was sitting safely inside the castle walls, laughing at them.

Just as she'd almost managed to convince herself their plan was a complete failure, she heard the noise she'd been waiting for: the grating screech of the iron portcullis rising.

Her muscles tensed in anticipation as she caught sight of her quarry. He moved as if carried by the wind, his blond hair streaming out behind him as the huge animal he rode galloped away at an ever-increasing speed.

Bridget scanned both sides of the castle, looking for any sign of the men who were to join her in the chase. Not a leaf or branch shifted out of place. Where *were* they?

Already, Torquil was disappearing into the distance. They would lose him if she waited, no matter what the plan had originally been.

With a switch of her reins and a kick of her feet, she was off.

HE WAS TOO late!

Damn the stubborn woman for not sticking to the plan. Damn his eyes for not finding the scrolls sooner. Damn the Norns for thwarting his every effort.

Hall wheeled his horse onto the trail to pursue Bridget, who was already shrinking in the distance. Leaning low over his horse's neck, he charged along, gaining speed and slowly reducing the distance between them. Behind him, he picked up the sounds of the others joining in the chase.

Northwest they rode, eating up the miles as they followed the Beast on a sure course toward the jagged cliffs overlooking the North Sea.

He hardly felt the sting of the mist turning to rain as it bit into his face. Hardly heard the distant rumble of thunder and the crackle of lightning. His whole focus and concentration was on reaching Bridget before she reached the Beast.

Ahead of them loomed the great cliffs where walls of jagged rock plunged straight down into the churning sea. One way or another, their wild flight would be ending soon.

Though he'd closed the distance that separated him and Bridget considerably, she had also closed the distance between her and Fenrir.

Hall skirted out to the side, hoping to cut her

off. Barring that, there was a chance he could insert himself between Bridget and Fenrir. He'd settle for any small favors he could get, but it appeared there were no favors in his future.

There was no way for him to get to her quickly enough.

Bridget charged across the last bit of open ground like a maddened Valkyrie, her hair billowing out around her as her arrows flew, swift and sure, toward her target. She rode without fear, without reservation, holding nothing back.

In that moment, Hall knew he must have her for his own—forever. She was his kindred spirit, his untamed warrior, the one woman who could ride at his side into eternity.

When this was over, somehow he would convince her to take him, no matter that his life was not his own. No matter that he was destined to spend his years protecting Mankind. He would do it without complaint, if he could have her at his side.

If she'd have him.

If they survived this battle.

BRIDGET STEELED HER senses and let loose her arrow, her only thought its intended trajectory. He was prey, like any other. Her arrow would find its target and bring his frenzied escape to a halt.

A second time she pulled back the heavy string and let go, knowing even as she did that she'd missed.

Think like the rabbit, her father had taught her. *Anticipate where the rabbit will turn.*

Hunting this Beast was no different than hunting the rabbit. He was simply a larger target to hit.

She tightened her knees as she urged her mount to another burst of speed with a kick of her heels. Quickly, she nocked another arrow into her bow. She was one with the animal she rode, feeling his movements beneath her as if he were an extension of her own body. One with the arrow in her bow. One with the target in her sight.

Lifting her arms, she pulled back, loosing the arrow. Following its trajectory to its target.

Success!

The arrow buried itself high in Torquil's leg, eliciting a scream of surprised pain.

"Yer pain has just begun, you filthy bastard," she murmured, lifting her bow again.

If she were to have any chance at the man, she needed him off his horse.

Two shots in rapid succession, one to his arm and one to split the reins in his hand. Another scream, this one a long, unearthly sound, such as she'd heard only once before. The night of the horrible storm when she'd first realized that Hall would not stay with her.

Torquil's mount, given his head by the loose reins, reared in fear of the approaching cliff, throwing his rider to the ground before racing away.

Brie slowed her approach, giving her prey time to realize he had nowhere to go but to face her. She tied the bow into the sheath on her back and drew the sword as she slid off her horse to confront her enemy.

The sword's song sang in her ears, giving her courage, urging her forward. Killing a man was no different than hunting her dinner.

Except that some small voice in the back of her head kept trying to convince her that it was different. She'd done it before, but that truly had been different. She'd done that to save Hall from an evil villain who'd closed in on him when he was defenseless.

Just as she closed in on Torquil now.

Didn't that make her the evil villain in this scenario?

This was no time to doubt herself. No time for her conscience to kick in. Not when her revenge was so near at hand.

Her only option was to drown out the voice in her head.

"Remember me, Torquil MacDowylt?" she called out as she approached the laird, sword held aloft in front of her. "Or perhaps you remember my father, Hamud MacCulloch. You hanged him for the crime of following yer brother, Malcolm, when he escorted Malcolm's wife to Tordenet."

That was it. That was her reason for her being here. Her justification for what she was about to do.

Torquil rolled from his back to his stomach and pushed up to his knees, managing to get unsteadily to his feet.

"Why would I waste my thoughts on remembering such an insignificant creature?" he returned, laughing in a booming, unearthly voice as he broke off the arrow that stuck out from his leg and threw it behind him. "Is that your best effort, girl? If it is, then you're lost, because your best is not good enough. Not by far."

Brie lifted the sword, gripping it with both hands as he charged toward her. Any doubt she had about her ability to strike a man down fled when his eyes began to glow eerie red.

It might look like Torquil MacDowylt she faced, but it wasn't. It was the Beast who charged toward her.

With all her strength, she swung the sword at his neck, connecting with his shoulder as he attempted to dodge her blow.

Another scream from her attacker, this one a thousand times louder than before. The screech echoed so loudly, she dropped the sword to cover her ears. The long, loud, rattling howl of a creature unknown to the Mortal world filled her mind and buffeted her senses as she stumbled back from the slumped shell of the man.

A cloud of black smoke wisped out of the gaping wound in Torquil's shoulder and swirled up into the air above him. A sickening, putrid smell reminiscent of rotted meat filled the air as the smoke gathered into a tightly swirling mass. It throbbed and pulsed before it stretched out, plummeting straight toward her.

Frozen to her spot, Brie could do nothing but watch in horror as the black mist engulfed her, cutting off her air, dragging her to her knees.

HALL KICKED HIS horse, demanding every ounce of speed the animal could give him.

"No!"

The cry of denial was torn from his lips as he watched Fenrir's essence drain from Torquil's body, gather its strength, and plunge down over Bridget. It encased her in its black mist and tightened around her, driving her to her knees before it suddenly puffed away.

The jewel's protection had held, but its effect wouldn't last for long. One single jewel was no match for the Beast.

Once again the black mist churned and gyrated, gathering strength for another onslaught. Bridget, unaware of the danger, struggled to her feet and picked up the sword, holding it point down to support her as she stood.

He was close enough now—he *had* to be.

Hall tore one of the scrolls from his bag and ripped the ribbon from around it, holding it up at his side like a knight carrying a banner into battle.

The mist pulsed as if it were being pulled apart before stretching out into a long, thin strand of black thread. It flowed toward him to cover the face of the scroll, a writhing, living mass. So much weight was added to the scroll, Hall was forced to drop his reins and use two hands to roll it back up. Once rolled, he dropped it into the bag and turned his horse to race toward the men who followed.

"Gather the jewels!" he barked at Eric, the first to reach him. "Put them inside the bag to secure the scroll. You must hurry!"

He handed off the bag, relying on his companion to carry out his instructions. It had to be done immediately, before the Beast could recover and escape.

Then Hall turned his horse to see Torquil on his feet, advancing on Bridget.

"I REMEMBER YOU," Torquil snarled, his eyes wild, but with the madness of mere man, not the Beast. "You tried to kill me, and then you escaped my vengeance."

"As you escaped mine," Brie replied, struggling to lift the sword.

Her encounter with the essence of the Beast had weakened her, as if the hideous mist that had engulfed her had sucked away her life force to bolster its own energy.

Even weak, she was still a match for the bastard advancing on her. One arm hung limply at his side, blood staining the shoulder of his tunic where her sword had already connected. His movements were further hampered by the arrow broken off in his thigh.

It would be easy enough to run him through, if only she could manage to lift the damn sword. Easy enough, had she not completely lost her appetite for killing this man. It was the Beast that was responsible for her father's death. The Beast that needed to pay.

The realization hit hard, clouding her eyes with welling tears. If she killed Torquil now, she'd be no better than him. No different at all.

"Stay where you are, MacDowylt. The time has come for you to answer for yer crimes. My friends will be here soon enough."

Torquil's face was distorted in a crazed grin, all his madness on open display.

"I may well travel to the next world this day. But I willna travel alone." He pulled a wicked-looking blade from a sheath he wore strapped at his side and lunged forward.

Brie sidestepped his attack, dragging the sword she still couldn't lift to circle around Torquil, her back now to cliffs. From this vantage, she had a clear view of her rescuers racing toward her. She had only to hold the madman off for a few minutes to allow them to reach her.

If only the madman would cooperate.

Already he lumbered toward her, blade raised, eyes glazed over with his madness, a cry of rage on his lips.

Brie struggled to lift the sword for her defense as the world around her slowed to a crawl. Though her muscles were weak, her senses seemed sharper than ever, as if the gods themselves wanted her to experience her last moments on earth to their fullest.

The ground under her feet vibrated with the pounding hooves that couldn't possibly reach her in time. Rain pelleted her face, and the sound of waves crashing on the rocks far below warred with a distant thunder rumbling in the heavens.

Torquil slammed into her and she dropped the sword to fasten both hands around his wrist, focusing all her energy on holding off the dagger he swung toward her face. As they struggled, her feet slid on the slippery ground and she lost her balance, tumbling backward.

The ground came up fast to meet her, slamming against her and stealing her breath. She managed to keep a tight grip around Torquil's wrist, though with him on top of her, his blade was mere inches above her shoulder.

His teeth bared, he looked more like a rabid animal than a man as he forced the blade closer to her body.

She'd underestimated her opponent. She wasn't a match for him in her current state. Unless she did something drastic, she couldn't hold on much longer.

Sometimes in life, you must let go in order to hold on.

Orabilis's words shimmered in her memory and she gave herself over to them.

"I pray yer right," she muttered, releasing one hand from Torquil's wrist.

Freed from her hold, the blade plunged into the top of her arm as she dug the fingers of her free hand into the wound on Torquil's shoulder.

He screamed with agony and threw himself back away from her, grabbing her braid as he rolled over the edge of the cliff.

Pain slammed into her as his weight dragged her toward the edge. Below her, the white foamy waves crashed onto the jagged rocks. She fought for a handhold on the wet stony ground, something—anything—to slow her slide over the edge.

"If I go, you go," the desperate monster of a man screamed at her.

With her fingers losing their grip on the rocks, and one leg already over the edge, Brie knew it was only a matter of *when*—not *if*.

HALL WATCHED IN horror as Torquil tumbled over the edge of the cliff, dragging Bridget along with him. He jumped from his horse and threw himself forward onto his knees to grab her hand.

He pulled and she screamed, leaving little doubt that Torquil held on to her still. One look over the edge, and Hall drew his sword and swung, slicing through the silken strands of Bridget's hair.

As the MacDowylt plunged down toward the raging water, Hall dragged her into his arms, crushing her to his chest as he moved back from the brink of disaster.

He'd almost lost her. The fear consumed him,

weakening his legs so that he couldn't stand, couldn't speak, couldn't do anything but hold her close.

She clutched his shirt as if she might never let go, whimpering in his embrace.

"I've ruined your hair," he managed, his mind still roiling with what might have been.

Her shoulders shook, and he didn't know if she sobbed or laughed. He didn't care which, only that she was safe in his arms, no matter what the Norns had woven into their tapestry as her fate.

Though he wanted nothing more than to hold her in his arms, there was still one last thing requiring his attention.

Releasing his hold on her, he lifted the makeshift necklace from over her head. The ruby was needed in the bag with the other jewels to secure Fenrir's imprisonment.

"Holy Mother," Jamesy bellowed, pulling Bridget away to wrap her in his own embrace. "Get my bag, Alex, she's bleeding."

With her brother taking charge, Hall rose to his feet and joined Eric, who stood near the side of the cliff.

"The last jewel," Hall said, handing it over to Eric, who added it to the bag tied at his waist. "We've no cause to worry over the Beast any longer."

"And what about Torquil?" Eric asked, turning his gaze to the rocks below. "What do you suppose became of him?"

"Fish food, likely," Finn answered, joining them. "No one could have survived that fall."

"As you say." Eric looked unconvinced. "I'd feel better, though, to see his body on those rocks."

"They're dead?" Bridget called out, wincing as her brother tightened the wrapping around the wound on her arm. "Both of them?"

"Torquil has been taken by the sea, and Fenrir is back in the prison where he belongs." Hall held up the bag Eric had handed him as proof before shoving it into the sporran he carried at his waist.

"Then feed the Beast to the sea as well," Bridget demanded, her eyes bright with tears. "Prison is not punishment enough for all the evil he brought into our world."

"Fenrir cannot be destroyed by plunging the scrolls into the sea. They would simply be tossed around by the waves until someday some poor innocent soul would rescue them from their watery home and start the process all over again."

They couldn't so easily pluck Fenrir's thread from the tapestry of the Future. That was why the Elves had imprisoned him to begin with. The ancient gods of Asgard refused to order his destruction.

"You will not destroy the Beast?"

Her gaze bore into his very heart, forcing him to steel himself against the pain in her eyes. It wasn't his place to defy the will of Asgard.

"No. This is how it must be."

"Then we are done here," she replied, turning away from him. "And all I fought for is truly lost."

Lost, indeed. Clearly, in that moment, anything that might have been between him and Bridget was lost as well.

The Beast, it seemed, had won after all.

Thirty-four

BRIDGET'S ARM HURT like hell; not even the honey ale she'd poured over the wound had helped. Maybe, as Hall had once claimed, she should simply drink the contents of the flask and be done with it.

Hall.

Would she ever be able to pass a day, even an hour, without having him invade her thoughts?

She groaned and scrubbed her hands over her face, thankful she was alone here by the river while all the men gathered in their camp.

After a day and a half on the trail, their little group had met up with Malcolm and Patrick and a company of men from Castle MacGahan. For the past hour, they'd been presenting their arguments as to what should be done next.

She couldn't care less what they decided. It meant nothing to her. All she wanted was to be left alone to wallow in her misery.

She'd taken her revenge on Torquil MacDowylt, and instead of the satisfaction she'd expected, she felt only a great, gnawing emptiness. Orabilis had been right. Revenge wasn't enough to give her life meaning. She wanted . . .

What she wanted didn't matter.

She'd spent her life doing what she wanted, and what did she have to show for it? The Beast still lived, so even in her quest for revenge she hadn't succeeded. The wound on her arm would be long in healing, and if not for Hall she'd likely have met her own end on the jagged rocks of the North Sea, along with the MacDowylt laird.

And as a bonus? Useless blue symbols stained the whole of her body. Symbols that Orabilis had warned her she'd regret.

All she'd managed so far was to prove that everyone else in her life was right. Orabilis, her brother, even Hall.

Her thoughts always managed to circle back to him. Hall, the thing she wanted most. The thing she could never have.

She reached for her bag and dug around until her hand closed over the flask of honey ale. After removing the stopper, she tipped back her head and let the brown liquid burn a trail down her throat.

The beverage flowed down into her empty stomach, lurching and sloshing around, creating havoc that she chose to ignore, following the first drink with a second.

She had a vague memory of an old man her father had pointed out to her once when they'd traveled to Inverness. A drunkard whose mind was long gone, his days spent sitting by a fire, drinking tankard after tankard of strong ale. It was his escape, her father had told her, from the pain of losing his wife and children.

Escape sounded more than a little attractive to her, and she downed another large swallow of ale.

But where was this lovely escape her father had claimed the liquor brought? Though her head felt heavy and her stomach churned, her memories of Hall hadn't diminished in the least.

She tipped back the bottle for a fourth time, emptying it, just as her brother pushed through the brush to join her.

"Here you are. I wondered what happened to you that you didn't stay to hear Malcolm's decisions."

She shrugged and stuffed the empty bottle into her bag. "Makes no never-mind to me. The laird will do what he will do, and I will do . . . nothing."

"With Torquil dead, Patrick will take a contingent of men and lay claim to Tordenet." Jamesy sat down across from her and scratched his stubbled chin. "Would you want to return there to live, do you think? It was our home as children."

"No." She didn't need to think about that one at all. She'd been but a small child when she'd lived there. Her only memories of Tordenet were more recent, and all of them involved Hall. "Never."

"Our uncle predicted you would say as much."

Jamesy nodded thoughtfully, focusing his gaze in the distance. "He also says it's time we settle on the question of yer future."

"My future?"

Her future was black. Black, nasty, and empty, like looking down into a well with no bottom. Why would anyone want to talk about the big, black, empty hole that lay in store for her?

"Aye, yer future." Jamesy stood to pace back and forth. "I'd hope that after everything that's happened, you've had yer fill of adventure. That you'll be ready to settle down to a normal life like other women."

"Normal life?"

"Exactly." Jamesy seemed to be warming to his subject, his face alight with excitement.

She remembered that look. It was the one he'd worn when he'd convinced her she wanted to stay home with her aunt instead of going hunting with him and Da. It had been what he wanted, not what she wanted. But with his enthusiasm, he'd convinced her to spend the most miserable week of her life.

"Give up this ridiculous warrior notion of yers. Take a husband and make me an uncle. Be normal, Brie."

So they'd planned it all out for her, Jamesy and Uncle Harald, sitting in the circle of men deciding who would go to Tordenet, who would return to Castle MacGahan, and, likely, what poor fool would take on the burden of wedding Bridget MacCulloch.

She reached again for her bag, remembering as her hand closed around the bottle that it was already empty.

Too damn bad, that.

"So, we're in agreement, then?" Jamesy reached for her hand to help her to her feet, drawing back as she stood up beside him. "You smell like a draught-house. What's wrong with you?"

"I hurt," she confessed simply.

Her body, her mind, her heart. They all hurt. And of the three, she was sure that only her body had a chance of recovering.

"Och, Bridget." Jamesy tried to pull her close but she pushed away.

His pity only made it worse. Especially since he had no idea what he pitied her for.

"As to any agreement—" She stopped, feeling the tears welling up from deep inside, waiting until she could force them back down. "Decide what you will for me. I no longer have any care how I spend my days."

Without Hall at her side, one day would be no better than another anyway.

Thirty-five

CASTLE MACGAHAN LOOMED ahead of them, the portcullis lifted in welcome so that the gates resembled a great mouth opened wide, waiting to swallow them at their journey's end.

"It's good to be home," Eric laughed as he rode next to Hall, his eyes shining with his excitement. "I feel as though I've been gone for a year."

Considering how short a time Eric had been wed, Hall understood why his friend was so eager to return.

For him, though, it was the beginning of an end he didn't relish.

His work here was done. There was no more rea son for him to remain at Castle MacGahan. Chase Noble was settled, so he'd paid back his debt to his Faerie friend to see after his son's welfare. Fenrir was safely returned to his prison, and Torquil Mac-Dowylt no longer threatened the future of Mankind. The task set him by Thor was all but complete. Once a place of safekeeping was decided upon for the scrolls, all that had brought Hall here would be finished.

All his missions completed, and what did he have to show for it? Indebtedness to two Faeries, and a broken heart. Little wonder his father had refused to carry the mantle of Thor's Rock.

Days like this, he'd gladly have given it up himself.

"I hope you'll no take personally my leaving you behind?" Eric's wide grin spoke of his excitement.

"Go. Else we're likely to have your fair Jeanne running out to meet us."

Eric's horse broke into a gallop and within minutes several other men, including their good laird, Malcolm, spurred their mounts to follow suit.

Off to one side, Hall spotted Bridget riding alone. He'd worried over her health for the past two days, though Jamesy had assured him she was recovering. It was only that, even from a distance, she seemed different. Her silence, the way she carried herself; nothing spoke of the vibrant, untamed warrior he'd come to know.

He turned his horse toward hers. Thanks to her brother's constant hovering, this was the first chance he'd had to speak to her alone. Yet as he drew his horse up next to hers, he floundered for something to say.

"What do you want?" she asked, her voice flat and dull.

Under any other circumstances, he'd have described her as defeated.

"What's next in your life, Bridget MacCulloch? Now that your revenge is complete."

"Is it?"

Of course it was. She'd done what she set out to do. "Torquil MacDowylt is dead."

She sighed deeply, staring into the distance. "So he is. But was it truly he who killed my father? Or was it the Beast? The Beast that still lives, there in the bag that you carry at your side." Bridget lifted a hand to brush her hair back from her brow, a movement that carried the frustration she obviously felt. "Once again I came so close, and once again I failed. In so many ways."

They rode into the gate, traversing the tunnel in silence to reach the castle bailey, teeming with excited, happy people.

"But you didn't fail. Fenrir is imprisoned."

"It's of no matter. Jamesy was right. I'm no warrior if I canna defeat even one enemy. Both he and my uncle Harald are determined that all I need to complete my days is a husband of their choosing to settle me down. So, in answer to yer question, I suppose that's what's to become of my life." She wiped the back of her hand over her eyes and turned her face away from him.

A husband of *their* choosing? For his Bridget?

Not likely.

Not while he breathed air.

If anyone was going to choose a husband for Bridget, it should be he who did the choosing.

He couldn't stand to see her spirit broken like this. The fire, the passion for life, was gone from her eyes. They would not do this to her.

He would not do this to her.

As they brought their horses to a stop in front of the stables, he quickly dismounted and reached up to help her down, fastening his hand tightly around hers.

He would see that sparkle of life back in her eyes, no matter what it took.

A quick glance around and he headed out, dragging her along behind him toward the workshops.

"What do you think yer about?" she demanded, running to keep up with his determined steps.

"Doing what needs to be done," he answered, more sure than ever about the course he'd chosen. "What should have been done long ago."

Heat billowed from the forge where the smithy worked his iron, shimmering in the air around them.

He had intended to consult with the Faerie, Syrie, to determine Fenrir's fate. As Orabilis had warned, the Beast could not be left in the Mortal world. The temptation for someone, at some time in the future, to call upon his evil power would be too great.

Wyddecol, the home world of the Fae, was a possibility, but who could say how the Faeries would respond to such a request?

No, now that he'd thought it through, this truly was the best option.

Hall pulled the bag with the scrolls from his sporran and held it up for Bridget to see. "Do you still believe annihilation is the necessary consequence for the Beast?"

"I believe it is the only acceptable consequence to guarantee the future of our world. If the Beast is imprisoned, we both know he will be found and released upon the world again. It's only a matter of time. Some other innocent like my father will die."

She was right. It was what the Elves should have done a millennium ago. What he did now would simply right the wrong they'd perpetrated. To hell with what the gods of Asgard decreed. There would be no escape for Fenrir this time.

With an arm crooked above his eyes to protect against the billowing heat, Hall leaned toward the forge and tossed the bag inside, into the flames.

Never again would Fenrir plague the world.

Overhead, the skies rumbled with a thunder well beyond Hall's control. The ground under their feet shuddered and rolled as if the planet itself responded to his action.

Hall wrapped his arms around Brie, covering her body with his own when they were thrown to the ground.

Lightning exploded through the heavens like some giant crazed spiderweb crackling across the sky as people in the courtyard ran for cover, their screams drowned out by a ripping, tearing noise that filled the air and buffeted their ears.

When the noise finally ceased, the silence was almost as deafening as the noise had been. Gradually, a hubbub of excited, frightened voices filled the silence as people picked themselves up off the ground to begin to seek some understanding of what had just happened to them.

Hall helped Bridget to her feet, taking care to avoid her injured arm. "That's that, then. Do you still feel as though you failed?"

Her mouth opened and closed twice before she managed to form words. "I canna believe you did that for me," she said at last, her voice trembling. "I canna believe you destroyed the Beast."

"Though I didn't do it solely for you, I want you to know that I would gladly move heaven and earth to return the light of possibility to your eyes." He lifted her hand to place a gentle kiss on her palm. "Seeing it shining there now assures me I did the right thing."

"What have you done?" Syrie ran toward them from the keep, her skirts gathered in her arms so as not to slow her down. "What have you done?"

The little Faerie halted in front of him, breathless, her eyes wide with distress.

"I did what needed to be done. We'll none of us ever have to fear Fenrir again. I destroyed the Beast by tossing the scrolls that bound him into the fire of the forge."

Syrie's hands flew up to cover her cheeks. "Do you have any conception of the magnitude of your actions? You've killed one of Asgard's own creatures!"

Hall understood quite well what he'd done. It seemed to him it was the Faerie who didn't understand.

"As one of Asgard's own myself, it was my right to do so. Free will, I believe it's called."

He was Thor's Rock, tasked with the well-being and security of those Mortals who'd found favor in Thor's eyes. And he'd just ensured the well-being and security of untold generations of his grandfather's followers.

Syrie took a deep breath, casting a worried gaze toward the sky before fixing it back on him. "Right or not, by your actions you've destroyed the tapestry woven by the Fates. You could well have changed everything—and you've certainly drawn the eyes of every god and goddess to this very place, to all of us. Your action has shaken the very foundations of the fabric of life."

Bridget nudged against his side, slipping her hand into his as if to give him strength in his confrontation with the Faerie.

"Perhaps you are correct, Syrie. I may well have drawn the combined ire of Asgard and Wyddecol. But in doing so, I made the Mortal world a better place, and I've saved the woman with whom I would spend the rest of eternity. The woman I would have as my wife." He lifted Bridget's hand to his lips and locked her gaze with his. "If she'll have me."

BRIE'S WORLD REELED out of control, as if she were caught in some amazing dream from which she never wanted to wake.

"If *I'll* have *you*?" she managed at last. "Why would *you* want *me*? Yer a laird, a landed man of wealth and position. I'm but a painted wildling with nothing of value to my name. I am no one."

Had he forgotten that he'd refused her for this very reason?

"Never say that. Never think it. You are Bridget MacCulloch, daughter of the House MacUlagh, descended from the Ancient Seven who ruled the land when not even the Roman invaders dared challenge all the way to the Northern Sea. You are the woman who has captured the heart of Hall O'Donar, lowly laird of the Thunder's People in the Land of Mists."

She'd captured his heart? Though that had been her dream, it was more than she'd dared to expect.

Syrie said, "Tell her what that really means, O'Donar. Tell her who your people are, who *you* really are, and what her life will be like if she agrees to your offer. She deserves that before she commits herself to you."

Hurt flashed in his eyes, followed by a complete masking of his emotions. Did he not realize she didn't care about any of that?

She said softly, "You've no need to tell me anything more, if you dinna choose to. I dinna care who yer people are. All that matters to me is who *you* are, and I already ken all that I need to about you."

"No." He squeezed her hand as the half smile she loved so much lifted the corners of his mouth. "The Faerie has the right of it. You deserve the whole of the truth. I am Thor's Rock, a living descendent of Thor himself. I am his champion in the Mortal world. I told you once before that my life is not my own, and that was the truth. I am bound to go when and where he directs me, to answer the needs of his true believers and to see to their safety."

"So yer the warrior I always thought you to be, am I right?"

"There's more," he said, as if once he'd started, he needed to unburden himself. "I am laird to a people and castle plagued by the Fae, as much as by the inhabitants of Asgard."

"I beg your pardon!" Syrie huffed. "The Fae do not plague a place. We grace it with our presence for a time."

"In that case," Hall chuckled, the light of hope returning to his eyes, "my home, the place that will be our home together, has been more than amply *graced*."

"It sounds to be an interesting place you promise as our home together."

"Interesting, perhaps," he agreed. "But I can never promise you a normal life. Many of my days, great swaths of months on end, will be spent away from our home in service to Thor. I cannot change this."

"I would never ask you to change it." Brie pulled her hand from his to cup his cheek in her palm. "But I would ask you to understand that though you may be away from the land and buildings you call our home, our *true* home will always be wherever we are together. And wherever you go, I will go, so you will never truly be away from home again."

"Then your answer is yes?"

"My answer is yes. With all my heart, yes."

Hall crushed her in his embrace, lifting her from her feet to twirl her around as he covered her lips with his, submersing her in the heady haze his touch always brought.

Could her life get any better than spending it with the man she loved over any other?

It could, and would. She would share her home with the Viking gods of her father's people, and with the Fae.

Her brother had been wrong. Not only had she not had her fill of adventure, the adventure of her life was only just beginning.

Thirty-six

HALL GLANCED TOWARD the western horizon, judging the position of the sun as it sank in the sky. He'd have to hurry to finish this task and still make it to the garden on time.

He didn't want to keep his bride-to-be waiting; the woman had a temper on her. A smile broadened his face at the thought of Bridget in a full rage. She should have been born a redhead.

He made his way across the bailey to the blacksmith's shed, where he peered into the forge. If his luck held, it wouldn't take overly long to find the treasure he sought. Heat wafted out in waves to greet him as he poked the smithy's tongs into the coals, digging around until at last he found what he hunted.

The soot-covered ruby glowed with heat as he pulled it out of the furnace and set it on the ground at his feet. Once it was cool enough to handle, he held it up to catch the day's last bright rays.

His inspection revealed exactly what he'd expected. The jewel hadn't escaped the effects of its time in the fire. A jagged white crack ran the length of the ruby, deep inside the interior. The heat had burst it from the inside out. Still, the jewel held together, strong to the last, even after its beauty and monetary value had faded.

This little bauble had protected Bridget in her battle with the Beast, as his rowan-wood goat had once protected him. It deserved a better fate than being discarded with the fire's ashes simply because its magic and value were gone.

Besides, it would make a perfect wedding gift for his perfect bride.

As he had done once before, he tied a long, thin strip of rawhide around the gem and finished by knotting the ends to form a crude necklace.

That would have to do for now, though he'd promise her better for later on.

Satisfied with his efforts, Hall dropped the gift into his sporran and headed for the garden to meet Bridget. His heart raced in anticipation of the rendezvous as if he hadn't seen her in days.

Since they'd made public their intention to wed, they'd been allowed no time alone together at all. Considering all the obstacles her brother and uncle had placed between them in the past two days, Hall suspected the two men still chafed over being denied the right to choose who would marry Bridget.

But his Bridget was an inventive woman, outwitting even her ever-present relatives. At the midday meal, she'd managed to whisper to him as they'd passed in the great hall, her message short but welcome.

The garden at sunset.

The remainder of the day had dragged for him as if the hours were weeks.

He rounded the corner of the garden wall, hardly daring to believe his wait was over, half fearing he'd imagined her words in his desire to be with her.

But Bridget herself sat on the garden bench. The sun shone around her like a halo, and just like that, nothing else mattered. Not her family, not the delay in seeing her, nothing other than this moment in time.

She spotted him immediately. Her face broke into the most beautiful smile he'd seen in days as she hopped up to run to his open arms.

Mindful of her bandaged arm, he pulled her close and breathed in the clean, sweet scent of her. "I've missed you."

"And I you," she murmured in return, her lips tracing a path over his cheek as her hand slid up his neck and into his hair. "I thought I'd never get away from those women. Syrie has hardly left my side, and the good Lady Danielle has her heart set upon something she calls a hen party for this evening. She claims it's a necessity before a wedding, though I've never heard of the like before. Only by asserting a great need for rest before we tackle the chickens was I able to sneak away."

Sneaking away had never sounded so good. As

it did every time Hall touched Bridget, his body responded immediately to the feel of her in his arms, and his mind raced, trying to imagine where they might find a moment of seclusion.

"Is there no place in the whole of this damned castle where we can be alone?" Bridget asked, proving once again how perfect she was for him, her mind and his in perfect sync.

"You've all the time in the world to be alone." Jamesy had somehow managed to arrive unnoticed. "*After* tomorrow. *After* yer safely wed."

"You do realize that we spent days alone together as we traveled?" The glare Bridget directed at her brother would have skewered a lesser man.

"I do," he answered. "And you will again, little sister. After tomorrow, and no before."

Hall's body ached at the prospect of letting this woman go so soon. "I suppose it would be bad form to murder the man who is to be my new brother?" he whispered in Bridget's ear.

"Mayhap," she answered on a sigh, resting her forehead against his shoulder. "But as he's already my brother, I could gladly do it for you."

"Come on with you," Jamesy encouraged with a broad grin. "I've no desire to stand out here shivering in the cold while the two of you anguish over one another."

With another heavy sigh and a roll of her eyes, Bridget turned to head toward her brother.

"Wait." Hall stopped Brie before she could leave,

remembering the gift he'd brought. "I have something for you. A wedding gift."

He pulled the necklace from his sporran and dropped it over Bridget's head, envying the jewel as it fell into place between her lovely breasts.

"Once we reach Haven Castle, I'll have a silversmith set it into something fancier and more permanent for you."

Her eyes sparkled as her hand tightened around the flawed jewel. "I'm amazed you were able to retrieve this little gem. It's perfect as it is, thank you. I'm only sorry I've nothing to give you. At least"— she grinned, nodding toward her brother—"nothing I can give you with him standing there, as he seems determined to do."

"Ahem," Jamesy said. "I can hear you quite clearly. I'll thank you to save that sort of blether for after yer wedding, when I'm no forced to listen to it."

"Who would have guessed my own brother would be such a maiden about this?" she asked with a chuckle.

"Have some control over yerself, lass!" Jamesy insisted. "We'll deliver you to the chamber yer sharing with Mistress Syrie, where I'm sure you'll be well looked after for the night. And then you and I, O'Donar, we've a none-too-patient group of men waiting for us in our laird's solar."

Jamesy claimed his sister's good arm, forcing Hall to walk behind them as they made their way into the keep. Her annoying brother even inserted himself between them as they said a chaste good night, and by the time Hall and Jamesy reached the laird's solar, his desire to do harm to the other man was ceasing to be a joke.

"Here they are!" Chase called out, shoving a mug into Hall's hand as they entered the crowded room. "I'd begun to wonder whether I should send out a search party. What took you so long?"

"I was only trying to speak with Bridget," Hall explained, lifting the cup to his lips.

Whisky. Smooth and strong. Exactly what he needed to tamp down his frustrations this night.

"And speaking is all you'll do with my sister until the wedding's done and over," Jamesy said, slapping Hall's shoulder as he passed.

"Hey, I totally understand what you're going through," Chase commiserated, his gaze following Jamesy's departing back. "Why do you think Christiana and I chose to marry as soon as possible? You think you have it bad? Christy has *two* brothers, and both of them were breathing down my neck."

Hall smiled in spite of his irritation. Chase Noble, the brother of his heart, always had that effect on him.

"A toast," Malcolm called out, raising his cup high in the air. "To a battle well ended with the aid of our newest kinsman."

As the cups were lowered, Eric lifted his again. "To yer wedding on the morrow, O'Donar, a day that equally marks the end of our troubles and the beginning of yers!"

"To Hall O'Donar and Brie MacCulloch," Chase yelled over the laughter as the jug was passed around the room for refills. "May they live long and prosper."

Chase ended his toast with a hearty laugh as if he'd thought of some private joke before draining his cup. "So, tomorrow the former Bridget MacCulloch will become Brie O'Donar and you, my brother, will have to come up with a naming gift, if I'm not mistaken. Have you decided on what you'll give her yet?"

"A naming gift?"

The thought hadn't crossed his mind, but Chase was absolutely correct. By their marriage he was giving Bridget a new name, and Thor demanded that a gift be exchanged.

By the gods. With less than twenty-four hours before they would wed, he could think of only one way to determine the perfect gift for the woman of his dreams.

He would have to ask her what she wanted and then, as he'd once sworn he would do, he would move heaven and earth to give it to her.

Thirty-seven

THIS HAD TO be the best idea any of those over-bearing women had ever come up with.

Brie lifted one foot from the hot water in which she soaked and propped her heel on the edge of the big wooden tub. Tiny dust motes danced in the sun-beam that washed over her foot.

Steam, thick with the scent of mint and balm, eddied up around her like a warm, moist pillow.

She couldn't remember the last time she'd felt so relaxed.

This latest "necessity" before her wedding was definitely an improvement over the ridiculously named hen party Lady Danielle had insisted on the night before. With not one single chicken in sight, she'd been forced to endure an evening of giggling women and their unending, unrequested, and com-pletely unnecessary advice.

Not that she didn't appreciate each and every one of them. She did. It was only that secreting her-self away with Hall would have been a much more enjoyable way to spend her evening.

But this? This had turned out to be one watery little slice of heaven. Best of all, once they'd pampered, petted, and smothered her with herbs and soaps for her bath, they'd said farewell and left her gloriously alone.

Me-time, Lady Dani had called it.

They'd be back all too soon, bearing bath sheets and the freshly altered dress she was to wear for her wedding, and all the babble and bustle would return with them.

A twinge of guilt stung her conscience. If she'd spoken her thoughts aloud, the world would surely have judged her an ungrateful wench. And rightly so. For all their efforts on her behalf, the ladies of Castle MacGahan were owed better than she'd given so far, and she vowed to do her best to join in their excitement over the dress and readying her for the ceremony. It was the least she could do, to thank them for all they'd done for her.

But right now, in this precious respite from their overly helpful ministrations, she would enjoy the peace and quiet of this delightful me-time.

Brie slid down in the tub, dunking her head under the fragrant water and emerging to brush back the hair from her face. Her locks, once so long and heavy, barely clung to her shoulders now, their bulk left behind at the bottom of the North Sea cliffs.

Jeanne had assured her they could dress her hair today so that no one would notice how short it was, while Lady Dani had hinted that she might find she enjoyed having it shorter.

She reached for the soap, delighted to find it had an entirely different scent from all the other items in her bath. It smelled of something light and floral that made her feel feminine and dainty.

Not that she'd admit *that* to anyone.

She scrubbed the soap along her arm, realizing with a start that the markings Orabilis had painted there had all but disappeared in places. Perhaps she wouldn't have to worry over her strange appearance embarrassing her new laird and husband after all.

"You sneaky old witch," she said with a laugh.

Now, *there* was a woman who had a way of obscuring everything she said. It would make perfect sense to her if Orabilis were indeed a Faerie, as Hall had claimed.

Hall.

Just thinking of her groom sent shivers of delight coursing along her skin. That she would be joined with him for life by the time this day's sun had set was almost beyond belief.

Everyone should have the chance to be as happy as she was today.

She'd just rested her head against the tub's edge and closed her eyes when a light knock sounded at the door.

She stifled a groan of disappointment and reached for the washing cloth to give her some measure of modesty before the women once again descended.

"Come in," she called as the door behind her creaked open, then said in her best cheery voice, "Have you brought the dress? I can hardly wait to see it."

Two large hands clamped down on her shoulders and water splashed over the sides of the tub as she started forward.

"No dress, I fear," Hall murmured, brushing his stubbled chin along the tender skin of her neck before stopping to nibble the lobe of her ear.

Had she thought herself in heaven before? She'd been wrong.

Her good sense almost deserted her completely when his hands slicked down her wet body to cover her breasts, his warm breath hitting the side of her face in rapid little pants.

What were the chances she could strip him bare, drag him into her bath, and have her way with him before the ladies returned?

Slim to none, the way her luck had been going. She hadn't even been able to manage a kiss in the garden before her brother had arrived.

"We canna do this now, my love. Syrie will have herself one full-out Faerie fit if she finds you here like this."

"I know," he answered on a sigh, slowly moving his hands back up to her shoulders. "It's not even why I came. But when I saw you thus, I couldn't stop myself. Have you any idea how badly I want you every time I see you?"

She understood his need all too well.

He dipped his head and covered her mouth with a long, slow kiss. His tongue flickered across her lips and she turned in the tub, rising up on her knees, ready to take what she wanted, the ladies be damned.

"By Odin's breath," he whispered, tracing a finger down the side of her face, "we will finish this tonight, I so swear it. But for now, I need to speak to you."

He rose to his feet and backed away, clear across the room, his face red as if with great exertion.

Or heat. Her own body felt hot enough to boil the bathwater.

"Then hurry up and speak yer piece before they return and find you here."

The fog had lifted from her brain as he'd put distance between them, and a scene with the fiery-tempered Faerie was something she'd prefer to avoid.

"A few hours from now, we'll wed and you'll take my name for your own. For that, Thor requires that I give you a naming gift. You've but to tell me what you want. Your heart's desire is what I would gift you."

If this was any harbinger of things to come, her life was shaping up to be an unending series of surprises.

"You already gave me a gift. I have no need for anything else."

His face broke into that most wonderful smile, and she very nearly climbed from the tub and went after him.

"Need is not a consideration, my love. The name change requires it, to honor Thor. It is the custom of my people and I cannot ignore it."

"With you to be my husband, I canna think of anything more in the whole of the world that I want. Unless . . . a dog, mayhap? I've considered one after seeing the kind beastie that travels with Finn. The two of them do seem to get on happily enough."

"A dog?" Hall's brow wrinkled in confusion. "That's it? That's the greatest desire of your heart? I offer you anything in all the world, and you'd ask for a dog?"

"Well, it's the only *thing* I can think of. If I could choose my heart's desire, though—if I had that sort of Magic at my disposal—I would wish that Jamesy might find the one person who would make him as happy as you've made me."

"So be it, my beloved. Consider it done."

The smile returned to his face, and she would have climbed out of the tub this time but for the door opening wide.

"What is this?" Syrie demanded, glaring at Hall. "Can I not trust you even for the length of time it takes your lady to bathe? Don't you have things you need to be doing to get yourself ready? What are you doing in here?"

Brie was amazed that the tirade could go so long without the woman seeming to need to stop for a breath, but Hall took the scolding in stride. If anything, his smile was even broader by the time Syrie paused.

"I came here looking for you, Elf. These are your chambers, are they not?"

"Faerie," she muttered, her eyes flashing as she crossed to the bed to drop the armload of fabric she held. "And what business, pray tell, could you possibly have with me?"

"I'd ask that you join me in the garden for a short talk."

"No." Syrie busied herself shaking out the dress from the drying sheets. "Can you not see I'm busy here? I haven't time for a talk. Say what you need to say now and have it done."

"Unfortunately, I cannot speak in front of her." Hall tilted his head in Brie's direction. "I need your help with a surprise to make this day special for my bride."

Syrie's lips pressed together, and Brie knew the woman would give in. If all Faeries were such romantics as this woman, Wyddecol must be a most fantastic place.

With a sigh of annoyance, Syrie tossed a drying blanket to the floor next to the tub and headed for the door. "Very well, Northman. For Brie's special day, and no other reason. And as for you, I expect you out and dried off by the time I return," she told Brie as she followed Hall outside.

With the door again closed, Brie slid back down into the water to steal a few more glorious moments, her mind filled with names for the dog Hall was no doubt on his way to get for her right now.

Thirty-eight

"ALL RIGHT, OUT with it. What do you want of me?"
Syrie waited, hands on her hips, and though
she tried to look angry, Hall knew he'd hooked her
when he'd told her he wanted her help for Bridget's benefit. Since what he planned to ask her to do
should be something she'd be happy to do, it was all
smooth sailing from here.

Then again, he could never be sure when it came
to the Fae. Just in case he'd read her wrong, he positioned himself at the opening of the walled garden
to prevent any hasty departure she might attempt.

"With our wedding today, I give Bridget a new
name. If I'm to honor Thor and keep him happy, I
need a naming gift for my bride."

And considering the havoc he'd just caused in
destroying Fenrir and the scrolls, he couldn't afford
to skip any step that might keep his grandfather
happy.

"Again, Northman, what do you want of me?"

"I wish to give my new wife her heart's desire.
As it so happens, her heart's desire is to have her

brother as happy as she is. I come to you to ask that you make that happen by finding Jamesy's Soul-Mate and reuniting them."

Watching the Faerie flounder for words, Hall wanted to remember this moment forever. The Fae were never caught without something to say.

"I . . . I . . ." she stuttered, her arms moving from her hips to cross protectively in front of her. "I cannot. What you ask is beyond my ability to give you. You'll have to find another gift."

She wasn't telling the truth, and he had no intention of letting her off the hook so easily. After all, he'd sworn to move heaven and earth to give Bridget her heart's desire. One small Faerie was not going to stand in his way.

"I know my history. It is the responsibility of the Fae to reunite those who should be together. And while the powers of most Faeries are limited while they remain in the Mortal world, you are an exception. You do have it within your power to do as I ask. I've seen the results of your having used those powers all around me."

"You don't understand. I'm forbidden from using my power while I'm here."

Obviously the two of them had very different ideas of what the word *forbidden* meant.

"Then how do you explain what you've already done? You brought Lady Danielle here. You brought my brother, Chase Noble, here. And not from a mere continent's distance, either, I might add. And those are only the instances I know of. It's clear enough to me, my lady, that though you scream a pretty argument about the integrity of the Norns' tapestry, you've pulled more than a few threads from it your ownself. Why will you not do this thing, which the greater good would deem to be your responsibility anyway?"

"As a matter of fact, I am expressly forbidden by my goddess and the Faerie High Council from doing exactly what you ask of me."

"To hell with your High Council." Those pretentious Faeries had always been a high-handed lot, eager to accept glory but slow to accept the obligations glory conferred. "Your people broke the world with their warring. Your people are responsible for reuniting the soul pairings that were torn asunder, thanks to their greed and lust for power. It *is* your responsibility to put things back as they belong. Yours and all your people's."

This was a perfect example of why he hated dealing with the Fae. Were it not for Bridget's desire to see her brother happy, he would wash his hands of these creatures forever.

"And what right have you to criticize me," Syrie demanded, "to order me to do that which I know I must not? Is it not bad enough that your rash behavior has called down the attention of every being in every world to what happens here in this very spot?

There are serious consequences for disobeying my goddess. Consequences I'd rather not pay, thank you very much."

"Consequences and your false goddess be damned!" Thunder pounded the sky above them and the earth trembled under their feet. He shouldn't allow his emotions to run wild, but for Brie he would do anything. "It is your duty. This is what you were born to do, Elf!"

"You well know I'm a Faerie, not an Elf!" she shouted back, her temper ignited by his. "None of you are ever satisfied! No matter how much I tread the line, no matter how often I give. Fine: I'll grant you what you want. But it won't stop with Jamesy. It never does. You say that's all you want now, but there's always another in need of their one true love. Malcolm, Christiana, now Jamesy. Next will it be all of his friends? And all their relatives? The friends and relatives of every man, woman, and child at Castle MacGahan? So be it, Northman. No matter the wrath of my goddess, may each of them find their own true SoulMate! There. There is surely nothing left for you to ask of me. Is that what you wanted?"

"It is, indeed, sweet Elf!" With a kiss to her forehead, he picked up the furious little Faerie and swung her around in a circle before setting her down to race off to the keep. He had no particular desire to be near her when she had a chance to reconsider the magnitude of what she'd done, or the full consequences of her tantrum.

Wedding Day

Syrie Aí Byrn ran her hands down the front of her dress, brushing away imaginary wrinkles. She needed something to keep her hands and her mind busy.

She wished, for perhaps the one hundredth time today, that Patrick were here instead of at Tordenet. As annoying and bossy as he could be, he was always sure to give her a platitude to console her or an argument to distract her from her worries.

And worries she had aplenty.

When the Tinklers had passed through the last time, Editha had carried a warning from the goddess herself. Danu had fixed her eye upon Castle Mac-Gahan and the Great Lady would brook no more indiscretions on Syrie's part. No more tinkering with individual lives. Bringing Dani here had been the gift she was granted when she'd been allowed to pass through the curtain separating Wyddecol from the Mortal Plane with her Magic intact.

She should have returned to Wyddecol as soon as her reason for being here was fulfilled, but she hadn't. She'd found pleasure in this world with these people. She'd felt needed.

But being needed occasionally led her to use her forbidden Magic, and because of that, the goddess was displeased.

So displeased, in fact, she'd sent Editha to inform Syrie that she was forbidden from returning to her home world until she could prove herself worthy of her powers.

And should she fail? Editha had been clear on that point, too. The goddess herself would see to Syrie's punishment if she used her Magic again.

All she had to do was mind her actions and go about her days as if she were a Mortal. It should have been so simple.

But today, guilted by that great oaf of a Northman, Thor's annoying grandson, she'd gone far, far beyond an individual bit of tinkering or indiscreet use of her Magic. She'd agreed to set to rights a great swath of what her people had broken well over a millennium ago.

While a tiny corner of her heart rejoiced at the virtue of her actions, her rest of her internal organs quivered in fear of the imminent consequences.

It was only a matter of time. There was no way something this large could sneak by unnoticed. Retribution would come, swift and sure, and Syrie's world would never be the same again.

MALCOLM MACDOWYLT, LAIRD of the MacGahan, skimmed his gaze over the crowd filling his great hall. They were his people, his responsibility, and for the first time since he'd made that claim, they were all safe from the evil that had hunted him.

A great weight had lifted from his shoulders with Torquil's death. The people of MacGahan could look toward a future free from the threat of his half brother's vengeance.

He felt ten years younger. Even the headaches that had plagued him for the past year were gone.

"Malcolm!"

He looked up to find his beautiful Dani running toward him, her cheeks pink with excitement. She'd been a whirlwind of energy over the past days, organizing what she'd insisted was a proper wedding for Hall and Brie. He'd never seen the like of what she'd planned, but it made her happy and that was all that mattered to him.

"Is everything ready in here?" she asked. "Jeanne is putting the finishing touches on Brie's hair, and then we'll start her walk down the aisle. Once their vows are recited, that's your cue to kick off the wedding reception, which will rival your old Odin's Feast. Ada's even serving up the bog myrtle beer, so there'll be a hot time in the old town tonight, if you know what I mean."

No matter how long she'd spent in his world, in his time, her strange way with words still brought a smile to his lips. She was the joy of his life, and he sent a silent thanks to Elesyria for having brought his Dani to him.

He snagged her hand and lifted it to his lips before tucking it under his arm. "Stop for a moment, love. Take a breath and enjoy what's been accomplished."

"I don't have time to take a breath. I've a million last-minute things that need doing."

"And they'll all still be here a minute from now. Relax. Enjoy what you've already accomplished."

With an arm around her shoulder to keep her at his side, he surveyed the room once more.

Hall caught his eye first, standing on the dais with Chase Noble at his side, impatiently drumming his fingers against his sporran as he awaited the arrival of his bride.

Impatience or nerves. It was, after all, the big warrior's big day.

Chase leaned away from the groom to catch Christiana's hand as she hurried by, no doubt on some wedding errand Dani had devised. Malcolm's sister stopped and shared a quick conversation with her new husband—and a not-so-quick kiss—before going on her way.

Christiana had blossomed into her own since she'd found her life partner in Chase Noble, smiling more than he'd ever known her to.

"We've a good life," Malcolm mused, tightening his arm around his wife. "Surrounded by those we love. Our family has certainly grown in this past year, has it no?"

"It has at that," Dani agreed, turning her radiant smile on full force. "And it's getting ready to do some more growing, my love." She pulled his hand from her shoulder and rested his palm against her stomach. "In about six or seven months."

Words deserted him as the blood in his body drained to his feet. He could only stare into her smiling face, doing his best to absorb the glorious news.

"A child?" he managed at last. "Are you sure?"

"Positive," she answered, her smile even broader than before. "I wasn't going to say anything yet, but I suppose a joyous day like this is as good a time as any to tell you, right?"

A child. His child. "How did this happen?"

The musical tinkle of Dani's laughter drew several sets of eyes to where they stood.

"Well, dear husband, we can't spend all our time acting like rabbits without producing a bunny or two, can we?" She squeezed his hand. "You happy about this?"

Happy? He was beyond happy. He was ecstatic. Here he'd thought the day he married Dani was the best of his life. He should have realized that with her at his side, his life could only continue to get better and better.

JAMESY MACCULLOCH SAT on the bench in the great hall, waiting for a signal from Lady Danielle for whatever new oddities she had planned for the day.

Already she'd ordered all the tables moved so that they lined the walls. The benches were left behind to form neat, angled rows of seating, reminding him of the pews in the cathedral he'd visited in Edinburgh. And considering the whole of the castle was gathered to witness the marriage of his sister to Hall O'Donar, he was forced to give grudging approval of the arrangement.

Eccentric little thing that Lady Danielle was, she must please his laird well enough, since Malcolm appeared more relaxed than Jamesy had ever known him to be.

Theirs was a happiness Jamesy might be tempted to envy, if he were a man with any interest in such a dull, domesticated life.

He wasn't.

He would, however, pray that his sister had found the same sort of delight. She certainly seemed well on target for it. He'd never seen her so contented as when she was in the presence of her groom.

As pleased as he was for his sister's happiness, his emotions were in turmoil as he waited for her wedding to begin. So much had happened in the last weeks to hand him the freedom he'd so long desired.

An immense sense of relief filled his heart. His days of worrying over Brie's rash behavior were quickly coming to a close. In an hour's time, his wildling sister would be O'Donar's responsibility. Though, as he'd pointed out to the big warrior last night more than once, Jamesy would gladly hand him his arse on a spit if he failed to care for her properly.

Jamesy fidgeted on the bench, anxious for the day's

events to get moving. The excitement coursing through him was more than relief. The exchange of vows was to be followed by a feast that would last late into the evening, though he planned to make his exit early.

Tomorrow would mark the beginning of a new adventure, and Jamesy was nothing if not a man who lived for the next adventure. With the security of both Castle MacGahan and Tordenet now assured, he was free to join his friends Finn and Alex in settling the problems that plagued the MacKillican clan.

Tomorrow the three friends would set out, beginning their journey with a short side trip to see Mathew and Eleyne safely returned to their home at Castle Glenluce. Once that task was out of the way, they would head for Alex's family home, where his friend would inform his father of his intent to join Finn and Jamesy in their search for adventure.

With the English rattling swords at the border, he doubted his peace and quiet would last long. A good thing, too, since, to his way of thinking, peace and quiet were highly overrated.

Lady Danielle's laughter drew his attention and she waved her hand in his direction, his signal to join her outside the entry doors so that he could walk Brie the length of the great room to present her hand to Hall O'Donar.

His wait was over.

CHRISTIANA MACDOWYLT NOBLE hurried through the great hall toward the kitchens to fetch a sprig from the rosemary plant Cook kept there. Dani had insisted that Brie must have something new to carry on her walk down the aisle. Apparently the old, the borrowed, and the blue items weren't satisfactory on their own.

Though she'd grown exceptionally fond of her sister-in-law, Christiana was utterly grateful to Chase for having insisted upon a quick, quiet, private exchange of vows when they wed. All this attention would have been far too much for her taste.

Brie, on the other hand, appeared to be floating through the whole experience, allowing others to set the terms and rules of her wedding, her eyes focused on the prize at the end of the day.

Christiana had known from her first meeting with Brie that she was an extraordinarily strong woman. Her good grace in the face of these festivities only served to solidify that opinion.

Ahead of her, Chase stood on the raised dais next to his friend and brother, Hall O'Donar. According to Dani, Chase served the purpose of best man in this ceremony.

She couldn't agree more with the title. Her handsome, wonderful Chase, the light of her life, was indeed the best man she'd ever met.

She could hardly wait to travel with him next month to take possession of Tordenet. Malcolm's home was a wonderful place, and everyone had gone above and beyond in their efforts to make her feel welcome. But returning to Tordenet was a dream come true. There she'd be close to Orabilis and surrounded by the things she loved.

Chase snagged her arm as she attempted to pass, and pulled her close.

"I canna dally, my love. The bride is waiting on my return," she said.

"She's waited all day. Another minute isn't going to kill her."

He dipped his head to kiss her, and for an instant, transported away by the feel of his lips on hers, she forgot that anyone else shared the hall with them.

Hall's pointed clearing of his throat brought her back to her senses, and her face heated rapidly as she realized the groom wasn't the only one who'd been watching.

By the old gods, Chase had the ability to steal away what little sense she'd been given.

"Save me a seat," he called after her as she raced away on her mission.

As if he thought he'd need to remind her to do such a thing. He was such a part of her now, she couldn't imagine not having him at her side. Thanks to him, and the Faerie who'd helped her find him, her life was every bit as wonderful as the charred runes she wore around her neck had foretold it would be.

HALL O'DONAR ALLOWED himself a wide grin as Christiana hurried from the dais. His debt to his old Faerie friend was settled well and good. Chase was safe and sound and, from the looks of it, couldn't be happier.

That this was due in part to Syrie's intervention only proved that what he'd done this morning in tricking her had been the right thing to do in the long run. Granted, it would take some time for the Magic to run its course for everyone concerned, but in the end, everyone in this room would benefit.

Even the hot-tempered little Faerie herself.

It was shaping up to be a banner decade for weddings at Castle MacGahan.

A hush fell over the crowd as a lone piper picked up the strains of a song unlike any Hall had heard before. All heads turned to the back of the room, toward the great entrance doors where Jamesy Mac-Culloch entered with the most beautiful woman Hall had ever seen in his life on his arm.

"Here we go," Chase whispered next to him. "Come on in, the water's fine."

Hall couldn't answer, could hardly breathe. All that was left to him was to stare at the woman walking toward him, her face adorned with a smile to match his own.

By some frippery known only to the fairer sex, Bridget's hair had been piled upon her head and surrounded by a garland of dried flowers.

She wore a dress of pale yellow, similar in color to the frock the Tinklers had given her, but the similarities stopped there. This garment had been fitted to his woman, baring her shoulders, hugging her breasts, and flaring over her hips.

A thin strip of rawhide circled her neck and disappeared into the lace and ribbons that contained her breasts.

She wore his necklace.

"I give unto yer care the well-being and happiness of my only sister," Jamesy said when they reached the dais. As he placed her hand upon Hall's, he whispered, "And dinna you forget the warning I gave you last night, aye?"

As if Hall needed his brother-in-law's admonition to watch after Bridget.

"You look . . ." He paused, awed by the moment.

"Amazing," Chase whispered loudly.

"You look amazing," Hall finished.

Perhaps this was why Lady Danielle had insisted that every groom needed a best man. To offer help when his words failed him.

He tried again on his own. "Your dress is . . ." Not like anything he'd ever seen before.

Bridget shrugged, her cheeks coloring a delightful pink. "A bit revealing, is it no? Lady Dani assures me it's quite modern."

"Beautiful," Hall assured her. "The gown is almost as beautiful as the woman who wears it."

"Oh," she breathed, her eyes filling with tears.

"Vows!" Chase hissed, with an elbow to Hall's back.

Vows. Yes. Everyone in the great hall waited for him to start.

He cleared his throat and squeezed the hand he held within his own two.

"I, Hall O'Donar, take thee, Bridget MacCulloch . . ." He began reciting the words that would change his life forever, setting him on a path to happiness far greater than he had ever expected.

Epilogue

BRIE UNFURLED HER blanket over the soft green grass and kneeled to unpack the basket of food she'd brought. Once the midday meal was laid out and ready, she sat back to await Hall's arrival.

As usual, she was much too early.

Not that she would complain about sitting here in the quiet beauty of this Irish hilltop, with the sun warm upon her skin and nothing but green as far as she could see. Far from it. Haven Castle had truly lived up to its name.

The spring and summer in her new home had been the most glorious months of her life, with each and every day bringing some new delight.

Saturday, as today was, had become her favorite day of the week.

With the arrival of warm weather, she and Hall had taken to meeting out here for their midday meal every Saturday, followed by her lessons. Between her determination and Hall's, she'd managed to turn her knowledge of letters into an ability to read and write over the past seven months.

More or less. Brie was the first to admit that she could decipher words much better than she could form them with the tedious quill and ink that often taxed her patience to its limit.

She might have mastered even more, had their Saturday lessons not always dissolved into unfettered lovemaking. Though, in truth, it was mostly the lovemaking that kept her coming back for the lessons.

A smile lit her face as she spotted her beloved husband in the distance. He rode toward her at breakneck speed, shirtless, standing in his stirrups, one arm raised in greeting.

Bare-chested! A shiver ran down her spine and ended up centering low in her belly. No shirt likely meant he'd stopped for a dip in the pond before coming to meet her. And *that* meant they might skip lessons altogether this fine day.

A perfect way to say good-bye to summer if ever she'd imagined one.

"We've a letter!" he called as he jumped from his horse and gathered her up in his arms to greet her with the kisses she so anticipated. "Fresh from the messenger's hands."

She'd been right about the pond; his hair still held water droplets. And his face was freshly shaved, just the way he knew she liked it best.

With his bare, warm skin under her hands, her mind wandered down paths that had nothing to do with the letter he waved over his head, and everything to do with how quickly she could climb out of her shift.

"Brie, love, lessons first, then dessert," he laughed, dropping to sit before pulling her down onto his lap.

Her man might have only the purest intentions about the lessons, but the bulge under his plaid bumping against her bottom told her his body had other ideas. Ideas to match her own.

"It's from Chase," he said temptingly when she tried to turn in his lap. "News from your home. For your lesson today, you can read the letter to me while I relax."

He scooted her off his lap and stretched out on his back, arms behind his head.

"Fine," she relented. The sooner she blundered her way through the missive, the sooner they'd get to the "dessert" she wanted.

Chase formed his letters in the strangest fashion, which slowed her reading. She was able to decipher a few words quickly enough to realize the main reason for the letter, though.

"Malcolm and Dani have had their baby!" She scanned over the chicken scratching for more recognizable words. "A boy. They have a son."

Damn her slow brain, but she couldn't figure out half of the words Chase had written. "I canna find the babe's name, Hall. Take this thing. Read it to me. Tell me what name they've chosen."

"Only because my brother has the worst handwriting anywhere." He hoisted himself up on one elbow and took the paper she held out, scanning over the whole of it before speaking again. "He doesn't give the name, love. Sorry."

"No mention of the name? Yer brother is an idiot, Hall O'Donar. Only a man would forget to share such an important detail."

"Then we shall consider this an opportunity."

There was mischief behind the smile breaking over his face. "And how would not knowing something be an opportunity for us?" she asked suspiciously.

"Because it will serve as a perfect excuse for you to practice your writing. You can send a note of congratulations to Malcolm and Dani and ask them what they've named their fine new son."

Her husband was a fiend for practice.

"I will, indeed," she agreed, turning to lean over him, one hand on either side of his body. "As you say, it's the thing to do. But no right now. I'm done with my lessons for this Saturday and I'm thinking, because of the frustrating nature of that missive, that I've earned that dessert you tempted me with, aye?"

"Aye," he agreed, fastening his hands around her waist as she straddled to sit on him. "We've both earned it."

She pulled the tie from her hair as his hands wandered up from her waist to fasten on her breasts, just as she liked him to do.

Yet in spite of the lure of his obviously ready

body, she could only picture a tiny nameless baby when she closed her eyes.

"I canna believe he did that."

"Let it go, love," Hall said on a sigh. "Later, when we pack up our blanket and return to the keep, you can busy yourself with planning the perfect revenge on my brother for having denied you that wisp of information that you wanted most out of his letter. I'll even help you. We'll think of something truly diabolical, if you like. Later."

He wrapped one hand around the back of her neck and pulled her head down for a kiss while, with his other, he tugged at the skirt wrapped around her legs.

"If we ever have a babe of our own, I'll see to it that yer brother doesn't learn his name until he's ready to take up arms of his own," she threatened.

There. See how Chase Noble would like that.

"When, not if," he corrected with a grin. "It will happen eventually. If we keep practicing your lessons, that is."

"Lessons, my arse," she replied, jerking her skirt out from under her so that she sat upon her husband, skin touching skin.

He closed his eyes, groaned, and slid both hands around her waist.

"If we do have children, I'd want them all to be sons," she said.

His eyes popped open and he dropped his hands from her waist. "Why would you say that?"

It should have been obvious enough. She'd been raised by her father and her brother. "I wouldna ken what to do with a daughter, or how to begin to raise one properly."

"You're jesting, right? You'll raise our daughters as you were raised. You turned out better than any other woman I've ever known, so why would we want to raise our daughters any differently?"

He reached for her again and she grabbed his hand.

"You'd no be ashamed of a wildling daughter, with no the first idea of how to put ribbons in her hair or what fancy gowns the other girls wear?"

Hall pulled his hands away and scrubbed them over his face.

"I'll be every bit as proud of them as I am of you, love. I'll be happy to have my keep filled to over-flowing with nothing but wee, wild, brown-haired daughters, all growing up to be fine, wild, untamed warriors exactly like their mother."

There wasn't another man in all the world like hers. "Maybe daughters wouldna be so bad after all."

"They will be wonderful. But"—he flipped her to her back in a move so fast, it took her breath away—"we'll never get that keep full of wild, untamed warriors if you don't quiet your blether and put your mind to the business at hand."

"I will," she answered, reaching up to tuck a

strand of hair behind his ear. "So that's how you see me? As a wild, untamed warrior?"

"Exactly how I see you," he confirmed, pushing her skirts out of his way to fit himself between her legs. "My own personal wild and free, untamed warrior, racing over the hillsides, bow drawn, arrow nocked. My perfect lifemate. I would have you no other way."

How could she have gotten so lucky? To find the one man on the whole of the earth who saw her exactly as she saw him?

Two untamed warriors taking on the world. Together. For the rest of their lives.

Because the best conversations happen after dark . . .

Announcing a brand-new site for romance and urban fantasy readers just like you!

 *Visit **XOXOAfterDark.com** for free reads, exclusive excerpts, bonus materials, author interviews and chats, and much, much more!*

XOXO **AFTER DARK**.COM